D1441198

THE 228 LEGACY

Jennifer J. Chow

Martin Sisters Publishing

Published by

Martin Sisters Publishing, LLC

www.martinsisterspublishing.com

Copyright © 2013 Jennifer J. Chow

Martin Sisters Publishing, LLC, Kentucky.
ISBN: 978-1-62553-039-4
Literary/Women's Fiction/Multicultural
Printed in the United States of America
Martin Sisters Publishing, LLC

DEDICATION

To my parents and my in-laws: for encouraging me in my stories and inspiring me with yours.

Lisa

Lisa watches her name get crossed off the payroll list. "Last one hired, first one fired," her boss says, adjusting the tortoiseshell glasses sliding down her nose. "Budget cuts."

Lisa holds back the tears, staring instead at the carrot orange stains covering her hands. How would she tell her daughter? Will Ma have to bail her out?

Her boss glances up. "What are you waiting for?"

"I was just leaving, ma'am." Lisa lowers her eyes as she backs out the door.

She makes her way down the dingy hall to the "employees' quarters," a tiny cubicle of a room adjacent to the kitchen. Gleaming metal lockers line one wall, but Monroe Senior Home didn't provide a unit for her belongings. Her battered brown purse lies in the corner, hidden by a hamper of dirty linens. She pulls off her own food-splattered emerald apron and drops it into the bin, feeling a twinge of regret; the fabric boasts one of the few colors that complement her yellow Asian skin.

As the apron lands there for the last time, she notices her nametag pinned to the fabric. It's a hideous beige plastic chunk with her name embossed in 40-point font, the letters already fading from a year's worth of service. Still, it's hers, so she yanks it off. She can add it to the collection of souvenirs from her other failed jobs: the parking attendant's neon orange vest, the grocer's puce uniform, and the frayed poodle skirt from the 1950's diner.

She passes through the dining room one more time before leaving. She hears the usual complaints from the grumpy residents about the filet mignon lunch: the bloody lump of meat, its rubber taste, and the home's lack of vegetarian options. Nobody seems to enjoy their meal at Monroe Senior Home. Instead, diners feel obligated to gripe about their entrees and demand customized food. For the amount their families pay for the private housing, she supposes that the residents have the right to alter their menus. As their grumblings fill up her head, she's glad she's no longer a kitchen helper.

She pauses at the receptionist's desk. Tina, a pert blonde, has always been nice to Lisa. Plus, the receptionist keeps an excellent stash of chocolate mints in her desk drawer which she's invited Lisa to share in. Tina's not around, and Lisa assumes that she's busy escorting a rich family for a tour of the grounds. It'll take a while because the two-story mansion boasts multiple private suites and an elaborate French garden.

Lisa grabs a handful of mints from the drawer. *Since they won't be giving me a good-bye gift, I'll get my own.* She spies two blank memo pads with the elegant Monroe Senior Home insignia and swipes them. She spots a couple of file folders underneath and takes those as well. She's always liked the client file folders with their creamy vanilla exterior and their multiple interior flaps. Maybe she could use one as a career portfolio. At thirty-two, she still has time to excel at something. In fact, she plans to polish her résumé at once. With the new elegant carrier, she's bound to secure a dozen job offers in no time. She smiles all the way back home, through the twenty-minute bus ride on the sputtering Fairview Express, the sole public transportation in town.

Her optimism diminishes as she enters her studio apartment. Tomato sauce-stained napkins from last night's dinner drown the coffee table. The nearby ratty black sofa that her daughter sleeps on remains clear and unsoiled, though. Lisa's own full-sized bed in the corner unveils rumpled bed sheets and a heap of old, unwashed clothes.

She walks over to the neglected (and therefore) gleaming kitchen. Perching on one of the barstools, she runs her hand down the cool, clean white-tiled countertop. *Maybe I'll use one of the creamy folders to store gourmet recipes. Abbey could use a decent home-cooked meal for a change.*

When she picks up one of the folders to start her recipe list, she's surprised to see the neat typewriting. "The Chens" covers the upper-right hand corner. Under the label, a large sticky note dated 3/18/80, from three days ago, reads, "Tina, Jack is missing. Please locate him."

The file contains information on Jack and Fei Chen, one of the few couples who live at Monroe Senior Home. Now that she thinks about it, Lisa hasn't seen Mr. Chen in awhile, but she remembers his yellowed tea drinker's smile. He was one of the few seniors who actually thanked Lisa for her efforts. She wonders if his gratitude had anything to do with her ethnicity, since Fairview contains few Asians. No, she's seen Mr. Chen complimenting the other kitchen helpers and staff around Monroe Senior Home, too.

She scrunches her eyes as she attempts to picture Fei Chen. She recalls an impression of a flighty woman with near-translucent skin stretched across her bony figure. She didn't see Mrs. Chen in the dining room often. Lisa asked Mr. Chen about it once, and he had shrugged his shoulders. "She doesn't like to sit still for very long," he'd said. Without fail, though, Mr. Chen always asked for a second portion of lunch to bring back to his wife.

She taps the closed file with her fingertips. *I'll need to let Tina know. She'll understand that it was all a mistake. I didn't take sensitive information on purpose. Besides, she shouldn't keep client info lying around in her drawer anyway.* She picks up the phone to call but stops when she hears the key turn in the lock. Her daughter enters with her shiny obsidian hair and high cheekbones, looking like a younger and more famished version of Lisa. "Mom, I'm starving," Abbey says.

Lisa peeks at the clock. It's six, and Abbey's spent the last three hours studying and completing homework after school was dismissed. She gives her daughter a guilt-stricken look and studies the refrigerator's contents. Nothing in there except a half-gallon of questionable milk. She opens the freezer to check its supplies and sees a package of fish sticks. She grimaces but turns to face Abbey with a fake grin, showing her the ice-covered box. "I can heat these up in the microwave real quick, dear."

Abbey tries to hide her sigh. "That's okay, Mom. I'll dial." Her daughter picks up the phone and proceeds to place their usual order with Antonio's Pizzeria. *I guess the gourmet meals will have to wait until tomorrow.*

Abbey

Abbey feels a tap on her shoulder and turns in surprise. She has no friends at school. "What are those dots on your face?" The question comes from the most popular girl in her year, Rosalind.

Rosalind's long, blond hair flows in ringlets down her back. She displays the signature California tan that Abbey's sallow skin lacks. In fact, Rosalind epitomizes everything Abbey desires. Rosalind's blue eyes sparkle while Abbey's dirt brown irises fade away. Rosalind has a sharp, Grecian nose rather than Abbey's own blunt, misshapen snout. Rosalind boasts full bow-shaped lips instead of a razor-thin mouth. The usual mantra pops into Abbey's head: *I don't belong here.*

Despite its small size, Fairview acts like a pompous place. It contains one elementary school, one high school, and one junior college. Every institution in town carries a famous name, even "Atchison Elementary K-8." Abbey frowns, remembering that the name of a debatable one-day U.S. president adorns the school building.

"Abbey? Hello?" Rosalind drapes a delicate finger across Abbey's cheek. "What are these dots?"

"They're moles." Uncomprehending fair faces, the slew of constant students attached to Rosalind, blink at her. "Don't you know what moles are? They're like freckles."

Rosalind raises one groomed eyebrow. "Oh, but they're so bumpy." She flicks back her hair and sashays away, the crowd following her. "Road bumps," she says in a mock whisper that reaches back to Abbey.

Abbey uses her hands to cover up the blemishes, but the great scattering of moles across her face means she can't block out every ugly mark. She puts down her arms in despair. *And I'm already an outcast because of my name.*

Her mom's Beatles obsession transferred over to Abbey's name, and she recalls hearing "Eleanor Rigby" sung to her as a lullaby. While adults view her name as "creative," peers find it odd. In the polished Fairview world, accepted girl names are ones like Susan and Mary. She walks to her locker and spins the dial, but her fingers slip on the metal. *Like it's not hard enough just being the only kid at school with one parent around.*

She enters the combination again, and the lock springs open. Abbey grabs the math book for her next class and tries to close the door, but it catches on something. She places the bronze medal back on the heaping pile of awards stacked on the bottom shelf.

She keeps all her accolades tucked away at school. She started the trend after she won her first ribbon in kindergarten. She earned it for "best handwriting," in printing her alphabet. Her mom complimented her on it, but then tucked it away once Ah-Mah (her grandmother liked to be called by her respectful Taiwanese title) came to visit. Abbey cried the rest of that day.

As she grew older, Abbey observed that her mom filed report cards away in haste and that Ah-Mah became stressed whenever Abbey talked about school. Abbey doesn't know the reason for the tension but understands enough to hide her awards away from home. Sometimes she wonders if her mom even knows about the achievements. She imagines that they would have been mentioned during the mandatory parent-teacher meetings. If so, though, her mom has never asked to see any of them. Her mom also never takes her to "Awards Night," the special evenings at Atchison Elementary held to commend its top students. Abbey must receive her certificates from Principal Marshall the day after the ceremonies.

Abbey shifts the math textbook from one hand to the other as she proceeds to class, since the heavy tome always strains her thin arms. The walk seems long despite its short distance. She passes by just two doors, for English and History, before reaching her destination.

She and her fifth-grade peers already segment their academic schedules into varying subjects led by different teachers. At Atchison Elementary, the students receive their grades on a 100-point scale in each subject. Their grade point average and their current class ranking are posted in the main hallway. Abbey's tied in the number one slot with Ara, averaging a 99% throughout her school years. She wants the valedictorian slot when she graduates, and she knows that he does as well.

She takes a deep breath as she opens the door to math class because Ara will be there. Their academic rivalry doesn't scare her. In fact, it's the reason he talks to her at all. He asks her about her test scores or the latest homework assignment. No, she needs to prepare herself because her heart flutters at the sound of his voice, like all the other girls in her year.

Although Ara matches Abbey's exoticism in this white-bread town, he seems to wield a shield of protection around him. Despite his Armenian heritage, nobody appears disturbed by his cultural difference. In fact, it makes him more appealing. She wonders if it's because he's a boy.

She walks into the room and spots a crowd near Ara. They linger on his words until the bell rings. It's difficult to concentrate in math class with him there. Fortunately, her knack for numbers saves her whenever she's called up to the blackboard because instead of listening to Mr. Malone, she spends her time sneaking glances at Ara.

His skin is the color of rich mocha. Thick, expressive eyebrows frame his hazel eyes. He's the tallest boy in their year and even made the tryouts for the school's seventh grade basketball team. Due to his height, his knees often bump into his desk whenever he moves them. He shifts them about every ten minutes—she's observed him and written down the times in her notebook.

Today, he wears a navy blue suit with a tie, his wavy hair slicked back. His attire always seems polished, and she's never seen him in casual wear. She supposes that the refinement is passed down from his parents, two well-respected town members. His dad, an esteemed pediatric dentist, works with all the Fairview Elementary students. His mom reigns as a top cardiac surgeon in her field.

When the bell rings in dismissal, Abbey jots down the night's assignment. It's the only part of the class worth paying attention to. Even the typically alert Michelle Adams must agree because she's snoozing away at her desk.

Michelle's a legend at Atchison Elementary. She created her own school newspaper in the second grade, and it's become the unofficial grapevine for all the students. She wears clashing clothes and mismatched socks under an oversized patchwork jacket, but her social nature compensates for her eccentric appearance. In fact, Abbey wonders if Michelle uses the odd clothing to put her interviewees at ease and gather more information.

Abbey considers waking Michelle up. As if in reaction to the unspoken thought, she sees Michelle jolt awake and swivel her head in alarm. To save her from any embarrassment, Abbey hurries out the door and over to the cafeteria.

She can find it just by following the pungent odor. The inferior food exists as the only mar on the school's reputation. She pulls the meal ticket out of her pocket, one of a dozen kids who receive subsidized food. The wealthier students open up their silver monogrammed lunchboxes packed with gourmet food from home or line up in the parking lot where the caterer vans show up.

Abbey takes her tray of slop. The food arrives in various geometric shapes. She notes, with relief, that the mounds appear dome-shaped and rectangular in form. Once, she received a hexagonal mystery meat. She tried to feed it to the squirrels on campus, but even they scampered away from it.

She heads outside to eat under the huge elm. The tree marks her usual lunch spot, and she enjoys lying down after her meal and watching the sunlight spear through its leaves. The downside to the place, and the reason why nobody steals the space from her, is its proximity to the trash cans. She swallows the only edible portions of her meal and places the tray to the side.

She lies down to watch the leaves fluttering beneath a turquoise awning of sky when a half-empty bottle of mango smoothie misses the trash can, and its fruity spray arcs in the air. She feels the gooey wetness land on her shirt. She sits up and spies Rosalind beside the dumpster. "Oops," Rosalind says. She gives Abbey a smirk and saunters away.

Abbey's so busy yanking leaves off the tree in an attempt to erase the growing orange blob that she blocks out the jingle of keys approaching. A creaky voice says, "Here, miss." She looks up to see a grizzled Asian man offering her a cloth and a bottle of clear liquid. "Try to pat off the mess, and then spray some solution on it."

She spots a workbox filled with cleaning materials at his feet. "Okay, sir. Thanks." She takes his tools and drops her own useless, crumbled leaves to the ground.

"I'm Jack, the new janitor here." The old man points to his blue uniform with the cursive letters spiraling out his name.

"Nice to meet you, Jack." She hands back his supplies and eyes his clothes. "Wait a minute. Our janitors don't have names embroidered on their shirts."

He traces the letters. "I've had this work shirt for a long time." He picks up the smoothie bottle and tosses it into the trash can. "Have a nice day, miss."

Abbey hears a faraway giggle as Jack walks away from the tree. She catches a glimpse of curly blond hair out of the corner of her eye. Her cheeks feel like flames. *Rosalind saw me talking to the janitor. She'll never leave me alone now. Plus, he's Asian. What if she thinks we're related?* Abbey squares her shoulders and makes up her mind to never talk to the man again. *But he does do his job well.* She fingers the imperceptible yellow smudge on her shirt, a remnant of the original garish mango stain.

Jack

Jack fidgets in the principal's office. A call from Atchison Elementary's administrator on the third day of work bodes ill. Maureen Marshall, a petite brunette with wire-rimmed glasses, wears a haggard expression. To compensate for her tired-looking face, she applies heavy makeup, which seems clownish under the fluorescent lighting. She tends to favor cheerful cardigan and skirt sets, and today's version doesn't disappoint with its lemon drop yellow color.

"Your work has been...slower...than we're used to at this institution. I know your age must play a factor, Mr. Chen." Jack feels his heart speed up because he can't lose this job. Then he would have to return to Monroe Senior Home.

"I hired you as a special favor to my friend Fred at the community college." Maureen rubs her eyes. He spies etched lines spreading out at their corners.

"I admit that I'm more used to a college campus, but I tried getting a job with him there, Ms. Marshall. And even with all our years together and his position as the admissions director, he couldn't hire me."

Maureen puts her palms up. They're smooth and plump, unlike Jack's own wrinkled and sun-spotted hands. "Please address me as Principal Marshall. I do understand Fred's situation. I know that they don't have any spots available."

Jack takes a deep breath and says, "Principal Marshall, I love my work. Cleaning is the only job I've ever had, and I'm good at it. A year off can make anybody rusty, but I'll get up to speed again."

Maureen tucks a lock of brown hair behind her left ear. He notices the grey roots showing at her temple line. "Okay, I'll give you another chance. You keep the same non-union wages and clean overtime next week. Our annual spring dance is coming up, and I expect you to work hard to get our school ready in time. The gymnasium floors need to sparkle, and the decorations should be hung up four hours before the event."

"Of course, Principal Marshall." Jack scrambles out of her office before she can change her mind. He's never been reprimanded about his work before. A lump, the solid ache of shame, stays in his throat as he drives back to his run-down hotel.

*

Jack hand-washes his work shirt and hangs it up on the line above the bathtub. He likes the way his name looks spelled out, although the "J" is fading after fifty years of use. He landed his first job on the spot when he was sixteen. At the time, he didn't have an English name, so when he donned the discarded blue shirt from its previous owner, he took on his new identity.

His parents' original plan had been to focus on his schooling, the reason for their immigration to the United States from China. When he was sixteen, though, his parents died within a year of each other, and the dream perished. Despite his previous five years of living in America, his English remained guttural and accented when he interviewed for the cleaning position. Over the years as a janitor at the local college, though, he polished his English skills until he spoke the clear, crisp diction of an American-born. It also helped that he had enrolled in an ESL course at eighteen.

That class was where he met Fei. When she sat down next to him, he watched as the yellow taffeta skirt swirled around her shapely legs. He was hooked from that first skirt twirl and married her within the year. He felt that Fei's passionate and impulsive nature challenged him and rounded out the jagged edges in his personality.

Fei loved to "live life," and she enjoyed exploring new places. Since they were poor, the couple couldn't afford exotic vacations. Instead, they traveled to various free venues, like museums, outdoor concerts, and even newly opened stores. In fact, she invented their weekly tradition, "Dates on a Dollar." They enjoyed many star-gazing nights wrapped together in a blanket, sharing a peanut butter and jelly sandwich.

Jack turns away from his dripping shirt and starts brushing his teeth. From the tiny bathroom, he looks into the main room. It brings a wry smile to his lips. Maybe Fei would appreciate his current adventure on the cheap. The squalid room sits on the third floor of a shabby hotel, but he imagines that in its heyday the place advertised elegance. Half-ripped gold paper peppers the walls. A wire outline that once housed a crystal chandelier retains a solitary dusty light bulb. He picked his current residence, far into the urban camouflage of Los Angeles, when he sped away from Monroe Senior Home.

He pictures his suite at the senior home, decorated in purple—or at least that's what he thinks it is. He never remembers, since Fei was constantly repainting its walls. For a woman who cleaned houses for her job, it seems ironic that so many boxes of cutesy figurines and glittering costume jewelry cluttered their room. He can't imagine living again in the space without tripping on one of her memories.

The black rotary phone rings in his room. Dust clings to his fingers as he picks up the receiver. Jack hears a tinny voice down the line asking for "John." The extended version of his name. Have they found him already?

"Is this John Roberts?"

Wrong number. Relieved, Jack hangs up, making sure to disconnect the phone. He double-checks the deadbolt on the hotel door and pulls tight the flimsy curtains. He doesn't want anybody to find him here, especially the Monroe Senior Home administration. He left without informing them, sneaking out through their back door. He wonders if he breached his housing contract.

They had been lucky to live at the senior residence, a place filled with splendid furnishings and competent staff. Even from the beginning, though, he had felt uncomfortable there. Fei's old employer's estate had paid for their rent. The late Mrs. Timothy Evans had left a clause in her will providing for their retirement in the posh home, a reward for Fei's long years as her housekeeper.

Jack examines his own uncomfortable hotel bed now, a far cry from cleanliness. Its gritty sheets rake at his arms. He pulls the musty covers over his head. In the darkness, Fei's image remains, and he knows that another long night awaits him.

Silk

Silk sits knee-to-knee with her granddaughter. She stares into Abbey's eyes, focusing all her energy on creating the intimacy needed for the best language learning to occur. She insists on intense concentration, wanting the Taiwanese language to bind to her granddaughter's heart.

"Abbey, tshiamng li si to-tah e lang?" Silk says. *Abbey, may I ask where are you from?*

Her granddaughter responds with her own melodious Taiwanese words. "Guasi Bi-koktshut-si e Tai-bi-lang."*I am an American born Taiwanese-American.*

Silk peers over her granddaughter's head to track Lisa's progress; her daughter flips through the battered index cards in her hand. Silk sketched the images herself during Lisa's childhood. They're now faded and wrinkled after decades of use. Lisa looks at one and says, "Gu." Silk remembers sketching a black and white heifer to represent the word.

Her daughter looks at the next image. "Tsa-po."

Silk peeks at the flash card. "It's tsa-bó. Girl, not boy."

21

"Don't correct me, Ma." Lisa creases the battered cardboard square with her tight grip. "I know. I'm a girl, tsa-bó."

"No, you should say tsa-bó-lang because you're a woman now."

Silk sees the heat rise up in her daughter's cheeks, a quick flood of red. "Ugh. I can't wait for this verbal torture to end," Lisa says.

Silk's hand twitches in reflex, and she can almost feel the smack of her hand against Lisa's cheek once more.

At seven years old, Lisa had been practicing basic vocabulary then, too, and she kept confusing the genders. The lesson culminated in Lisa saying, "I'm a boy," with Silk laughing at the mix-up. A blushing Lisa scattered the cards back then and yelled, "I don't want to learn Chinese anymore!" Silk struck Lisa in the face—not because of her unwillingness to study, but because she had used the word "Chinese" instead of "Taiwanese."

She sees fear flit across Lisa's adult face, along with a widening of her chestnut eyes. She didn't know that Lisa still carried the childhood memory with her, too. Silk controls her trembling hand and excuses herself to use the restroom. She hurries into her master bedroom and locks the door.

She sits on the bed, smoothing the quilt in a repetitive motion, and peeks out the window. The sky seems shrouded in dark clouds, ready to rain. For a minute, she wonders if the gloom seeped out of her recurring nightmares to take physical form in the daylight.

Silk shakes her head to clear it. She needs to act normal for the routine get-together. Despite their turbulent history, her daughter Lisa never fails to visit on the designated Saturdays. *I named her well, and there's a lot of meaning behind a name.* Her daughter was named after this country. The letters squashed together resembled "USA" and reminded Silk of her start in this new land. She considers her granddaughter's name Abbey, rolls it around on her tongue, and spits it out in confusion.

Silk embraces her own name. She knows that most people picture silk as a delicate fabric and realizes that her name might suggest a weak constitution. However, she knows the true story behind the production of the smooth material. Raw silk from the cocoon changes to a fine fabric only by undergoing rough treatments through boiling water and harsh soap. She has already experienced her own transformative trial back in Taiwan.

She forces her mind to think about more peaceful memories from her home country, to dwell on Lu. Her husband's name also held extreme significance. He insisted everyone call him by his last name, Lu. His first name was Tarou ("eldest son"), a proper name during the Japanese reign over the island. Even as a young boy, though, Lu wanted to remain true to his Taiwanese roots and refused to acknowledge his Japanese-influenced first name.

Lu and Silk met at Yangmingshan Park by accident. She went to the park every year during the cherry blossom season and sat in one specific spot to admire the flowers. Her family usually accompanied her, but since she'd turned twenty-one that year, Silk insisted on going alone.

Her bench overlooked a nearby pond, and she could see the pastel petals reflected a thousand-fold on its glossy surface. That fateful day a strong voice broke into her reverie.

"You look so lovely. May I sketch you?"

She turned to see a young man, a couple years older than her, holding a pad and a pencil. "No." She returned to stare at the water, its reflection now revealing the stranger's shoulders hunched in sadness.

He reminded her of the type of cherry tree with clustered petals that droop down its frame. "*Shidarezakura*," she whispered.

"The weeping cherry tree," the young man translated.

"You know that term?" She looked up at him. "A fellow nature admirer. Okay, I give you permission to draw me. Is there anything special I should do?"

"Act natural, and keep sitting still."

She stayed rigid for ten minutes, but instead of concentrating on the natural beauty around her, her gaze flickered toward the young man. She liked his chestnut-colored eyes, his strong square jaw, and the cleft in his chin.

The stranger grinned. "All done."

She even liked his smile, the lopsided curve of one corner dipping a little more than the other. "May I see it?"

She peeked over his shoulder at the drawing, breathing in his heady soap scent. She could see the curve of her face on the paper: the familiar bent nose, the high cheekbones, and the narrow top lip. The proportions appeared a bit off (her eyes slightly wider apart than in real life) and the edges blurry, as though the artist seemed uncertain of his strokes. "Are you an art student?"

He laughed. "Thankfully not."

"What do you do then?"

The man ran his fingers through his choppy hair. "Nothing yet, but I studied chemistry. I just graduated from university in Kaohsiung, so I'm taking a little break. I couldn't resist seeing the cherry blossoms at this time of the year." He offered his hand to her. "My name's Lu."

She studied the chapped, rough lines sunken into his calloused skin. A fisherman by birth, she guessed, one of many from the port town. Yet he'd studied at a university and sketched in his spare time.

She took his hand and despite its rough appearance, it felt warm and smooth. Lu's contradictory qualities endeared him to her. "I'm Silk," she said.

"Silk, you can keep this." He offered the drawing to her.

"No, you take it, so you can remember me."

"I don't need it," Lu said. "I intend to draw many more pictures of you."

Lu kept his promise and ferried between Kaohsiung and Taipei to court her. They married within the year. Once Lu had secured a position as a lab assistant, she relocated down south.

She didn't keep in touch with her family because the custom was that when girls married out, they broke off contact, but she didn't mind the move. She knew that her presence burdened her parents too much. She remembered countless days eating the dregs of their rice pot, chewing the crusty vestiges that clung to its rusty sides. Plus, she liked the change of scenery. Sometimes she sat staring into the harbor, ignoring the speeding vessels and the scurrying people, and felt the same peace she always experienced at Yangmingshan Park.

Silk reaches for the memory box under her bed to revisit the tangible reminders of her marriage. A banging on the bedroom door interrupts her.

"Ma, are you okay?"

"I'll be out in a minute. I'll meet you in the kitchen." Silk pushes the box far into the back corner. She's never shown the container to Lisa, and she wants it to remain that way.

Lisa

Lisa watches as Abbey sets out the plates and utensils for their traditional post-language-lesson Taiwanese lunch. Her daughter places trivets down on the table to prevent heat damage. Lisa wonders where Abbey inherited her obedient nature. Not from Lisa, that's for sure.

Lisa never complained again after Ma slapped her in the face, but after the second grade, she pleaded to be bused out of Fairview to attend a Los Angeles school and "experience more culture." Her mother, busy with long hours at the vineyards, agreed to the request.

In reality, Lisa longed for the double freedom of being away from her mother and not needing to fulfill the intense academic rigor expected in Fairview. She maintained a C-grade average, with the occasional D tossed in; she figured that as long as she didn't fail, she was completing her education appropriately. As for culture, the only exposure to novel experiences was her use of marijuana.

A fellow student named Mary Jane introduced the drug to her in junior high. Lisa thought that kids with two-part names carried a bit of country about them; when the teacher called roll, she imagined Mary Jane as a girl in overalls with two fire-red plaits on the sides of her head. Mary Jane turned out different from her imaginings. She was Indian, with not one trace of whiteness about her. A true Native American, Mary Jane wove dream catchers in her spare time, as Lisa later found out. Her real name meant "fast salmon swimming up a rippling stream," but she chose Mary Jane as a tongue-in-cheek nickname. Lisa didn't know why Mary Jane approached her that first day of school, but they soon bonded behind the bleachers smoking weed.

From that day on, Lisa tried every substance under the sun but always reverted back to her first love. She stocked up on breath mints and air fresheners to cover the smell and practiced the lies she would tell her mother. Lisa was open to anything done to her own body, but she drew the line at practices that affected other people. She knew friends who invited her to shoplift, paint graffiti, and cause general mayhem, but she always refused.

When she graduated from high school, she took on odd jobs while staying rent-free with her mother. Lisa's laissez-faire attitude fit in well with the hippie era. In 1969, she hopped on a bus, and after two route changes, attended a Woodstock-wannabe concert. She met Paul her first night there. He was one of a handful of Asians, but he stood a head above the others, and she liked the way he tied his long hair back into a sleek ponytail. He offered her a drag of his joint, and she thought she had found true love. They spent a lot of that weekend enclosed in the backseat of his used Edsel.

Nine months later, Abbey arrived in her life. She's amazed that one weekend produced such a wonderful girl. Her daughter acts smart and responsible, and seems more of an adult than Lisa in every way.

"Are you listening to me, Lisa?" Her mother's voice breaks through, and Lisa's mind returns to the present. Her training chopsticks, the two poles tied together by a plastic connector to prevent slippage, sit untouched near her plate. Ma and Abbey, on the other hand, click-clack their way around the food dishes with a swivel of their fingers.

"Uh-huh." She nods her head to cover herself and glances at Abbey to gather a clue about the current topic of conversation. Her daughter's head lowers, and she looks preoccupied with her stinky tofu.

Ma clears her throat. "I asked, 'How is your job going?'"

"Well, it *went*." Lisa's laugh falls flat.

"Do you mean you lost another job?" Her mother counts off Lisa's previous job felonies on her fingers. "Dented a car's bumper, broke eight dozen eggs, swiped the tips from the share jar. What is it this time?"

Lisa crosses her arms against her chest. "I didn't do anything wrong." Except take an important file folder, but that was after being fired.

"What are you going to do?" Ma asks.

Lisa shrugs. The truth is she doesn't know. She wants to hide from reality. In fact, she's still holding onto the folder on the Chens, hoping that Monroe Senior Home hasn't noticed its absence. Most of the time, she ignores her faux pas. However, a part of her wants to claim that she found it somewhere, return it, and receive a reward. Maybe they would even offer her old job back, but the monotonous work would bore her.

She feels unclear about what occupation would really fit her best.

"I'll give you three days. Then I'll call up Gus," Ma says.

"No, Ma, I'll find something." There's no way she's working for Gus alongside her mother. Her mother has worked at Lincoln Vineyards for thirty years now, one of her first jobs after immigrating to the United States. Her mother receives a fancy bottle every year she works at the vineyard. She even installed a bonafide wine closet to keep them organized in a wooden rack behind glass doors.

Her mother dragged her into the vineyards once during Lisa's childhood. She hated everything about it. She detested the blazing sun, the dirt on her palms, the grime on her clothes, and the ache of her fingers afterwards. Her mother, on the other hand, hummed through the whole experience. Her mother loves manual labor; the dirtier, the better. Lisa can't understand it.

Lisa makes a show of looking at the clock. It reminds her of past schooldays, counting the seconds and waiting for dismissal time. Release from her mother arrives at noon. She watches the hands collapse on top of one another. "It's time to go home, Abbey." She gathers her purse. "Thank you for having us over, Ma."

"Thank you, Ah-Mah." Abbey chimes her goodbye using the proper, respectful title. She twists a lock of hair around her forefinger. "Before we leave, though, it's been three months. May I have another fact, please?"

Lisa notices her mother's slight pause before she says, "Fisherman hands."

Abbey

"3. Fisherman hands." Abbey reviews the latest entry on her list, received from Ah-Mah two days ago at lunch. The other two read: "1.Used last name only, 2. From Kaohsiung." She records the phrases in a notebook labeled "Genealogy," from a recent school project. Despite the end of the assignment, she still carries it around and likes to look over her grandfather's information.

For the class assignment, the teacher had required her students to draw their family tree. Abbey couldn't list too many names. She didn't have a collection of history like some of the other kids who could trace their roots to the Pilgrims. She was also the only one who appeared descended from a single line of women. The male side of the tree contained her grandfather's surname and her father's first name, with no other information accompanying them. The blank spaces looked kind of funny, but she hadn't felt like laughing; she had felt like crying during her presentation. She realized that she didn't know anything about the men in her family.

She didn't care much about her father. She knew that Paul had served basically as a sperm donor. Her mom had told her about the accidental pregnancy.

On the other hand, Abbey did want to know more about her mysterious Ah-Gung ("grandfather" in Taiwanese). He must have been a decent man, since Ah-Mah had married him, but nobody gave her any specific details about his life or his death.

She couldn't gather any info from her mom. Her mom didn't know anything about him except that he had died in Taiwan. Mom claimed that it was never a subject of conversation between her and Ah-Mah. Her mom had no memory of the man and couldn't be bothered to investigate.

"Don't you ever wonder about him?" Abbey once asked.

Her mom shook her head.

"Well, do you have a photo of him, at least?"

"No. I never saw any even while I was growing up." She shrugged. "They're probably all in Taiwan."

After that unenlightening conversation, Abbey had approached her grandmother. Her original idea involved conducting a thorough interview with Ah-Mah. She had written down pages of questions to ask, but her grandmother refused to answer a single one. Finally, Abbey finagled a deal—if she mastered all her Taiwanese phrases on each Saturday visit for three months straight, she could get one detail about her grandfather. Receiving a factoid every quarter of the year meant that it would take decades before she would learn anything substantial about her Ah-Gung.

Abbey closes her notebook and sighs. She looks around the empty campus. It's a half-day at school today because of teacher in-service. She's already completed all of tonight's assignments, but her mom still hasn't arrived. She bets her mom doesn't even remember the shortened day, even though she insisted on picking Abbey up in Ah-Mah's car.

Mom borrowed the car from Ah-Mah the other day to go grocery shopping because she wanted to try out some gourmet recipes from the newspaper. Her mom gets in these domestic moods when she's in between jobs. The only reason they can afford the fancy ingredients is because Ah-Mah slips her mom a red envelope with "lucky" money during every monthly visit. Embarrassed, Abbey pretends not to notice each time.

Abbey checks her wristwatch. She can't take the Fairview Express home. The next bus arrives in another hour, and all the other students get picked up, so there's no school bus to take her home, only public transportation. She digs in her pocket for some spare change. She'll need to use the pay phone to call her mom.

As she moves down the hallway, she glances at the bulletin board on the wall. She's still tied with Ara for the number one spot in her grade. Half covering the list, an orange flyer announces the spring dance scheduled for this evening. It's no wonder that she hasn't heard about the event. No one's asked her to it. Nobody would, so she never pays attention to the social events held at Atchison Elementary.

She groans. The sole pay phone at school is located in the gym where the dance will be held. She doesn't need to be reminded of her loser status. The building lies separate from the rest of the school, but its size takes up a quarter of the Atchison Elementary compound.

She enters the polished floor of the structure and notices the decorations inside. Cheerful balloons in lime and lemon float along the ceiling. The scent of jasmine wafts in the air.

She places two dimes in the pay phone's slot. The line rings five times before her mom picks up, and she sounds like she's just woken up. Her mom curses, promising to come right away.

After Abbey replaces the receiver, she hears giggling. She turns around and sees Rosalind and a couple of groupies enter. They make their way to the corner of the gym where a huge backdrop stands. Two tall foliaged trees are knotted together by their branches. Brilliant flowers dance across the entwined natural bridge. Professional photographers will capture beautiful couples and gaggles of best friends in front of the display tonight.

Rosalind puts her hands in front of her, as though framing the scene. She tilts her head to one side. "I'm going to buy a lavender dress to match the color scheme."

The other girls squeal their approval, and they make plans to head to the mall.

Abbey rolls her eyes. She can't imagine having so much money that she'd buy a new dress for every dance. She watches Rosalind and her crew hurry out in excitement. Abbey follows behind unnoticed. She sees Rosalind bump into a ladder Abbey's sure wasn't there before.

She sees Rosalind rub her shoulder in irritation. When Abbey looks at the ladder's top rung, she finds the old Asian janitor up there plastering a banner above the archway that reads, "Love Blossoms At The Spring Dance." She watches in horror as time slows down and the old man totters. He hits the ground, and she hears the loud snap of bone against concrete.

Jack

A sharp pain sears through Jack's body. He remembers falling from the ladder but nothing afterwards. No, that's not right. His mind flashes back to a face—the image of a kitchen helper from Monroe Senior Home bent over him. What does she have to do with Atchison Elementary? He ponders this curious picture. Is he suffering from brain damage? Or maybe he's dead. That brings a smile to his face. Perhaps he would see Fei.

The day his wife died, they were taking a joyride in his Rambler, which he often did to get out of Monroe Senior Home. Though he was proud that he could still drive, they didn't venture far. They would stop for a cup of coffee nearby or cruise downtown and return.

He remembered that she had rolled down the window on the passenger side. She liked putting her hand out and mimicking waves in the rushing air; sometimes she urged him to do the same. One minute her face lifted up toward the sun with a huge smile. The next moment, she shook all over and slumped down in her seat.

His body spasms with the memory, and he winces. No, he must be alive. He clearly feels the pain concentrated in his right leg. He opens his eyes to blank white walls. The smell of antiseptic burns his nose. A young man in doctor's attire walks into Jack's hospital room as if on cue. He appears adolescent in Jack's eyes; not a trace of five o'clock shadow touches the youngster's face. Jack looks around the room in search of a senior doctor when the man speaks.

"Mr. Chen? I'm Dr. Salzman. It looks like you've had a nasty femur fracture on your right leg." The doctor holds out an X-ray for Jack to examine.

Jack squints at it. "What's that supposed to tell me?"

Dr. Salzman takes out his ballpoint pen and taps several locations. "This is your hip. Here is your knee. Between them, you can see the complete break that occurred from your fall."

"That doesn't look good."

"No, it's not. We'll have to operate, and I'd like to schedule the surgery for tomorrow morning."

"That soon?"

"It would be the best choice for you."

Jack eyes the young doctor with distrust but nods his head in assent after a moment. The doctor takes out a bunch of forms and places them on the bedside table. "Please sign these."

Jack fills out the paperwork. As he finishes, he asks, "How did I even get here?"

"You don't remember? A mother from the elementary school where you work drove you here. Do you have any other questions?"

Jack hesitates before he asks, but he feels worried. After all, he's only been in the hospital once in his life, as a child to get his tonsils out. "Dr. Salzman, you're not one of those student doctors, are you?"

The doctor bristles. "No, I'm not." He closes the chart with a snap and adjusts the morphine setting. "Good day, Mr. Chen."

Jack succumbs to the quick numbness that pervades his body.

When he opens his eyes, he sees a Chinese mother and daughter sitting two feet away from his bed. He recognizes the woman's high cheekbones and warm chestnut eyes. "You're from Monroe Senior Home." *I'm not going crazy.* A second later, he panics. "How did you find me?"

"I don't work at the home any longer." The woman blushes a deep ruddy color. "I used to be there as a kitchen helper, but there were some cutbacks. My name's Lisa, and this is my daughter Abbey."

"Hello." The girl raises her head, then drops it down again. She tries to cover her face with a layer of ebony hair, but he manages to catch a glimpse of its triangle shape and sallow complexion. He realizes that it's the girl he's seen eating alone by the trash cans at Atchison Elementary.

He clears his throat. "Thank you for bringing me to the hospital, Lisa."

"It's no problem at all," Lisa says. "Abbey witnessed the whole terrible incident. I arrived right after the ordeal, and we rushed you here. How are you feeling?"

"Fair, I guess. I'm supposed to go into the operating room tomorrow. After that, who knows how long it'll take to heal?"

"Good luck with your surgery." Lisa writes down her phone number. "If you need anything, feel free to call me."

"Thanks again, but I should be fine."

They exit the room after bidding him farewell, leaving him to count down the hours before his surgery.

*

His operation runs smoothly. The bone appears re-aligned, and the metal plate and screws seem positioned in the right place. He feels buoyed up after the surgery. He could get around with a brace on his leg, and it shouldn't take too long to recover. Besides, he injured something trivial, not like his right hand, which he uses all the time. He attempts to swing himself out of the hospital bed and collapses in agony. Maybe he's misjudged his ability.

He wants to go home, though. He sighs, remembering that his car remains parked at Atchison Elementary. He also recalls that he does have a dominant *right leg* when it comes to driving. Determined, though, he signals for a nurse.

"I want to be discharged," he says.

She looks through the paperwork. "You're all set, Mr. Chen. You read the fine print, right? In your condition, someone needs to pick you up and take you home. I know it won't be a problem for a sweet old man like you."

"Of course it won't," he says. The nurse made a mistake, though, because he has no Fei, no friend, and no family member, to help him. He grits his teeth and locates the number for the taxicab service in his wallet. When he arrives home, he slumps down in his chair.

Poor health scares him. He played rough in his younger days but came back with nothing more than minor scratches. He's never broken a bone in his body before. He used to attribute it to a superior build, but now he deems it sheer luck.

He's accustomed to his body responding to his mind's commands. Part of the reason why he loves being a janitor comes from his enjoyment of moving around to clean and fix things. He groans. He won't be able to work for a long time; he practically crawls to move around the room. *At this rate, I'll need a wheelchair to get around.*

He feels his bladder complain, and he moves at a snail's pace to arrive at the toilet. He props up the lid, sweat forming under his armpits. He stands, but his weak leg trembles under his body's weight. Defeated, he snaps the seat back down. He can't even piss standing up anymore. When he's done, he inches back to the bed and searches for Lisa's phone number.

Lisa

Lisa doesn't know why she offered to help Mr. Chen because she has no experience in caretaking. She should just tell Tina the receptionist at the senior home his whereabouts. The Monroe Senior Home staff will take good care of him. Maybe there would even be a reward. However, she resists telling them because, based on the scared look she'd seen on Mr. Chen's face, she knows that he doesn't want to be found.

She worries about the old, fragile gentleman recovering on his own. So when Mr. Chen calls and asks for her help, she jumps at the chance. At his new residence, it takes a few minutes before he answers her knock. When the door opens, she sees him leaning against the jamb, panting from the exertion of letting her in.

She's used to seeing a glowing Mr. Chen at Monroe Senior Home, not this broken man in his run-down hotel room. She knows that he has no children and no nearby relatives from reading his file. She can't imagine being so alone; she knows that her mother and Abbey will always take care of her.

Mr. Chen's hands cover his face, and something about the gesture tugs at her heart. His hands look rough and calloused. They strike her as testimonies of hardship, like a fisherman's hands.

She ponders over what her mother told Abbey at the last family lunch. She can't believe she doesn't know something so simple about her father, the tough texture of his hands. Then again, they didn't talk much about her father in the past. Her mother worked all the time when Lisa was younger, and Lisa had spent her days partying in a substance-induced haze. *If you can't even talk to the living, then how can you connect with the dead?*

Mr. Chen lifts up his head slowly and meets Lisa's eyes. "I could use a little help, but I won't be able to pay you," he says.

"That doesn't matter. What do you need, Mr. Chen?"

"Please, call me Jack." He runs one hand through his wispy grey hair. "First, I need my car back."

"Sure, Jack." She'll need to leave her mother's car here and retrieve it later once she drops off his vehicle. "I'll go to the school right now. They're probably wondering how you're doing, anyway."

"Thanks." He hands the keys to Lisa. "It's an old blue Rambler. It'll be easy to spot in the line-up of sports cars."

His light joking lifts up her spirit as she exits his room. He must be feeling better. She doesn't even mind the clunky Fairview Express ride to the school.

*

Lisa arrives at Atchison Elementary and spots the Rambler right away. She's about to open the car door when the principal shows up in a tangerine orange cardigan and skirt set. "I'm so sorry to hear about Jack's accident. How is he doing?"

"He has a broken leg, but is fine otherwise. Of course, he'd like to return to work as soon as possible," Lisa says.

Maureen waves the comment away. "Oh, Jack shouldn't worry about that. Tell him to take all the time he needs to heal properly. We've already hired a temporary replacement for him. Could you please inform him that his short-term disability benefits will start soon? The check should arrive in the mail anytime now."

Maureen looks at Lisa. "I assume that you're a relative?"

Lisa's not surprised the principal doesn't recognize her as Abbey's mom, since she hasn't attended many school events. She plays along with the woman's assumption. "Yes, I'm his daughter."

"Indeed, I can see the family resemblance." Maureen hands over an envelope with Jack's name on it to Lisa. "Rosalind Lucent informed her family of the accident, and they'd like to financially assist with Jack's healing process."

"That's very... kind of them," Lisa says. She heard Abbey's account of Jack's "accident," how Rosalind bumped into his ladder and caused him to fall. Rosalind's mother, Crystal Lucent, a top Fairview lawyer, would want to avoid a lawsuit. "I'll be sure that Jack gets the money."

Lisa turns to leave, but Maureen clears her throat. "You know, we've done all we can to aid in this unfortunate matter."

Lisa senses Maureen's worry about any negative impact on the school from the incident. "I'll inform Jack about your concern," she says. Lisa's statement could refer to the principal's worry about Jack's condition or the school's reputation. In any case, Maureen looks relieved and turns to go.

On the way back to Jack's hotel, Lisa picks up some fast food. She doesn't know when he's eaten last. His eyes mist up with gratitude when he sees the meal.

To her surprise, she enjoys his dependence on her. She likes the feeling of being needed. It's a novel situation for her. Her mother never required a child's help, and Abbey acted like an adult almost from birth. Lisa and Jack eat together, perched on his mattress, in harmony. Oily wrappers litter the scratchy bedspread, and a companionable silence fills the air, broken only by the occasional lick of fingers.

"You're like the daughter I never had," he says.

She stops in mid-bite. "It's funny that you would say that. Principal Marshall assumed that I was your daughter today. I didn't bother contradicting her, and she gave me this." Lisa pulls out the sealed envelope from the Lucent family and hands it over to him.

When he opens it up, he whistles. "You're still looking for a full-time job, right? How would you like to be my paid caregiver?"

She bites her lip. "Are you sure you don't want to return to Monroe Senior Home? The medical staff there has better credentials than me."

He shivers. "No, I can't imagine going back right now. My wife just passed away, and there would be too many memories of her. I don't know if I'll ever go back."

She places a gentle hand on his shoulder. "I would love to be your caregiver then, and I promise not to tell Monroe Senior Home where you are," she says. "I feel guilty about lying to Principal Marshall, though."

He shakes his head and places his rough hand on her back. "I would be proud to have you as a daughter."

An inner wall she didn't know about collapses inside her heart. This kind, sweet man could be the dad she never had. She indulges in the fantasy of a real, complete family at the dinner table. She pictures succulent seafood dishes, a signature Taiwanese spread, fanned across expensive porcelain plates. She imagines the smiling faces of Jack, her mother, and Abbey seated around a feast. It could happen. Jack needs a loving family to surround him, and Lisa knows that her mother would respect a fellow manual worker. Above all, Abbey could find the grandfather figure that she's been seeking.

Silk

Silk stares at the strange man across the table and remembers how she landed in this predicament. Her daughter had called out of the blue and said:

"Guess what, Ma? I have a job now."

"Good for you, Lisa."

"I help this nice old man. I'd really like you to meet him."

"But I've never met any of your employers before."

"This is different, Ma. I work only for him. The man's lost his wife and has no family here. Please do this favor for me."

Lisa's pleading resulted in this contrived meeting at Silk's house. Silk picks at the greasy pizza slice in front of her. Her daughter offered to provide the meal, unfortunately, in gratitude for her acceptance. Silk sees her granddaughter use her napkin to blot off the piles of oil on the cheese.

However, the newcomer, Jack Chen, inhales the pizza. Silk observes a trail of tomato sauce sliding down his chin. He's a man who's aged hard. She sees the wrinkles etched deep into his skin, like fissures in a rock. His tanned skin looks like layered sandstone, and his yellowed teeth hint at filth.

She realizes that she's staring and decides to start a conversation to ensure a bearable meal. "Mr. Chen," she says.

"Call me Jack."

"Mr. Chen. What did you do before you retired?"

"I've always been a janitor, and I'm still working at Atchison Elementary now." Interesting. She assumed he'd stopped working at his advanced age. She does admire people who keep themselves busy even as they grow old. Plus, he seems to respect the hands-on labor that she values.

"Lisa told you about the accident, right?" Jack asks.

She gives Lisa a penetrating look, and the story falls from her daughter's lips. Silk issues sympathetic murmurs when she hears about Jack's fall and his leg fracture. She wants to know more about this resilient man, so she asks him about his background.

He launches into a story about his English name—and her shoulders stiffen. He picked his name by happenstance? Names define a person's path, and he chose his by wearing someone's discarded old shirt? She sees Lisa encouraging the old man with her nods. She knows that her daughter can get carried away by her fantasies and probably imagines them all together for the holidays. Silk sighs. She'll have to find out more information about this new infatuation of Lisa's. She decides to explore Jack's history. She can learn a lot about somebody from their past.

"Mr. Chen, where are you from?" she asks.

"I'm from mainland China, but that was a long time ago, although I still understand the language. I pretty much grew up in the U.S. What about you, Silk?"

"I'm from Taiwan."

He flashes his canary teeth. "We're the same, then, both Chinese."

With one word, the images of the Chinese Kuomintang soldiers from the massacre assault her. She sees the crispness of the men's high-collar military shirts, the glare of their helmets' sun symbol, and the thrust of their menacing rifles. All their seeming trappings of order and authority disappeared with every wail of a woman raped. Lucky for her, she escaped that terror by hiding in the locked confines of her home. The one or two times a soldier found her, he left in disgust when he saw her ripe belly.

She stares Jack down. *"We are not the same."* She speaks the words to him in Mandarin, not wanting her daughter and granddaughter to understand.

She notices the sudden lull in eating and feels the weight of Lisa's and Abbey's stares, but the memory flashes continue. She recalls the piles of detached heads littering her homeland, evidence of the soldiers' brutality. *"Chinese and Taiwanese people are not the same. If you can't understand that, then you need to get out of my house."*

He attempts to apologize, but she cuts him off. She thrusts her index finger out and points to the front door. Her daughter and granddaughter both wear bewildered expressions on their faces. Even though Lisa doesn't know Chinese, her daughter can understand body language. Lisa scrambles to grab Jack's manual wheelchair, but Silk stops her. "I need to talk with you in the kitchen first."

Behind the closed door, she issues a command to Lisa. "Never bring that man here again."

"What are you talking about, Ma? Jack's like a father to me."

"You don't know a single thing. He's nothing like your father."

"I like helping him, Ma, and Jack's done nothing wrong. You're the one who's rude, and I don't know why." Lisa narrows her eyes. "Is this because of a stupid political stance?"

Silk cares little for the battle of political right. She doesn't concern herself with the legal issues surrounding Taiwan standing as its own nation rather than as a snippet of China. Jack's ignorance itself riles her up, his attitude that Chinese equals Taiwanese. That absolutist viewpoint leads to trouble. It's a belief which, magnified a thousand times, results in silencing people who disagree with the notion, like during Taiwan's massacre in 1947.

That blindness can take away a beloved husband's life, her precious Lu, and create a lifetime of emptiness. Silk refuses to tell Lisa, though. Her daughter, unaware of how her father died, needs to stay innocent. She doesn't need to be plagued by the same nightmare images that haunt Silk. She must protect her daughter from this stranger and his dangerous beliefs. "I don't want you working for that man," Silk says. "Quit the job, or I'll disown you."

"I'm not going to leave him helpless for no solid reason," Lisa says and bangs the kitchen door on her way out. Silk can hear Lisa calling out to Abbey to put on her shoes to leave. She opens the door to find her daughter wheeling Jack out of the house, with Abbey trailing behind them. She wants to call Lisa back, but what would she say? She can't and won't unearth a lifetime of hidden secrets.

Abbey

Abbey hates war within the family, and she despises her role between her mom and her grandmother. They refuse to talk to one another and send her as a go-between to relay any essential messages between them. Then, at other times, they see her as a child and ignore her altogether during this feud. She tries to bridge the gap by tempting both sides to reconvene (more Taiwanese lessons for Ah-Mah, home-cooked meals for Mom) but she's told "to stay out of it." She can't, though, not when she's the messenger.

On top of the family drama, she's been pulled into the life of the ancient janitor from her school. She likes being dropped off and picked up in a car by her mom, courtesy of old Mr. Chen's clunker, but it requires her tagging along on all of his errands as well. She once waded through cramped aisles of medical equipment, too narrow for her mom to fit through, to get to the pharmacy and hand over a doctor's prescription. The mystery note read, "HHU." When Abbey received the item, she looked at the misshapen plastic bottle in confusion. She must have stood too long at the counter because the pharmacist dismissed her by saying, "Good luck with that hand held urinal!" She almost dropped the thing in disgust.

Her mom calls Abbey her "special helper" now. Abbey provides an extra pair of hands to pick up groceries or toiletries at the store. She can unfold and fold up the wheelchair in a flash. She's become so connected to the old man's life that the receptionist at his dingy hotel hands her his mail. She thinks her mom sees this connection and incorrectly labels it as intimacy.

Now, as her mom drops her off at school, Jack Chen sits on the passenger's side. Mom requests that Abbey say, "Have a good day, Grandpa" as Abbey heads out the door. Abbey doesn't want to, but she knows that the first period bell will ring in a minute, so she parrots the words without emotion.

As she enters school, Abbey sees Rosalind lingering on the front steps chatting with her girlfriends.

"Hey Abbey," Rosalind says. "I didn't realize the janitor's related to you."

"No, no." Abbey holds up her hands in protest. "I hardly know the man. It's our nickname for him."

"Really? I don't call every elderly man on my street 'Grandpa.'" Rosalind's steel blue eyes challenge her.

"In our culture, it's a sign of respect to be called by a family title," Abbey says. "It's like calling older people 'aunties' and 'uncles' to honor them."

"If you don't know him that well, then how come he was in your car?" Rosalind asks. She flips her hair and walks away from Abbey without looking back.

By noon, everyone at school's heard about Abbey's comment. They all assume Jack Chen's her real grandpa. Students give her odd looks and snickers. She isn't just the poor girl who eats subsidized lunches by herself anymore; she's now the girl who's related to the guy who scrubs their toilets. Her teachers are worse—they act sympathetic and ask after the old man's health. Some even offer extensions on her assignments during this "rough time," although she refuses any displays of assistance.

She walks into Mr. Malone's classroom and waits for his reaction. To her relief, he doesn't seem to care, and for once, she has a reason besides Ara to enjoy math class.

She watches Mr. Malone's bald head as he moves about the room. She listens as he draws up an equation on the blackboard and solves it. Then he swivels around and claps his chalky hands once. "Pop quiz," he says with glee.

A collection of groans rise in the air while she hides a secret smile. She can lose herself in the numbers. She whizzes through the work and double-checks her answers. Her sheet's done in ten minutes' time.

Her stomach turns over as she imagines herself submitting the work. She knows that when she approaches the wire basket to hand in the paper, the other students will glance up and murmur beneath their breath. She's used to the snide looks from her classmates because of her obvious outsider Asian appearance, but not because of fake family connections.

Today, though, she's an outcast because of her "blood tie" to the old janitor. She starts to stand, but notices Ara glance at her and mumble, "She's done already? I wish she'd stop messing the grading curve and give everybody a break for once."

She feels a flush of embarrassment spread through her body. She didn't realize that the other kids had an issue with her grades. True, she always got the top marks in Mr. Malone's class. Everybody knew it, too, since he read the test grades out loud, but she competed against herself during every test. She sought to challenge her mind and tackle the math problems to the best of her ability.

Since Mr. Malone graded on a curve, though, everyone else's ranking must depend on her score. In an already competitive school, maybe her perfect math tests created even more stress and tension for others. She sits back down and thinks of a way to redeem herself.

She looks at her paper and picks several exercises, then writes in minor errors that alter their answers. She leaves one problem blank. Abbey waits until the last minute to turn in her work, when Mr. Malone says, "Pencils down!"

She walks, dragging her feet, to drop her exam in the full wire basket. She sees Ara staring at her in surprise. He, of course, finished long before. She feels a mixture of guilt and pleasure under his extended gaze.

Jack

Jack knows that he introduced a wedge into the Lu family. Although Lisa supports him, he feels unnerved at being kicked out of Silk's home. He likes to think of himself as a knowledgeable person despite his lack of a formal education. In fact, he picked up many tidbits of information while working at the local college. He didn't mean to offend Silk. He wanted to establish a common ground and recognize the Chinese heritage underlying Taiwan's people.

He recalls that the vast majority of Taiwanese citizens descend from the Han Chinese, who immigrated in the 18th century or arrived in a massive wave after World War II. He thinks about the mainland Chinese face, fair and delicate, and he compares it to the darker, flat-nosed appearance of Taiwan's indigenous people. *Lisa resembles the former. After all, most Taiwanese are not the true native island aboriginals.*

He wonders how to make amends. He prides himself on his easygoing nature and hates making waves. He tried to apologize numerous times after the occasion, to no avail. He obtained

Silk's phone number and left a dozen voice messages. He even ordered a bouquet of yellow roses sent to the home to symbolize his intended friendship. The florist told him that the flowers were refused at the doorstep.

He knows that Silk's not the only member of the Lu family disturbed by his presence. The girl Abbey doesn't like him, although she assists him at her mother's behest. He can read meaning into the silence and stiffness of the girl's attitude. Maybe if Fei and he had raised any children, he could connect with the girl better...

They tried so long to have children. In their quest, they hunted down auspicious dates, tried fertility diets, and embraced new maneuvers in bed. After an exhausting fifteen years, Fei finally found out that she was expecting. She surprised him with the news by using one of their Christmas traditions.

They didn't have much money, so instead of buying Christmas presents for each other, they substituted stocking stuffers. She enjoyed delicate scented soaps with fruit segments, specks of cinnamon, and so forth. He got itchy woolen socks, first as a joke, and then as a standing ritual. He didn't mind because he suffered a lot of wear and tear in his socks from walking around the college grounds attending to his duties.

As a Christmas custom, his wife changed the appearance of their stockings every year. She would add a tiny alteration in the middle of the night and see if Jack noticed in the morning. Over the years, their plain red stockings overflowed with buttons, ribbons, glitter, and bells.

On the 15th year of their marriage, the surprise came not from his own stocking, but through the additional tiny sock snuggled between the two big ones labeled "Jack" and "Fei."

After telling him about the pregnancy, Fei glowed with an inner joy. She hummed and waltzed around their apartment.

After three days, her happiness crashed. He found her in the corner of their bathroom, curled in a fetal position, rocking on her heels and moaning.

She sobbed, the tears puddling on the floor. "I lost her."

He went over and enveloped her fragile, trembling body with his long arms. "Do you mean—"

"Yes, our daughter's gone." His wife was convinced the baby would be a girl.

"It's okay," he said. He patted her shoulder.

"Don't belittle our child like that! You say that whenever I lose my keys. She's not a hunk of metal."

"I didn't mean it that way. Besides, maybe this is for the best."

"For whom?" She wept into her hands, and he noticed the blood marks on her fingers.

"We need to get you to the emergency room," he said.

"No, I can't leave her here."

She refused to move and at the end of the day, he had to pry the blood-stained panties from between her clenched fingers.

They never experienced another close call after that. An understanding grew between Jack and Fei that they would always be alone. Therefore, it surprises him now that he has a pre-made daughter in Lisa. He sees her as a sort of Athena, sprouting full-formed into his life. He calls Lisa a blessing long-postponed, and he craves any attention from her.

He enjoys her physical contact the most: the arms of support, the hugs, and the pecks on his wrinkled cheek. He delights in the unintentional connections that spill out from her. On reflex, she brushes crumbs off his stubbly chin and smoothes down his unruly white hairs.

Other people don't touch him anymore. He receives no handshakes, no pats on the back, nothing. He wonders when it happened, when he got so old that people avoid looking at him. He even likes it when Lisa rests her palm on his wheelchair while waiting for the elevator. The device seems almost an extension of his physical body nowadays.

Except that he doesn't need it. After Lisa paid a visit to the hospital to work out the insurance tangles, he received paid-for in-home physical therapy. Those were tough sessions, but he pushed through with his usual willpower. Lisa ran errands or took personal time during those hours because he had insisted on it. As a result, she didn't realize the amazing developments he'd achieved.

After the series of visits finished, Jack remained in his wheelchair on purpose. Lisa posted the physical therapy instructions all over his tiny room. She even tried to assist him once or twice with some of the exercises. "You don't want to stay in this ugly thing forever," she says every time she sees him in the wheelchair.

Unknown to her, though, he completes his exercises with vigor in her off-hours. He can even glide around with a walker now, and he doesn't doubt that he can transition to a single-point cane soon. However, he stays in the wheelchair whenever she's around.

Any recovery means decreased doting and affection from her. Healing would result in less overall time with her. It all translates to losing her, and he can't sever a tie to the only daughter he's ever had.

Lisa

Lisa's uncertain how long the division between her mother and her will last. Both refer to themselves as "ice queens" when angered. In Lisa's younger years, her mother not only put up a wall of silence, she even avoided entering any room Lisa inhabited.

Lisa, on the other hand, likes to pretend that a dispute's not happening. She imagines herself on an extended vacation. In the past, she's the one to give in, but she plans on holding out this time. Ma's approval, so important during her childhood, no longer applies to Lisa.

Sometimes, though, Lisa wishes they could connect as two mature adults. Each time she reached major milestones in her life, Lisa thought their relationship would change. She believed it when she graduated from high school, when she landed her first full-time job, and when she delivered Abbey into the world. She imagined that something magical would occur, and the two of them would finally be able to share heart-to-heart. Of course, that never happened.

On the other hand, Jack has allowed Lisa into his world. He's told her about his struggle growing up in between cultures, having emigrated to the U.S. so young. He's discussed his deep devotion to his deceased wife. And he's spoken a lot about his former work. Every day, she receives another anecdote from his days at the community college.

Today's story revolves around somebody who tried to make Jack a plate of chocolate chip cookies from scratch to thank him for his work. However, the student didn't add in eggs and butter and burnt the whole batch. They ended up tossing the hard wafers around as mini Frisbees on the green lawn.

She can tell that Jack misses his work. It must be frustrating for him to be stuck in a wheelchair, but his confined condition's starting to grate on her nerves, too. It's not just the manual exertion that annoys her. Of course, she doesn't like the constant shuffling in and out of the car, not to mention the folding and unfolding of the wheelchair.

Little things irritate her as well. She hates the scent of his deodorant; he applies the stick with liberal strokes because he dislikes showering even with the new bath chair and grab bar. She gets aggravated by the extensive time it takes to use a ramp instead of moving straight up the stairs. When she's at a store, she frowns at the other people who walk through the doors without needing to account for the dimensions of a wheelchair.

She's glad for the break she received when the physical therapist made home visits to Jack. The first few sessions, she indulged herself. She splurged on a massage and a manicure. In time, though, she realized that she yearned for the more simple pleasures, like relaxing with a cup of coffee without guilt.

What with shuttling both Abbey and Jack to and fro, Lisa feels like she's turned into a chauffeur. At least, Jack responds with gratitude to her gestures. Abbey's been distancing herself. Lisa knows that her daughter feels frustrated about not visiting Ma more often because of the current conflict.

It's the first Saturday of the month, and she finds Abbey sulking in their apartment.

"I don't know why I can't visit Ah-Mah," Abbey says.

Lisa glares at her daughter. "You know why. She's being so mean to Jack."

"I can see why she's angry with him. Remember, during the meal Jack referred to her as Chinese instead of Taiwanese? Even though Taiwan's a stone's throw away from China, it's still a different landmass, a separate country."

"What's wrong with mixing the words 'Chinese' and 'Taiwanese'?" Lisa shakes her head. "Ma has to get over that national identity obsession. She's got Chinese roots herself." Ma had told her that her ancestors had moved to Taiwan a long time ago, around 1644, with the Manchu invasion of China.

"I get what Ah-Mah's thinking," Abbey says. "Sometimes I feel so Taiwanese when I speak the language."

Lisa disagrees with her daughter. No matter how many times she practices the words, she fumbles at the foreign-sounding language. Born and raised in the U.S., Lisa labels herself a pure American, no hyphenated identity for her. "Ma's still not acting very nice. After all, Jack's tried to apologize to her so many times."

"Ah-Mah has strong opinions," Abbey says. "Plus, I still don't know why I can't visit Ah-Mah by myself. I can use public transportation to get there. I ride the bus all the time to school."

"That's beside the point," Lisa says. "Whose side are you on, anyway?"

"Are there supposed to be sides?" Abbey bends a school notebook marked "Genealogy" into a spiral with a sharp twist of her arms.

Lisa sees Abbey carry the thing everywhere. Sometimes her daughter focuses on her schoolwork too much. In the past few weeks, though, Lisa has spotted a change in Abbey's behavior. Her daughter seems to be talking more to the other kids at school. In fact, Abbey's been hanging out with Rosalind Lucent, and she's been coming home in new clothes and fancy makeup. Before, Abbey hadn't expressed any interest in her outer appearance, but Lisa supposes it's all a part of growing up. She's sad to lose her little girl, but she's excited that Abbey's finally making friends at school. Besides, it'll take her daughter's mind off the battlefront at home.

Silk

I'm right, and she's wrong. Lisa has been spoiled by growing up in the United States. She doesn't understand her Taiwanese roots. Silk shakes her head in exasperation. Based on pure facts, she's shocked that Lisa could defend Jack Chen and his wrong viewpoint equating Chinese and Taiwanese people. The difference between the two cultures is quite clear. In fact, the two countries remain separate geographic entities, divided by the Taiwan Strait. Despite the island's small size, Taiwan's heritage involves influences from the Native Aborigines, Dutch, Spanish, Japanese, and Chinese. With all the sway of those conflicting but splendid cultures, how could a Taiwanese and mainland Chinese person be the same? Moreover, her daughter's support of a stranger enrages Silk. *How can Lisa take sides against her own mother?*

This thought repeats as Silk goes through the mechanics of her annual physical exam. One of the reasons she picked Dr. Eggleston is because of the woman's shyness. Silk doesn't like doctors who babble. She doesn't want a friend for a physician;

she would much rather have the medical officer concentrate on the task at hand. Dr. Eggleston moves the cold stethoscope around Silk's chest, tests Silk's knee reflexes, and starts the breast exam. Silk returns to thinking about her fight with Lisa.

Dr. Eggleston's unimposing with her small 4'8" stature. In fact, she's half-hidden in the white folds of her medical smock, so it's no wonder that Silk doesn't hear the doctor until her fourth "ahem."

"Did you say something, Doctor?" Silk asks.

"I feel a small lump here," Dr. Eggleston says.

Silk's eyes rivet to the hand on her chest. "Please check it again."

"I've examined it twice." Dr. Eggleston looks away and seems to shrink even more into her oversized lab coat. "It's probably nothing, but we'll have to take a look."

Silk makes her way to the radiology unit two floors above. She's ushered into a windowless room with harsh white walls that remind her of bleached bones. She eyes the rectangular x-ray box with suspicion before she undresses in a separate cramped, curtained area. It's her first time baring her breasts to a machine, and she's uncomfortable with the notion.

She tapes the little asterisks with the silver balls to her nipples, so that they can better orient and review her breast images for an accurate diagnosis. She watches the technician position her breasts onto the platform. She feels detached from her body as her chest becomes squished and distorted by the clear paddle. The two fleshy hills seem foreign to her, and Silk realizes that she's never paid any attention to them. She sees them for a few moments when she soaps up in the shower or wears the obligatory bra. Now she scrutinizes the ivory color of her sun-shy chest, the freckles that splatter across the mounds, and the tilt of her curves.

"Thank you, Mrs. Lu. We're done here," the technician says.

Silk wraps the thin dressing gown around herself to cover up. "What are the results then?"

"The radiologist will show the outcome to Dr. Eggleston, and she'll discuss them with you."

*

Dr. Eggleston recommends a biopsy for Silk at a premier facility that provides same-day results. She doesn't tell her family about the appointment. When she finishes the procedure, she awakes groggy, clutching her sore and bruised breast. The confusion doesn't wear off. At the day's end, she's lying across two empty chairs in the waiting room recuperating, when the masked surgeon whisks in and shakes his head. "I'm afraid it's cancer," he says.

Fifty-five years old and her body's breaking down. She doesn't catch his next words, shrouded in medical jargon. While nodding in time to the pauses in the man's speech, she thinks about her breasts. She can't believe that she's never appreciated these appendages that signified her womanhood, sparked desire in Lu, and sustained Lisa as a newborn.

"...essential to fight breast cancer early on... chemotherapy...opt for reconstructive surgery..." The surgeon's voice drones on.

She's not interested in the man's advice. In case of any medical crisis, she's always counted on following Eastern medicine for relief: she'll drive into the city and visit the best herbalist to brew a restorative concoction. She'll attend weekly—or even daily—sessions with an acupuncturist to manipulate her *chi*.

She knows that the disease is a result of her karma. She understands that decades of pent-up emotion have weakened her immune system. At first, she considered the recent fight with Lisa as the impetus for the disease, but she has since ruled it out. In her heart, Silk believes that it's her ongoing fear from the 228 Massacre, when her husband was killed along with tens of thousands of innocent Taiwanese civilians, that's created the cancer.

They had been married less than a year when her tranquility shattered on February 28, 1947. The previous day a police officer hit an elderly woman when she refused to turn over her black market cigarettes. A riot ensued, and gunshots were fired at civilians. Silk had skimmed over the news article that morning.

She knew people called the new regime corrupt, but she refused to involve herself in politics. She didn't much care that fifty years of stable Japanese leadership had passed on to turbulent Kuomintang (KMT) rule from mainland China. Her days remained joyous simply because of her husband's presence. As far as she was concerned, the government existed in a separate bubble from her life.

Other Taiwanese, though, thought differently. They rebelled and instituted martial law in Taiwan on February 28 or 2-2-8. They even created a Settlement Committee to negotiate with the KMT rulers.

Lu heard about the group from a distant acquaintance at a local teahouse. Silk remembers standing in the restaurant's shadows, pouring tea into their cups with a delicate flick of her wrist.

"Our local leaders plan on giving the government a document to help them change their backwards ways," the companion said. "Let me show you a copy of the 32 Demands."

Lu scanned the list. "Yes, we do need autonomy, free elections, the army's surrender ..." His fingers skipped down each item. "These will all help us as Taiwanese people spread our rightful influence over the new rulers."

"I'm glad you agree with us, Lu." The acquaintance stroked his chin. "We need more avid supporters like you."

The next day, her husband disappeared. The leaders had responded back to the suggestions with violence. Cleansing rampaged throughout the nation during the 228 Massacre.

Silk recalls packing a bento box of rice and pickled radish for him the morning he vanished. "Have a good day at work," she said. She didn't realize those would be her last words to him.

She should have known that Lu would be one of the first targeted. Despite his ranking of "lab assistant," he was a scientist and therefore one of the elite academics. Plus, he'd always been open about his hope for a native Taiwanese-ruled country, even in public places like the teahouse. As the month dragged on, the killings appeared increasingly random. She escaped the day she identified a mangled corpse in the street as a middle school youth.

She didn't know she was pregnant until after her husband died. She's glad that she has a remnant of Lu in Lisa. Something tangible besides the old mementoes stowed away in her wooden box.

She's spent a lifetime in fear of a recurrence of a similar tragic event, even in the United States. She knows she's discouraged both Lisa and Abbey from pursuing anything academic because she still remembers the massacre's targeting of intellectuals. More regretfully, though, she realizes that she's erased Lu from their lives because of her inability to deal with the past. In essentially obliterating his life from Lisa and Abbey, Silk thinks it's understandable that her own life should be destroyed as reparation. Whatever fate has in store for her, she will accept. Acceptance is what she's always done.

Abbey

Abbey can't believe she's friends with Rosalind. It's amazing to be part of the popular crowd. Abbey receives smiles and kind words from the other students all day long. At lunchtime, she now sits on the coveted knoll in the middle of Atchison Elementary's courtyard. It boasts lush green velvet grass sprinkled with daisies. The sun shines bright on the place, a natural spotlight for the favored students of the school.

Abbey isn't a bosom buddy with Rosalind, but she's not a groupie either. Rosalind doesn't share any intimate details or secrets with Abbey, but she seems to desire Abbey's presence. Rosalind has even asked their family caterer to provide a second lunch for Abbey, so that Abbey doesn't have to swallow the dreaded cafeteria food. Yesterday, Abbey ate the most delicious meal: mussels with Roquefort sauce, truffles, and a handful of madeleines.

Abbey's tummy grumbles in anticipation of today's lunch as she walks down the school hallway to her locker. She thinks of the next class period with Mr. Malone, and a smile flitters across her face. She can't believe her new status is the result of a math exam. She received her marks back on her botched pop quiz, and for the first time in her life, she scored below 100%.

Like usual, the test scores were made known to the entire class. It's a method to help students strive for excellence, says Mr. Malone. To the kids, it's a tool used to torture the person who sets the grading curve.

"What happened?" Ara asked Abbey when he scanned the list of the exam results. She shrugged. He didn't delve any deeper. He probably imagined her sliding down to the number two spot in the class rankings, guaranteeing his valedictorian status. At any rate, he invited her to join his usual crowd for lunch that day. When he led her to the hill, Rosalind adopted Abbey on the spot.

Abbey eyes her new face in the mirror set into her locker. Her hair falls in tight spirals around her neck. She dislikes the smell of the chemicals from the perm, but she does possess those envied curls now. She looks at her blood-red mouth, her clumped eyelashes from the mascara, and the diagonal berry stripes down her cheeks. She frowns because she would never have worn makeup before this year. It makes her feel too old—like those girls who enter beauty pageants at age four. Sometimes she feels like she's a project, a moldable sculpture in Rosalind's Pygmalion efforts.

A voice startles her. "Nice trophy."

Abbey finds Ara examining her haphazard array of awards on the locker's bottom shelf. She slams the door shut. "It's a mess in there. Is there something you wanted, Ara?"

"I'm on my way to math class, and I thought we could walk together."

"Sure, why not?" She attempts nonchalance, but she knows that her beet-red face gives her away. Her palms sweat on the cover of the math textbook.

Ara pauses at the door to Mr. Malone's room and turns to her. "My parents are away at dual medical conferences next weekend, so I'm hosting a party. I've invited everybody within walking distance, but I wanted to invite you, too. Feel free to come by Sunday morning at eleven if you want."

He walks to his desk, which is already buzzing with his usual admirers. It isn't until after another student bumps into her that she realizes she's still standing in the doorway. *Did Ara just invite me to his house?* It's fortunate that Mr. Malone doesn't call on her because she's in a daze for the entire class period.

Jack

Jack thinks you can sense the brittleness in somebody when you've been with them awhile—it happened the same way with his wife. He could predict Fei's behavior based on her breathing patterns. When Fei was angry, she employed short, hopping breaths, and when Fei was happy, she emitted whooshes and soft snorts.

With Lisa, he diagnoses based on the shuffle of her feet. Today he knows there's trouble brewing when she walks in with the precise clip-clip of high heels. She's dressed in a faded grey suit, its power shoulder pads dwarfing her sweet and delicate frame. Her shoulder-length black hair is captured in a bun, highlighting her beautiful chestnut eyes, now glinting with seriousness. Heels always mean business and professional distance. Plus, it forebodes a trip to one of the multiple government offices which control his life.

Lisa tells him that Medi-Cal didn't cover some of his recent medical equipment, and she wants to contest their decision. They head into Los Angeles to find the appropriate office. Lisa spends twenty minutes circling the miniscule packed lot before she parallel parks several blocks away on a hill.

They hike to the building, Lisa breathless with pushing him in his wheelchair, and stop to marvel at its façade. The modern mesh of metal and glass radiates studied efficiency from the outside, but the interior proves otherwise. They talk to the disinterested brunette receptionist who cross-references his name to the assigned caseworker using a giant directory. She runs a lazy finger down the tiny print: "Your worker is Timothy Abbott."

He looks at Lisa to confirm the name. She gives a slight shrug of her shoulders. He understands; his case workers change so often that it's hard for her to keep track of them. Letters are sent to notify any changes, but sometimes they're lost in transit. Plus, with his dual residency at the hotel and Monroe Senior Home, he might have missed the correspondence.

The receptionist hands him a numbered ticket. He must wait in line behind twenty other elderly persons lounging in the lobby. Two hours later, Lisa takes a bathroom break, and Jack snoozes by accident. When she returns to prod him awake, he realizes that the number being called is higher than the one in his hand, and he must have missed his turn.

He apologizes to Lisa, who stifles a groan and stamps her foot down hard on the tile. Her heel breaks off, and she swears. She hobbles over to the receptionist to plead his case. Through her threats to call on the Legal Aid Foundation for assistance, she finagles directions to Timothy Abbott's office and barges into the closed room. The caseworker and his current client, a sharp-nosed elderly woman, protest their arrival.

"You can't interrupt me like this," says the portly case worker. Jack notices no other detail besides the man's girth overflowing a wheeled metallic office chair.

"It's my turn now." The lady screeches and swats at Lisa with an enormous paisley bag.

Lisa doesn't flinch. "Excuse me, but it's actually our turn. My friend's number was just called."

Timothy glances at Jack's direction, and his expression softens as he sees the wheelchair. "Let's take a look at your number," he says. The caseworker remains in his seat and pushes himself over to Jack's outstretched hand. He checks the number on the slip and looks at his fuming client. "She's right, Mrs. Jenkins. Can you please wait a moment?" The woman turns her back on the worker.

"Now, what's his name?" Timothy asks Lisa.

Jack clears his throat to signal his presence. "I'm Jack Chen."

Timothy opens a steel cabinet and looks at his files. Thick bifocals slide down his greasy nose. "Nope, the name's not here."

Lisa edges near Timothy to look over the case worker's shoulder. She glances back at Jack and shakes her head.

"He's not mine," Timothy says to Lisa. "You'll have to talk to his actual worker."

Lisa gives an exasperated sigh. "You've got to be kidding me. The receptionist downstairs told us you were the case worker."

"I'm not his worker, and I handle hundreds of clients. I can't be expected to add random people to my caseload. Those are the rules." Timothy's about to turn his attention back to

Mrs. Jenkins when he notes Lisa's stock-still figure. "Do you require assistance to leave?" He starts to pick up his phone.

"No." She keeps standing there, though, and the silence stretches. "At least you can tell me the name of Jack's real case worker."

Timothy opens his hands in a gesture of defense. "I don't know. You can ask the information desk out front."

Lisa pushes Jack's wheelchair extra hard back to the receptionist. Once there, the brunette apologizes without emotion, runs her finger down the page, and says, "Oops. I meant that Wendy Brown's his case worker. She's not in today. She'll be on vacation until next month."

Lisa hobbles up the hill back to the car, grunting under the weight of Jack's wheelchair. When she reaches the Rambler, she removes her hands from the chair's handles to unlock the car doors. Jack rolls backwards down the hill because the wheelchair's brakes are off. In panic, he jumps out of the chair. He gasps as he sees it heading toward a shiny new Mercedes. Hobbling, he barely reaches the wheelchair in time to stop the collision.

After he secures it, he turns to grin at Lisa, but he finds her scowling back at him. For a moment, he thinks that she believes the wheelchair crashed into the expensive car and is angry about this turn of events. Then he notices her eyes fixed on his mobile legs.

"I can explain," he says. "I didn't tell you because I didn't want to lose you. Plus, it's still healing, really." These statements reverberate in the frosty car ride back with no response from Lisa.

When he gets settled into his hotel room, she hurls the wheelchair into the corner. "I can't believe you lied to me. I hate people who lie." She slams the door in his face.

Lisa

The last time Lisa suffered so much hurt from a lie was when she was three months' pregnant. Before that date, she had pretended that the baby wasn't real. There really was no disruption to her life—no prolonged bouts of nausea, just the tranquility of not dealing with a period. When Lisa heard Abbey's galloping beat on the Doppler, though, she couldn't deny the truth any longer.

Something changed in Lisa when she knew she was bringing another life into the world. She quit drugs cold turkey and tried to climb the corporate ladder at her job—a sorry attempt in the diner industry. She did start saving some money, though.

She earmarked part of the stash for moving out of her mother's house. The other half she spent on a private detective named Ted Hollock. He was an unremarkable man of medium height and build with a bland face—somebody you would pass by on the street without looking at twice, which made for an excellent private investigator. He came recommended by a fellow waitress of Lisa's.

Ted completed his assignment in two weeks. He tracked Paul down in San Francisco. She had dreamed of reuniting with the father of her unborn baby. She wanted to provide the ideal white picket fence life for her child. She remembered the results of the investigation in vivid detail:

"I found him," Ted said.

"Already? How did you do it so quickly?"

"I'd like to take all the credit." Ted propped his dirt-encrusted sneakers on the tabletop. "But the concert you attended had all the registration records handy. It took one glance at the roster to spot a Paul with an Asian last name."

"How did he look?" Lisa ran her fingers through her own hair, greasy from the diner's constant deep-fried dishes.

"He was different from how you described him. No ponytail. Military short hair."

Clean-cut. All the better for a life with kids. Maybe he had stopped his marijuana habit as well. "What else did you find out?"

"He works as a medical equipment salesman."

"That's a respectable job. Where does he live?"

Ted reviewed his notes. "It's a two-bedroom apartment in The Tenderloin, a seedy neighborhood, but there are bars on the windows."

At least, he's living on his own, not at his mother's place like me.

"There's something else you should know." Ted rubbed the back of his neck. "He's not alone."

"He has roommates? That might be a problem, but I'm sure they'll understand."

Ted smoothed his report page. "There's a wife, a son, and two cats."

She blinked at him. "Whose wife, son, and cats are they?"

"Paul's." Ted paused. "The boy's already two years old."

"I don't understand," she said.

Ted filled her in, using information from one of Paul's talkative neighbors. Apparently, Paul had experienced "an early mid-life crisis," resulting in a month-long hiatus from his family. After a reckless weekend of drugs and rock-n-roll in Southern California, Paul had purged the rebellion from his system. He chopped off his long hippie hair, mended his ways, and settled down.

Lisa couldn't believe that Paul was married. She hadn't seen a ring on his finger, and he had assured her he was "unattached." One thing she couldn't imagine herself as was a home wrecker. She had endured too many lonely days as a child without a father to inflict that on another person, especially a little boy.

She took the results from the investigation and burned them. As she watched the embers fly up from the flames, she thought about her own moral code. She never undertook anything that would harm other people. Until that day, though, she hadn't known how devious words could inflict harsh damage. She moved lying high onto her list of forbidden vices then.

Silk

Silk looks over her calendar, where every day's filled with activity. She's taken a leave of absence from the vineyards, but she's busier now than when she was working. The days are color-coded for cancer management: yellow for acupuncture, green for medicinal tea, and orange for meditation. Monday through Sunday divide up into these requisite thirds, much like her breakfast, lunch, and dinner times.

She forces herself to eat those three necessary meals because of her poor appetite. She finds it hard to cook anything tasty anymore, so she stocks up on the "healthy" frozen meals found at the grocery store. She doesn't know why she bothered preparing food before. It's so much more convenient to heat pre-made items in the microwave. Eating takes up a mere five minutes at every meal, so she can concentrate deeper on her therapy.

She starts with acupuncture. Since it's impossible to find an acupuncturist in Fairview, she travels to Los Angeles every morning. She's used to the easy traffic in Fairview, so she times her trek to miss the rush hour of the imposing city. It still takes her forty-five minutes to arrive at the clinic, though.

She saw an advertisement for Sunny Days Clinic in a Chinese newspaper she picked up months ago. She felt obligated to go, if only to use the 50% off newcomer discount. She remembers the newsprint smudging off on her hand and transferring over to the acupuncturist, Dustin Ho, when they first met.

She'd expected a middle-aged man wearing traditional silk robes, speaking Chinese in quiet, respectful tones. Instead she got young Dustin with his plaid button-down shirts and jeans, booming words in his loud American voice. Silk realizes, though, that she finds his talking helpful because it's so distracting. Besides, she doesn't have to respond at all. Dustin's able to uphold conversations all by himself. She has learned about his four older brothers, his pet Doberman Spike, and the lackluster love life of an acupuncturist. Something about mentioning his desire to stick needles in them scares the girls away.

She can't say that she feels better after her visits, but she doesn't feel any worse. Plus, Dustin put her on a frequent visitor program, where every tenth session comes free. He also recommended an herbalist to her. If their surnames weren't different, she might have thought the shop was owned by one of Dustin's brothers.

Ed Su also has a penchant for plaid clothing and displays the unnerving American habit of looking someone straight in the eye. Instead of a loud, crisp speech like Dustin's, though, Ed hides his voice in slurs. He employs odd rhythms, combining words together in haphazard ways, like, "Here are your twopackets of tea that youwanted."

Sometimes it takes her several minutes before she comprehends his meaning. Ed doesn't seem perturbed by her silence—he continues to smile at her. In fact, she watched him grin through many awkward moments, like when a woman's three-year-old switched all the labels on his ingredient bins, so that he had to close up shop to re-organize them. She wonders if the calm composure keeps his customers returning, as his store's always packed when she visits.

She used to show up after every acupuncture visit, but Ed decided to decrease her traveling time by concocting bulk-sized orders of her medicine. Now she goes once a month for a refill. She rotates several teas during the week. She doesn't remember what each brew does, but they all emit an earthy smell and range from beige to red in color.

At the end of every day, she meditates. She clears her mind and tries to think of serene things: leaves rustling in the wind, gentle rain pattering on panes, and oceans composing lullabies. This exercise lasts for a short time before she tires of it. She prefers manual over mental labor and enjoys seeing concrete results. In fact, her attraction to vineyard work comes from its required constant physical activity and the tangible grape harvest. Recently, she's tried to incorporate a rotation of religious traditions into her quiet time. She tries various chants, burns special candles, and plays spiritual melodies, but she continues to find peace elusive.

It's during one of these attempts to find solace that the phone rings and offers a welcome distraction.

"I imagine you're stepping out of the door soon, Mrs. Lu?" Dr. Eggleston's voice sounds sweet with its tinge of deference.

"What? Oh, of course." Silk recalls the appointment card floating on the refrigerator door entombed in a swarm of magnets. She's supposed to go in for the results of a follow-up examination. "I'll be right there."

*

Silk's back aches in the cracked pseudo-leather chair of Dr. Eggleston's office. She's turned her chair, so that both she and the doctor face the open door. Silk hears the pathologist's laugh as he walks down the hall.

The results are good. My treatment plan worked. He'll come in and say I'm cured and ask, "How did you do it?" I'll smile and tell him not to underestimate alternative Asian therapies.

"Where do you come up with these great jokes, Brenda?" Silk hears as the pathologist nears the office. She realizes that the man has been speaking with the sultry receptionist out front.

Once the pathologist enters Dr. Eggleston's office, the man's face transforms into a grim and composed mask. "I'm afraid I have some bad news, Mrs. Lu. The cancer has spread and is affecting other areas of your body now."

Silk holds onto a silent scream for the duration of the visit. She doesn't realize how much hope she's placed into her regimen until this decisive pronouncement. Still, she refuses chemotherapy and what Dr. Eggleston labels as "modern treatment."

When Silk returns home, she rips up her precise and colorful schedule. She dumps the rest of the tea leaves in the toilet and flushes them down, not caring about the precarious rusting pipes in her house. She wanders around her home in a daze, circling, until she stands in front of the wine closet.

The organized bottles, in their neat rows, comfort her through the glass door. She sees the years of her life stretched across their shiny labels, each wine an annual accolade from

Lincoln Vineyards. She opens the door to touch them. She caresses the bottles with her fingers, and the tips of her nails clink against them in a mesmerizing cadence.

Abbey

Abbey dresses up for Ara's party on Sunday, selecting a turquoise butterfly shirt and velvet navy bellbottoms. She admires how the top flutters over her emerging curves. She says she's going to watch *The Empire Strikes Back* with Rosalind and her parents. She wonders if her mom can hear the lie in her voice, but her mom nods and lets her go.

She's the lone passenger on the bus that stops near The Bluffs. People who can afford to live there don't require the Fairview Express for transportation. The Bluffs is the most picturesque location in town. It boasts houses hoisted on a hilltop, although the view encompasses only other Fairview residences down in the valley.

She doesn't need directions to locate Ara's house. It's the tallest and most formidable edifice in the area. A fountain bubbles in the front, surrounded by a blue flower perimeter. Granite columns run down the side of the second story windows, and she can see the speckled rock glint in the afternoon sun. A massive stained-glass doorway looms forbidding in the center. She hears laughter from the interior and is steadying her nerves to ring the doorbell when a man rushes down the pathway from behind her.

He yanks the door handle and leaves it open as he carries in two heavy brown bags. "Honey, I'm home!" the man says. All chatter inside the house dies down as everybody wonders if Ara's parents have returned home early from their conferences. She feels the thump of her heart as the silence expands.

Then a flying figure knocks into the man. "Uncle Vance," Ara exclaims. The grocery bags drop onto the shiny marble floor with hard thuds.

The two embrace in a tight bear hug. Ara's hurtle into his uncle's arms has left Ara's polo shirt crumpled. With a smile, Abbey notices that its color matches the shade of her pants. She thinks that Ara looks even more handsome dressed in casual wear instead of his usual formal school attire. She marvels at his muscled arms, exposed by the short sleeves, and gazes at the snug drape of his jeans.

Vance punches Ara in the arm and pretends to wince. "Ouch, those biceps are huge. Look how big you've grown in three years."

"I thought Jess was watching me today."

Vance shakes his head. "Your babysitter had a stomach bug, so your folks called me."

"They did?"

Vance chuckles. "Consider it an olive branch to rejoin the family. Besides, they were pretty desperate. Your *hayr*'s a keynote speaker, and your *mayr*'s receiving an award at her function."

"Well, I'm glad you're here. Jess is pretty laid-back about friends coming over, but you can really party."

"In fact, I brought you something to increase the fun."

Ara looks in the bags. "You're the best, Uncle Vance."

"Hey, it's only a kicked-up version of juice."

They start to carry the bags away. Abbey steps inside the house and closes the door. At the sound, Ara turns around and sees her. "Abbey, I'm so happy you could make it." He flashes her a full-wattage smile.

She helps them unload the bags in the kitchen, an enormous cavern of shiny steel appliances set against glistening jet black tiled counters. As she pulls out a case of wine coolers, Ara drapes an arm around Vance's neck. "Abbey, this is my favorite uncle in the world. You should get to know him better." He swipes the alcohol and disappears into another room. "Guys, guess what I have?"

Vance looks like a half-finished man to Abbey. His broad shoulders promise height but end in stout legs. His hair is glossy black, but she sees grey at its roots. His eyelids droop, and he seems half-asleep, although he's looking right at her.

She feels compelled to speak, though she doesn't usually talk to adults. "It seems like you and Ara have a good relationship."

He glances at the adjoining room. "I love that kid. We don't see each other often enough."

"Why is that?"

"My brother—Ara's dad—doesn't think too much of me. I'm the black sheep of the family."

"Oh, I'm sorry to hear that."

"We live our separate lives, and I prefer it that way. Of course, I still enjoy visiting Ara."

She hears a crash from outside the kitchen. The noise makes for a good excuse to leave and find Ara. "Maybe I should check that out. It was nice meeting you, Vance."

She makes her way out to the living room. The walls, floor, and ceiling are pure white, but metallic art pieces dot the space. The modern creations come in bronze, silver, and gold, but she's uncertain what their twisted lines and edges represent. Two overstuffed cream couches have been moved to the corners of the room to make way for all the kids, the popular crowd at Atchison. Boys roll on the pale carpet, wrestling one another. Actually, she spots a couple of athletic females in the mix as well. The other girls, crammed at the opposite side of the room, shout encouragements. She spies Rosalind in a lavender twin-set clapping her hands and cheering on Ara. Opened wine cooler bottles and flimsy plastic cups litter the room's perimeter. The combined smell of sweat and alcohol depresses Abbey.

She heads back to the kitchen and finds a red-headed girl sitting at the counter talking to Vance. He looks up. "Abbey, you're just in time for my story."

A door off the kitchen opens up, and Michelle walks in. She pulls off her iconic patchwork jacket and drapes it over a high-backed stool. "Did you say story? Love them. I'm Michelle, intrepid school reporter." She offers her hand to Vance.

The red-headed girl at the counter introduces herself as Tanya. She's a cousin of Ara's basketball teammate, visiting from New York.

"Ladies." Vance bows down low as though starting a theatrical performance. "You don't want to miss this story. Do you know how Ara got the nickname 'Superman'?"

Abbey nods. Everybody at Atchison Elementary knows that Coach Henkins named Ara "Superman" for his extended hang time before dunking. Apparently, even Tanya the cousin knows the story and tells it to Vance.

"No, Ara received that nickname long before he played basketball." He leaned closer to them. "I called him 'Superman' when he was five years old. It was the day after a nasty storm, and my brother had called me to patch the roof. I fixed half the shingles by noon and then took a break for lunch. After my meal, I wanted to take a siesta, so I headed upstairs. When I reached the guest room, I spotted a tiny figure outside my second-story window.

"Ara had decided to climb up my unattended ladder. I opened the window and saw him at the top of the roof. He positioned himself, with his small tummy resting on one of the highest rungs. Ara closed his eyes and stretched his arms and legs out. Unbalanced by his weight, the ladder tilted away from the house. I reached out to snatch it. Ara hung balanced in mid-air, wiggling his arms and legs, as I slowly placed the ladder back. After a minute more of squirming, he opened his eyes and darted down. He never knew how much real air-time he experienced. It's a good thing I saved his neck that afternoon. Otherwise, there wouldn't be a Superman on the basketball court today."

He winked at the girls. "Let's keep this story between us. Ara would be embarrassed by the truth."

After the tale, Abbey relaxes around Vance. She can tell that Tanya and Michelle also settle into his company because they stay to chat. He offers them soda pop and his "famous" fudge chocolate chip cookies, which are the size of drink coasters. She sees the other girls gobble the whole portion, but Abbey can only finish half of it. Not wanting to disappoint Ara's uncle, she hides the rest of the rich gooeyness in a napkin. As she tosses the bundle away, a wave of dizziness assaults her, making her clutch the kitchen countertop.

*

Abbey hears water. Behind her closed eyelids, the sound transports her to a rare pleasant memory of her mom. She remembers skipping up the dirt path at Yosemite, her mom chasing her and telling Abbey to slow down. She runs faster until she faces a giant burst of water. Frightened at the sight, she slips and bangs her knee against a sharp rock. Her mom catches up to her and finds her crying. After a round of kisses, tissues, and bandages, she's able to face the forceful waterfall holding tight to her mom's hand.

The second before she fully wakes, Abbey swears that she can feel the aches of that long-ago tumble. When she opens her eyes, though, she realizes that her body's pain comes from her awkward splayed state on the tiled floor. She stretches her limbs and sees the source of water: a trickle leaking from the polished copper faucet. The bathroom is illuminated by a single tall pillar candle that emanates vanilla. The gleaming marble counters and potted orchid plant remind her of where she is— at Ara's house.

I can't believe I fell asleep in the bathroom. Was I trying to wash my hands when I conked out? In fact, she can't remember much beyond conversing with Ara's uncle, Vance.

She turns off the dripping water and hears new noises. One is a soft whistling coming from the oversized bathtub in the corner of the room. She investigates the sound and finds Michelle, the school's renowned journalist, snoring away. *That's odd.*

The other noise comes from beyond the bathroom door. It's a muffled weeping, a soft groaning mixed with tears. She strains to catch the repeating words, "Please stop." It's the voice of Tanya, the redhead from New York.

"Hush, my child," Vance says. "Uncle Vance will be real gentle with you."

Tanya's crying intensifies.

His voice hardens. "I don't like tears." Abbey hears a sharp crack resound. "Did you see the bedpost splinter? Now I don't want to use my belt on *pretty you*, but if I have to..."

The tears stop.

"That's better. If you're really nice to Uncle Vance, I'll make you another one of my fudge chocolate chip treats."

The cookies. He must have drugged us. She turns to Michelle slumbering in the corner and shakes her, but Michelle continues sleeping. She tries pinching her, tickling her feet, and even splashing cold water on Michelle's face. Nothing works.

Then Abbey remembers that she ate only part of the cookie while the other girls consumed the whole gigantic treat. She tries the bathroom door. Thankfully, it's unlocked, but she would have to pass by Vance to leave. She looks around the bathroom for an alternate escape route, but no windows exist in the room. Instead, the design boasts an enormous skylight, which creates a tranquil starlit setting impossibly out of arm's reach.

She starts to panic, eyeing the dim space for a feasible weapon when she hears the knocking. She freezes and stuffs herself in the corner near the door hinges. The sound repeats, and she realizes that it's coming from far beyond the bathroom door.

"Uncle Vance, open the door. It's locked."

"I'm busy." Vance's voice carries a tinge of command.

"It's the neighbors," Ara says. "They're talking about calling the cops—"

"What do you mean?" She hears the door open, letting in a stream of loud music and raucous laughter.

"The neighbors," Ara repeats. "They say we're too loud, and they'll call the police. They say we're disturbing the pea—" Ara emits a strange noise, like a distorted hiccup.

"Ugh." Vance's voice bellows in indignation. "Clean up that mess!"

"I'm sorry I can't help it." Abbey smells the rancid aroma of vomit now and hears Ara retch again. "Open the door wider, and let me use the bathroom."

"No, I'll help you in the hallway bathroom. Give me a minute to get dressed. I was, um, taking a nap." She hears Vance throwing on his clothes and leaving the room, cursing under his breath.

She waits a few moments before opening the bathroom door. She sees Tanya tied to the bed and tugs at the coarse ropes, but they don't give way. Abbey runs over to the bedroom door and locks it. At least Vance can't get in now without breaking the door down. With all the students drunk downstairs, though, she isn't certain if anyone would notice the crashing in of a door.

She assesses the master bedroom and spies the window. She yanks it open and gulps in fright at the distance to the ground. She needs to get out, though, so she creeps onto the ledge. Luckily, there's a huge column nearby that extends down the house. She shimmies down the pole but miscalculates the slickness of granite. She hurtles toward the ground at an alarming speed and at a jagged angle.

She braces herself for the impact and closes her eyes. "Got you! Now what do you think you're doing?" At first, she thinks that it's Vance talking. Then she looks and exhales in relief at the uniformed police officer who's caught her. "Crazy kids," the man says. "It's no wonder that the neighbors have called us."

The officer does a double-take of her terrified face. "Are you okay?"

With those words, she pours out the recent events. He hustles her into his police car. "You've been through enough today. Let me take you home, kid. My partner will take care of the rest of the situation."

Lisa

Lisa's frightened when the police officer knocks on her door. Her mother raised Lisa to be an obedient Taiwanese child, and she never provoked the law's wrath. Despite her rowdy teenage years, she maintained a clean record. Back then, she labeled it skill. Now, with a better perspective, she knows it was luck that she didn't get caught using an illegal substance in her youth.

Lisa's heart hammers at the sight of the dark blue uniform. For a moment, she believes that the visit's related to Jack. Maybe he injured himself or passed away, and the police are coming to her door blaming her for neglect or abandonment. Then she notices a slight movement from behind the police officer and sees the shivering figure of her daughter.

"What's wrong?" Lisa scoops Abbey into her arms, as though she's still a toddler.

"Your daughter's been through a shock, ma'am," the policeman says. "It might take her awhile to overcome it."

"Thank you for taking her home, officer." Lisa ushers Abbey into the security of their home.

It takes over an hour before her daughter's shaking subsides. Lisa makes cup after cup of steaming jasmine tea before Abbey decides to speak. "I didn't go with Rosalind and her parents to see a movie, Mom. I went to Ara's house instead."

Lisa listens to Abbey's account of the party with growing fury. "They need to lock that crazy man up!"

"It's okay, Mom. I told the police the entire story, and I think they rescued the other girls."

"Maybe I should take you out of Atchison," Lisa says. "We can find a place for you in the city—"

"It's not the *school's* fault." Abbey looks contrite. "It's my fault for going to that stupid party, anyway."

Lisa grabs Abbey by the shoulders and commands her attention. "Listen to me. It's not your fault. It's that horrible man, Vance, who has a problem. Maybe I'll talk to Ara's family…"

"Mom, that's not necessary. I really want to let the authorities sort it out."

Lisa sees Abbey's panic and backs down on her stance. "Okay, I'll honor your wish." She runs her hands through Abbey's silky hair and touches her daughter's cheek. "If anything had happened to you—"

"Thankfully, nothing did," Abbey says, but her face turns pale.

Lisa changes the topic to distract Abbey from dwelling on the day's events. "Abbey, I want you to keep a log of all your activities from now on. I need to pay more attention to your comings and goings. Plus, I want the phone numbers of all your friends."

Abbey hangs her head. "I'm sorry about lying to you today, Mom."

Lisa shakes her head. "I would have known if I'd been paying more attention to you."

She puts her daughter to sleep with the nightlight on, a childhood trick for creating a sense of safety. Lisa's words to Abbey tumble in her own head all night long, making sleep impossible. In the morning, she comes up with a resolution.

*

Lisa shows up at Jack's place while Abbey's at school. (She can't believe her daughter wanted to return so soon, but Abbey insisted on "going back to normal.") She wants to turn in her resignation to Jack. To her surprise, though, he's not in his room. The receptionist reports that he's at the local convenience store stocking up on supplies. In fact, the hotel staffer asked Jack to pick up a pack of cigarettes for him as well.

She feels bad leaving her letter at the front desk. She likes complete closure at the end of her jobs, but she has other things to do today. She scribbles a note to give to Jack: "Please call me later. We can talk more in depth about my decision."

After the hotel visit, she waits at the bus station. It'll take a while before she reaches her mother's house using urban transportation, but it'll help her to form the right words. She knows that her mother would want to hear about Abbey's experience yesterday. Plus, her daughter's brush with danger compels Lisa to put aside trivial arguments and cling to her family, her constant source of support. She's still revising the words of her apology and softening Abbey's story when she arrives at Ma's house.

She sees her mother's car in the driveway and is relieved that her mother's at home. The owner of Lincoln Vineyards insisted that Ma take an extra day off on Mondays, ever since her mother started experiencing back pain at work. She's glad that her mother hasn't decided to use the spare time to run errands.

Lisa turns her spare key in the lock. When she opens the front door, a stuffiness claws at her nostrils. She enters the house—and steps back outside to double-check the address. Her mother's house has warped into a den of pandemonium. Bowls pile up on the coffee table, with scraps of food clinging to the chipped porcelain. She follows a trail of half-eaten food to a mountain of dirty dishes in the sink. She looks in the cabinets, but not a single clean platter can be found. She eyes the kitchen trash can, where greasy paper plates and foam take-out boxes bulge out.

"Ma?" Lisa calls out but hears no reply. She turns to leave the kitchen and bumps into the glass door of the wine closet; it's ajar. She sees the heaps of empty bottles and sprints to her mother's bedroom.

She winds her way around the wrinkled clothes littering the floor. She doesn't find Ma in the unmade bed. She discovers her mother in the bathroom, collapsed on the mosaic tile.

Silk

Silk hates the gown scratching against her skin and the breeze blowing on her backside through the rear opening. She walks down the cold linoleum hallway and can feel the grit gathering on her bare feet. *I need to tell Lisa to fetch my clothes and slippers when she visits next.*

It's the second day of her detox program, and she despises the place. In addition to the hospital-like setting, she abhors the lack of privacy. She knows that the constant monitoring is for safety, but she bristles at the invasion of her freedom. She realizes, though, that even if she were being treated at an island resort, she would still hate the place.

She passes by an open door and sees a man convulsing, a writhing mass of skin and bones. He's the same one she saw yesterday running into a wall, convinced by his hallucinations that he could pass through solid matter. A familiar stench follows her even as she moves away from the room. It's the acid smell of vomit—one of the things, along with the sweats and tremors, that she's already experienced in this place.

She agreed to the program to serve as an example to her family. She had railed against this type of behavior in her own daughter, and she didn't want to act hypocritical about her own drinking. Moreover, she wanted to instill a sense of propriety to her granddaughter Abbey about the morals in the Lu family. At least, that's what she told both her daughter and granddaughter.

In truth, there's a deeper, darker reason she doesn't divulge to her family. She's uncertain that she can battle the siren call of alcohol. The ironic thing is that she doesn't even care for the taste or smell of wine. She even dislikes the giddiness it provokes because what she craves is its oblivion. In the nothingness, she finds liberty. In the emptiness, she can't relive the ravages of the past or experience the problems of the present.

What helps her re-focus and concentrate on sobriety is the image of her granddaughter. She carries the memory of Abbey's first birthday in her heart. She remembers preparing the mandatory long noodles for longevity, the red eggs for new beginnings, and the glutinous rice for good fortune. Lisa and Abbey smelled the delicious food and wanted to start eating right away, but Silk had stopped them.

"Before we eat, Lisa I want to do the 'one-year-old catching'."

"What is that?" Lisa asked.

Silk placed the hand-selected items down on the floor, several feet away from the baby. "Abbey needs to 'catch' one of these things. Whatever she grabs will symbolize her future career."

Lisa frowned at the array: a book, a spoon, thread, money, and a bowl of sliced grapes. "What do all these mean?"

Silk touched each item. "The book means a scholar, the spoon a cook, the thread a seamstress, the money an accountant, and the grapes a laborer—you know, a physical worker like me."

Abbey crawled toward the grape pieces and popped one into her mouth. "That's the perfect choice," Silk said. She felt a wave of relief wash over her.

"Um, sure," Lisa said. "Let's go eat."

After the extensive meal, Silk also served a homemade birthday cake. Abbey dipped the tip of her pinky into the frosting and tasted it. She turned toward Silk with glee and said, "Ah-Mah." It was the first word Abbey had ever uttered.

Silk values her connection to Abbey, and her love for her granddaughter has increased every year since her birth. She enjoys imparting her wisdom to a new generation and loves seeing the bright optimism and innocence found in Abbey's youth.

Silk halts her walk down the freezing corridor. Lately, though, her granddaughter's hope has flown away. Silk sees it in Abbey's slow steps and her cautious observance of strangers. She wonders what's causing her depression. Maybe Silk's alcohol issue troubles Abbey. That's why Silk puts her hand on the doorknob in front of her, turns it, and walks into the Alcoholics Anonymous meeting.

She hears the speakers' testimonies, and the beginning of the second speech touches her: "My name is Nancy, and I'm an alcoholic. Nobody else in my family is alcoholic, but I am. Sometimes it's the hardest thing to admit." Silk feels that way about being labeled an alcoholic, and she's glad that the woman speaks with such honesty.

All the stories told involve perseverance and the human will to succeed. The members don't refer to themselves as ex-alcoholics. Instead, they call themselves sober alcoholics. The idea of taking things one day at a time, one drink at a time resonates within her. After all, living in the moment is all that she has.

Silk doesn't raise her hand or signal that she's a newcomer to the group. She doesn't speak when sharing occurs. She decides to skip the refreshments and the chatting. At the end of the meeting, though, she picks up a brochure and skims through the twelve steps. She's surprised at the audacity of the goals listed. She's not sure that she likes the way A.A. attempts to deal not only with drinking but with people's emotions and their entire lives. She vows to participate, though, as long as A.A. keeps her accountable and fully present in the life of her granddaughter.

Jack

Jack feels uncomfortable despite wearing his familiar blue employee shirt. Usually the inspiration for his name soothes him, but today the fabric itches and chafes his chest. Perhaps it's because he's been spoiled by months of sweatpants and soft sweater vests during his recovery. He glances in the mirror before leaving. The clothes still fit, but the man reflected seems different from his memory. There are more wrinkles and sunspots on his face, a slight stoop to his posture, and a faint lean to the left because of his leg injury.

He turns the key to his Rambler several times before it catches and the engine starts. He's glad that his job has been preserved at Atchison Elementary. The principal, Maureen Marshall, was true to her word and kept his position open using floaters and existing staff to cover his duties.

Before he crosses from urban Los Angeles into suburban Fairview, he stops at a red light. This particular traffic stop infuriates him; on a good day, he catches the green, but on a bad day, he needs to wait an entire ten minutes before the color changes. It's an area tangled with stoplights and turn signals. The traffic light appears to be set on a prolonged timer instead of a weighted sensor, perhaps because the stop serves as the last barrier between Los Angeles and Fairview. Whether the division stems from the suburbanites blockading the city folk, or the urbanites shunning the city's outskirts, he can't tell.

He spies the verdant hills of Fairview through his dusty windshield. Typically, he runs through a mental list of to-do items left over from the previous day's work as he waits. Today, though, since it's his first day back, his eyes flick back and forth from his watch to the light. When he tires of ping-ponging his eyes, he looks around and notices the homeless guy.

Jack has seen him before: he wears a tight-fitting Army jacket over jeans two sizes too big for him. The homeless man uses a belt to resize the pants to his waist, but the pant legs still flare out. He holds the same sign every time: "Open to Any Type of Work." Jack has never noticed anybody stopping and talking to him.

He takes a good look at the man's face. In spite of the grime, the wind-whipped hair, and the stubble creeping across the lower portion of his chin, the homeless guy turns out to be a handsome, young man. With the right set of clothes and a shave, he could pass for a Fairview Community College student. The man must feel Jack's intense stare because he locks his cobalt eyes onto Jack.

Jack feels pressured to say something, since the man has singled him out. Anyway, with Lisa gone, he understands the pang of loneliness that the stranger must feel. He rolls down his window. "Hi, there."

"Hello." The homeless man's voice is softer than Jack imagined it would be. It has a timid quality to it, maybe from the lack of regular use.

Jack introduces himself. "I see you whenever I go into Fairview."

"I've noticed you, too, but I haven't seen you in a couple of months." The man smiles, showing slightly brown but even teeth. "I'm glad you stopped to chat. My name's Will."

Jack jerks his thumb at the man's sign. "What's your story?"

"My brother died in 'Nam. I protested the war, and Mom lashed out at me afterwards, saying my 'lack of patriotism' dishonored him. She kicked me out of the house and insisted I be written out of the will."

"She was kidding, right?"

"No, but Dad humored her at the time. He said that Mom's rage would subside in a week, and I would receive my share. They died in a car accident two days later."

"So you were left out here on the streets."

"Yep, all their money and assets went to charity. I looked for work, but people wouldn't hire me. Would you?" Will opens up his jacket. At first, Jack's eyes are arrested by a delicate steel chain resting against his shirt, but then Jack notices the telltale lump under Will's collarbone. Jack's seen a pacemaker in many of his peers before but never in a man this young. Will traces its outline near his shoulder. "I was born with an arrhythmia the doctors couldn't fix. It got me out of the draft, though."

Jack points to the glittering silver looped around Will's neck. "What about selling that fine piece of jewelry to get you on your feet?"

"Never." Will rubs his fingers against the fragile necklace. "I carry my family through the things I wear: my brother through the jacket, my father through the jeans, and my mother through this necklace."

"I'm sorry, Will. It sounds like you've had a rough life." Jack doesn't know what else to add, and at that moment, the light turns green. Honking blares from the car behind him, but Jack ignores it. He reaches over to his passenger seat and passes over his brown bag lunch. "It's the least I can do for you, Will. I'll come back to talk to you soon."

*

Jack shows up at Atchison Elementary in a frazzled state from his conversation with Will. He tunes out Maureen Marshall as she congratulates him on his return. He's slow attending to his duties in the morning, with his mind distracted, but the principal attributes his sluggishness to the injury and tells him to make sure and take breaks.

He takes her advice and decides to pause for a moment by the old elm tree. He's surprised to see a girl eating under its shade. He peers into the interplay of shadows from the tree and sees that it's Abbey nibbling away at a sandwich.

He's reminded of the phone call he placed to Lisa when he received her letter of resignation. "Hello, Lisa? You said I could call?"

"Oh, yes. Who's this?" Her voice seemed detached.

"It's Jack. You left me a note in the morning while I was out at the store."

"That's right." Lisa's voice turned business-like. "According to our agreement, I would help you until your recovery. It appears that you're walking fine now. You can even go to the store by yourself."

"Yes." He paused. "I'm sorry I didn't tell you about my physical progress earlier. I really couldn't have done it without you, Lisa."

"Just doing my job," she said.

"I thought perhaps you could visit me when you're free?"

"I don't believe that will be possible. I'm quite busy at the moment."

He backed off. "Maybe sometime down the road?"

"Probably not. You should consider returning to Monroe Senior Home. They'll take care of you there."

"You know I don't want to go back, Lisa."

"Well, I'm not sure what to tell you then. I've realized that I haven't been paying enough attention to the correct priorities in my life. I need to take care of my family right now."

He was stung. *Wasn't he family?* He thought he had treated Lisa like a daughter and that she considered him to be a father figure. *Had it always been a job to her?* Over the phone, though, he said, "I understand. I wish you the best of luck in everything, Lisa."

"Likewise, Mr. Chen." Then she hung up.

The afternoon light shifts, and Lisa's image dissolves. Instead, he sees Abbey looking morose and stressed. She hunches over her lunch, as though, by drawing up into a ball, she can hide from the rest of the world.

Abbey

Abbey munches her soggy tater tots in contemplation. She's resting against the ancient elm tree on day five of her imposed solitude, counting from when Ara's group first banned her from lunch with them.

Her peers started avoiding her the first day she returned to school. People slid their eyes away from her as she walked down the silent hallways. She knew that the rumor mill had started churning the day before, maybe even minutes after the police had shown up at Ara's house.

She gave them the benefit of the doubt. They're probably in shock. Goodness knows that she was pretending to continue a normal existence in order to survive. She believed that with scheduled activities, her thoughts would disturb her less. Emotions still seethed within her—anger, sorrow, and guilt—but she attempted to display a calm exterior. She knew that the hurdle of the day would be at lunch when she gathered around the hill with Ara and his friends.

When she arrived at her typical lunch location, she noticed that the group was bunched together. Ara set his lips in a tight frown and turned his back on her. She stiffened at the slight, but she forgave him. She supposed that he adored his uncle Vance and didn't like the negative spotlight.

She turned to Rosalind instead and spoke. "Hi, Rosalind. Could you move over a little? It's hard to squeeze into the circle today."

Rosalind didn't respond until Abbey had tried several times to get her attention.

"Are you talking to me?" Rosalind asked in surprise.

Abbey hesitated at the coldness in Rosalind's tone. "Didn't you hear me? There's no room for me to have lunch with you guys."

Rosalind's eyes flashed at Abbey. "We don't *want* to eat lunch with you."

"I don't understand," Abbey said. "We always eat lunch together."

Rosalind's eyes swiveled to Ara for a second before turning back to Abbey. "Not anymore. Now go away."

At first, Abbey thought the other kids didn't want to talk to her because she reminded them of that terrible night. Over the next few days, though, she noticed that their behavior didn't change around Michelle, the junior journalist. Nobody distanced themselves from Michelle, and they still allowed themselves to be interviewed for her articles.

Still puzzling over the discrepancy in their behavior, Abbey dumps her tasteless food into the trash and heads to the bathroom to wash the grease off her hands. She's in one of the bathroom stalls when she hears two girls enter. She recognizes Rosalind's clear, commanding tone at once.

"Let me see the list again," Rosalind says.

The other girl's voice squeaks. "Yes, Rosalind. Of course, Rosalind."

Abbey hears the rustle of paper.

"Ara wanted everyone in our grade to sign it. After you get the stragglers, I'll submit it to Principal Marshall. Then she'll have to take action."

"Yes, Rosalind, but I need to use the bathroom first. I'll see you in English class, okay?"

Abbey hears the door clang shut as Rosalind leaves. The other girl heads to the toilet on Abbey's right. She lays something down on the floor near the stalls' divider, an English literature book. A lined piece of notebook paper sticks out from between the pages. "Petition," it reads. Abbey bends over to look closer.

"Petition to expel Abbey Lu from school," the title announces. "Abbey has been telling lies about Ara's uncle Vance—"

The rest of the page is obscured by the book, but Abbey knows that it contains the majority of her fellow classmates' signatures. More disconcerting to her, though, is the recognizable neat, square handwriting of Ara, who must have drafted the petition.

Lisa

Lisa grips the doorknob of her mother's house in fear. In her rational mind, she understands that the house is neat and clean. A ridiculous thought remains, though, that she will find her mother collapsed on the floor once again despite Ma's current stay at the rehabilitation center.

Lisa reminds herself that she hired a maid service to clean everything. She couldn't handle tidying up the mess after delivering her mother to the hospital. She didn't want to see the empty bottles and breathe in the stench of depression. She had lied to the company when she asked them to clean the place. She told them renters had trashed the house.

She takes a deep breath and walks in. The house has miraculously transformed itself. Sunlight reflects off the white-washed walls, and she smells lemon drifting in the air. The kitchen gleams spick-and-span; the dishes have returned to their rightful spots, and the countertops sparkle. The wine closet's door is locked, and the racks seem lonely with only two bottles to adorn the space.

She turns away from the sight and moves on to her mother's bedroom. The room seems dust-free and pristine. The covers are pulled tight over the bed, and the pillow is fluffed and ready for use. *It seems like a hotel room now.* Her mother's brush, comb, and cosmetics are laid out in a straight line waiting for their user.

She heads toward the walk-in closet, but then changes her mind. *I should get the underwear first before I forget.* She pulls on the shiny knobs of the dresser. *How much should I pack? I wonder how long Ma will be in rehab.*

She sorts through the drawer, moving aside the silk pieces and selecting the practical cotton ones. Comfort prevails in a hospital setting. As she moves the underwear and bras around, something hard pokes her hand. She retrieves the offending item and finds a small silver key. *I wonder what that's for.* She puts it back in the dresser.

She places her selections on the kempt bed and walks to the closet. She sees the meticulous hand of her mother in the arrangement of the clothes. Ma's wardrobe is sectioned off by fabric and color. Lisa takes some casual outfits and places them on the bed with the underclothes.

She realizes that she's constructed quite a pile on the bed now. She goes back to the closet to find an overnight bag with no success. She decides to search underneath her mother's bed for one. She finds the handle of a dusty suitcase—her mother rarely travels—but its back wheel catches on something. She yanks hard, making the bag and a wooden box fly out.

The container has a keyhole in the front. *What could Ma be hiding in there?* Lisa wonders if the silver key from the dresser will work on it. The key fits in the lock, and she unveils the contents of the box. She finds a spray of faded cherry blossoms on the very top. Unwittingly, her fingers crush them to pieces as she puts them to the side.

Next, she finds the love letters tied up by a weathered blue ribbon. At least that's what she assumes they are, since she can't read the Chinese characters. She didn't know that her mother was so sentimental.

Then she discovers the sketches of Ma. She finds younger, kinder versions of her mother. The woman drawn beneath the cherry trees epitomizes innocence. It's not just the age lines carved in Ma's current face that differ from the portrait. There's a hardness to Ma's features now, something closed off to everyone around her. It's a steel core that locks others out, that doesn't even tell her own daughter when she started drinking and why.

Lisa continues looking in the box and discovers a photograph of her mother and a man holding hands. She assumes that it's her father. The man is tall, with a strong build and a square jaw. She tries to find a connection to this stranger by memorizing his features. Even in the fuzzy photo, she can distinguish the same cat eyes that adorn her own face. She wonders if his eyes were chestnut-colored, too.

She recognizes the promise of protection in the man's tight grip on his wife's fingers. He advertises a competence that skipped a generation and passed down to Lisa's daughter, Abbey. Lisa can imagine the confident man fishing, pulling in an abundant catch with his chiseled arms.

The newspaper article she finds right after, though, dissolves this image. Her father is standing, smiling brightly, and holding a medal in one hand. He stands beside a shorter man, toothpick-skinny, who sports thick spectacles. She's shocked by the award, but more surprised by their attire. Both men wear laboratory coats.

This is my dad? I thought Ma told Abbey that he was a fisherman. Lisa's mind whirls in confusion. *I don't understand. Ma loves manual labor and talks about the value of physical work all the time. Why would she marry someone so different? And why would she lie to us?* Lisa stuffs the clothes into the bag and places the box under her arm. She knows where to find the answers to her questions.

Silk

Silk dodges her own clothes as Lisa hurls them at her head. She recognizes the box in an instant, along with the silver key gripped tight in Lisa's hand. It's the container of her memories, the prison for her ghosts.

Silk confronts the contents of the wooden box. *The truth will out.* She takes a deep breath and tells Lisa about Lu. She tries to keep it all factual, to distance herself. She has tried to encapsulate Lu so long in silence, though, that he bursts forth now. Revealing the details of her past, she revives not a dull memory in her mind but her husband's vibrant self.

"Your father's name is Lu. Actually, it's Tarou Lu, but he never went by his first name." She fingers one of the drawings from the box, tracing the markings, trying to remember her younger self through its lines. "I used to go to Yangmingshan Park all the time to gaze at the cherry blossom trees. Your father found me admiring them when I was 21, and he sketched me. He courted me, and we married within the year. I moved from Taipei down to Kaohsiung—"

"C'mon, Ma. Save me the history lesson. I want to know about this." Lisa drops a faded newspaper article on Silk's lap. It shows Lu receiving an award. "You told Abbey that my father had 'fisherman hands.'"

"Well, your father did work on a boat for a while. He also studied chemistry at university. He received a medal for finding a new chemical compound. Or was it a chemical reaction?" Silk wrinkles her brow. "I could never keep track of his work."

"Why didn't you tell me before?"

"I didn't want to burden you, Lisa."

"All those years, and I never knew the real story." Lisa trails off, and Silk can see a new hardness emerge in her daughter's eyes. "I deserved to know about my own father."

Silk nods, but before she can speak, Lisa says, "And Abbey needs to hear about her grandfather, too. All this time, I've tiptoed around her academic achievements because you always stressed physical worth. Abbey's even scared to display her awards. I think she hides them from you and me. Abbey should feel proud and understand that her grandfather would have loved to see her shine in school."

Silk smoothes the wrinkled newspaper and places it back. "I didn't want to think—or speak—about all that's happened with your father."

"What are you talking about?"

"Your dad died in the 228 Massacre."

"That sounds like a bunch of numbers to me."

"It's much more than that." Silk feels her heart speed up, like a trapped bird flinging itself against the caged door of her chest. She calms down by concentrating on her daughter's needs. "I'm sorry, Lisa, about not telling you about your dad."

Lisa looks startled. "You've never apologized to me before."

"There's a first time for everything." Silk opens up the Alcoholics Anonymous pamphlet on her bedside table. "These meetings have been helping me, and I've been thinking over the twelve steps recently. Step eight talks about making a list of people we've harmed and making amends to them. I'm glad you found the box, Lisa. It's time to make things right for you and Abbey."

Lisa snorts. "It's a little too late for that."

Underneath the harsh words, though, Silk senses the potential for forgiveness. She knows a crack occurred in the wall between them when Silk surprised Lisa by apologizing. It's the first step toward letting Lisa into her world and treating Lisa not like the wayward daughter, but as an equal adult.

Silk hears Lisa clear her throat and check her watch. "I need to go, Ma. I want to be home when Abbey gets back from school."

"Of course, Lisa. There's one more thing, though. Since it appears to be the day for telling the truth, I want you to understand everything that's going on in my life."

Lisa gives her a questioning look, and Silk proceeds to tell her daughter about the cancer diagnosis.

"Ma, why didn't you tell me this before? You needed me, and I didn't know about it. I should have quit my job even sooner."

"No, Lisa. You were right to help Mr. Chen—"

"Don't talk to me about that man. He took away precious time from you and Abbey. If I'd been more aware of what was going on, you wouldn't be here. Maybe Abbey wouldn't have almost gotten hurt."

"Something happened to Abbey?"

"She went to a party I didn't know about, and a man there tried to take advantage of her."

Silk gasps. "Is she alright?"

"She's coping well. She's tough, takes after you."

"Maybe I've been too strong in my life. I kept this secret inside me, and to what gain?" Silk notices a dried cherry blossom petal stuck to one of the memory box's crevices. She picks it up and crumples the flower remnant, sending it back to dust. "Don't blame yourself, Lisa, for doing noble things. Only regret your poor decisions. With Mr. Chen, you were assisting a hurt, old man. There's no shame in that. Besides I wouldn't have accepted your help. I had it all planned out. I went to the herbalist, the acupuncturist—"

"The herbalist? The acupuncturist? Please." Lisa rolls her eyes. "You need to get real medical assistance, Ma."

"I figured the cancer was due to karma, a sort of payback for all those years of secrecy. The best way to deal with that kind of attack is through holistic medicine."

"Oh, Ma."

"I thought the alternative medicine would work. When I found out it didn't, I discovered the alcohol."

"What about now? Do you think you'll try chemotherapy?" Lisa asks.

Silk opens her mouth to talk about fate, but she stops. It's been a freeing day for her after all. Maybe she should escape the fetters of her past, including her view on destiny. She agrees to her daughter's suggestion.

Jack

Jack stands in front of Monroe Senior Home. It's a modern building attempting to masquerade as a European vacation house, with its eclectic mix of anything faintly foreign-sounding: French doors, Greek columns, and Italian fireplaces. It's a mishmash of styles under one roof, but its eclectic architecture is the closest he and Fei ever came to international travel.

He hadn't expected ever returning, but he had received the message yesterday from the hotel's front desk. "Tina from Monroe Senior Home called. I tried to connect her to your room, but your phone's not working." He still kept the phone unplugged as a deterrent to unwanted contact. "She expects you at the residence tomorrow at 9 am sharp. If you're not there by that time, she'll send the transportation van to pick you up."

He knows that Lisa must have given his information to them. Nobody knew where he lived except for her. A sour taste rises in his throat as he thinks about her betrayal. He swallows it down and turns to focus on the task at hand.

He squares his shoulders before entering the home's wide doors. He's ready to do battle with the staff. He doesn't want to live there, and they can't make him stay against his will. He's prepared to check out of the place and remove his belongings. He hasn't cleared anything out since Fei's death, and he took only the bare essentials when he left. He plans to justify his moving out to the administration by telling them, "It's only right to not take up space and open the room to new residents." He's sure that Monroe Senior Home has a wait list a mile long.

The receptionist Tina, to her credit, doesn't even blink when he walks in.

"Hello, Mr. Chen." She greets him with a smile. She doesn't stare at the slight hesitation in his walk. He's picked up the habit of testing his feet against the ground, in fear of another misstep and subsequent fracture.

"It's a nice day outside," she says. She acts like Jack's just returned from a walk around the facility. *That's one thing I'll miss about this place. The way they treat you like a king, even if you've been gone for months.*

"I won't be staying here," he says. "I'm going to my room and taking my things."

"As you wish, Mr. Chen." As he turns away from her, his peripheral vision catches her reaching for the phone. He can hear the beginnings of a whispered conversation with the administrator as he moves away. They might try to keep him here because they want the easy money from Fei's old employer, but that won't change his mind.

The second floor houses Jack and Fei's corner suite. Although he could use the elevator or ramp, he ascends the elegant spiral staircase instead. They used to take the steps together, since they were one of the more mobile residents in the facility. Plus, his wife sometimes liked to hurry to the top, spin around to face him, and perch on the balustrade. "I feel like Scarlett O'Hara," she would say.

He pauses on the threshold of the door. *I've forgotten about the good times I've experienced here.*

Inside, despite his mental preparation, the purple walls of the suite still surprise him. "It's lilac," Fei had said. "I painted it to match the flowers from the garden." He had acquiesced to the change from the previous bland white with grumbling. "If I wanted to be outdoors, I'd go camping."

He heads now toward the old oak dresser in the corner. The top portion holds his shirts, pants, and boxers. All the clothes are rolled and tucked in tight to fit the cozy compartment. The other drawers of the dresser were reserved for Fei.

The middle one was for her undergarments—bits of silk and lace that made her feel feminine. He thought she looked pretty enough in faded plaid pajamas, but he indulged her. The bottom drawer she kept for her treasures. She would squirrel away seashells from the beach or art projects from the home's daily craft time. He would joke that they could decorate the room for any holiday from the things in her drawer because she kept miscellaneous items forever.

He surveys the room. *Fei was a pack rat.* Besides the accoutrements of any woman (clothes, makeup, purses, and shoes), he sees boxes of papers. She saved faded photographs, old Christmas cards, and cutesy calendars from every year of their marriage. They were two years shy of their fiftieth anniversary when she died, so they had accumulated a lot of boxes.

He sighs and pulls out a large black garbage bag. He decides to start with the dresser and bangs his shin against the bottom drawer, which is ajar. One of his pet peeves about Fei was her habit of not closing anything properly. She left caps of toothpaste half-twisted. She closed Tupperware containers with a corner still popped up. She reserved a half-inch crack of space between dresser drawers and their frame.

He bends down to examine the jutting drawer. He puts the various knickknacks he finds in the garbage bag. At the very bottom, he discovers a heavy white scrapbook. The tome reads, "Forty-Eight Years and Beyond."

It's the scrapbook that they had always joked about but never had a chance to make. They had spent all their lives working hard and couldn't find the time to capture their memories in black and white. Whenever they hit a milestone, they would pretend to click an imaginary camera by miming with their hands: "Here's another one for the scrapbook."

Fei had a gift for recall, and she used it well during their arguments. Apparently, she had also used this talent for the scrapbook. She had marked down and described every key event of their lives together on the pages. She had even substituted stick-figure drawings for the missing photographs.

He turns to the end of the book, which details their life at Monroe Senior Home. He reads all about the crafts' circles she participated in, the special dances they attended, and the expense-paid casino trips they enjoyed.

She had tacked a note onto the last page, written inside a giant pink heart: "Happy 48th, love! Here's to more fun as we head toward the finish line. Remember, I'll wait for you there, Tortoise."

Fei had called herself a rabbit because of her natural high energy—actually undiagnosed hyperthyroidism, as the coroner told Jack during the autopsy report—and she labeled Jack a turtle. She always boasted that she'd make it to the afterlife first because of her speed. He would remind her of Aesop's fable, but she would say, "My dear, I'm not going to rest on my journey at all."

Fei never paused. She embraced every moment of her life. He knows she had no regrets when she passed on. With this certainty, he feels a peace pervade him. In the intimate space of their old bedroom, he can almost hear his wife chide, "You old fool. You've wasted all this time moping for me when you've got a life to live and adventures to explore." He chuckles at himself, and he can't remember when he last laughed.

He wanted closure today, but he didn't realize he would find serenity. He ties the garbage bag with a firm pull and shoves it under the bed. He climbs up and tucks himself underneath the fluffy covers, faint with Fei's lavender scent, and falls into the sweetest sleep.

Abbey

Principal Marshall steeples her fingers together, elbows against her polished mahogany desk, and purses her lips. The wild magenta mouth matches her cardigan. Abbey almost laughs at the outrageous color despite the principal's somber look. Principal Marshall's green eyes flash onto her for one second before they swerve back to Abbey's mom.

"Mrs. Lu, you do understand that I cannot ignore this situation, right?" Principal Marshall taps the petition filled with the names of Abbey's classmates. "The entire fifth grade—even Michelle Adams, our junior journalist who was at the party—signed it."

Michelle supported the petition? How could she?

"Principal Marshall, I believe my daughter is telling the truth." Abbey sees her mom clench her fists underneath the table.

Principal Marshall waves a magenta-manicured hand in the air. "That is neither here nor there, Mrs. Lu. I am not questioning your faith in your child, and the actual charges are for the police to investigate. I am talking about the well-being of the fifth grade class at Atchison Elementary."

"I understand that you're concerned about the reputation of *the elementary school*." Abbey's mom flashes a fake smile at the principal, but her eyes swivel to the multiple "Principal of the Year" certificates lined on the wall above the desk. "However, I am more concerned about the education of my daughter."

The principal nods her head with staccato bursts. "That's exactly what I'm talking about here. The tension that has been introduced into our rigorous academic environment is poisonous. It makes our students lose focus on their learning. I'm sure it must unsettle your daughter's studies as well. Therefore, I suggest a leave of absence for Abbey until things settle down."

"Are you telling me that I should take my daughter out of school for being honest?"

"No, I would never do that. I'm suggesting that Abbey take an early summer vacation for emotional health reasons. I'm only thinking about what's best for her."

"What about all the time away from class? How will she learn her subjects?"

That's right. Abbey would lose her valedictorian status for sure…along with a sense of normalcy to the world. She couldn't think about seeing her grandmother suffering without her schoolwork to buffer the pain.

"You can always hire a tutor. That's a common supplementary practice for our parents even during the academic year." Unlike the rest of the Fairview residents, Abbey's sure her family can't afford private sessions. Indeed, her mom gives Principal Marshall a blank stare, and the woman backpedals. "Of course, that's a route taken only by some of our parents. If you really want to continue her education, you could enroll Abbey in a more"—she spits out the next words like a sour lemon—"liberal school."

"I don't follow you, Principal Marshall."

Abbey sees the principal thumb through a directory on her desk, scribble some names onto scratch paper, and hand them to her mom. "These are some schools in the Los Angeles Unified District."

Abbey hears her mom's voice rise to a chalkboard-scraping pitch. "You want me to send Abbey into the city to finish her school year?"

Principal Marshall looks at Abbey and says in a quiet voice, "Perhaps Abbey would enjoy going to a more diverse school with people of her own type."

No, I wouldn't. I've lived and breathed this school for six years. Even though my whole class turned on me because of peer pressure, I'm not giving up.

"I am not sending Abbey into a different city for her schooling. I'm a taxpayer of Fairview, and my daughter deserves an education here." Abbey's mom pulls back her chair. "Good day, Principal Marshall. Abbey, you can return to your class."

*

Abbey's unsettled by the meeting with the principal, but not because of the adults' conversation. She knows that her mom will not back down. It's a strange feeling seeing Mom's strength emerge. Abbey used to think that Ah-Mah was the tough one. After all her grandma was the one who lugged crates of grapes at work in the vineyards. She was the one who carried Abbey when her little girl legs tired, while Abbey's mom trailed behind. Abbey doesn't like seeing Ah-Mah sick; Abbey only sees her during the in-between times, when she's not at her medical appointments. If Ah-Mah's feeling well, she'll ask for a story about her grandfather. If not, she'll soak in Ah-Mah's presence, finishing her homework in the same silent room.

Abbey looks up and realizes she's overshot her classroom while she's been lost in her thoughts. She turns around, but then changes her mind. She's confused and hurt that Michelle signed the petition, and even if she has to skip class, she'll find out why.

She locates Michelle interviewing a water polo player as he practices in the pool. When Michelle closes her notebook, Abbey beckons to her. Michelle glances at her wristwatch. "I've got five minutes to talk, Abbey. Then I need to write up this quick article and check the formatting of the paper before I send it off to the printers."

"I'll make this fast then. Why is your name on the petition?"

Michelle fumbles her reporter's pad but catches it. "What petition?"

"I think you know what I mean. The one to have me kicked out of school."

"How do you know about that?"

"I had a meeting with the principal and my mom."

Michelle's jaw drops. "I didn't think Principal Marshall would act on it. You've got rights to attend this school."

"Principal Marshall doesn't want any trouble at the school, and she really cares about its—and her own—reputation." Abbey leans closer to Michelle. "Why did you sign it?"

Michelle looks away. "I wanted to write again. Nobody in the fifth grade would let me be interviewed without Ara's approval. It's hard when you're up against the popular kids, so I decided to go with the flow."

"But you lied," Abbey says. "You were there, and you know exactly what happened."

Michelle shakes her head. "Actually, I only remember having a nice conversation with you, Tanya, and Vance. Then I recall a cop waking me up in Ara's bathroom. I figured I must have passed out, which is not uncommon." She drops her voice. "You know, at the party, I was taking a walk by myself for a reason. I've been diagnosed with narcolepsy—they're trying to find the right medication for me—and I thought the cold air would help me."

"Narcolepsy? What's that?"

"It's when you get really drowsy during the day. Sometimes you get sleep attacks and conk out for periods at a time."

Abbey remembers Michelle sleeping in Mr. Malone's class. "So you don't remember anything?"

"It's all hazy." Michelle looks into Abbey's eyes. "I'm sorry about the petition, though. I didn't mean to hurt your feelings, and I don't want you to leave the school."

"I understand why you signed it," Abbey says. "You wanted to keep the newspaper going, and you weren't clear about what happened that day."

"I'm not sure if you know this, but...Ara started the petition."

"Oh, I know, alright. In fact, I think I'll have a chat with him about it right now."

*

Abbey corners Ara at the end of math class. His groupies look on during the confrontation. Even Mr. Malone forgets to reprimand her for coming late to class. Instead, he stops grading his papers and peers their way over the tops of his wire-rimmed glasses.

"I can't believe you started that petition to get me kicked out of school."

"I'm trying to save my uncle's reputation."

"Vance's sick. I think he needs therapy or something."

"You left early, Abbey. The police investigated your outrageous lies." Ara's brown eyes emit ice at her. "Michelle's denied your allegations in black and white. And I've talked to my basketball teammate. His cousin Tanya told the cops that you misinterpreted the scenario; my uncle and she were playing a game."

Abbey shakes her head. That can't be right. She remembers Tanya's cries and her requests for Vance to stop. "I don't know why, Ara, but she's lying. What I do know is that your uncle drugged us and dragged us to a bedroom. We were trapped in the bathroom, for crying out loud. What honest man takes three unconscious girls into a bedroom?"

"I didn't see any of that."

"Yeah, you were too busy downing—"

"Shh!" Ara glances Mr. Malone's way, and his face flushes crimson.

"Look, I'm telling you the truth, Ara." Abbey locks eyes with him. "We were friends once. Please believe me."

"You better watch your mouth. That's my uncle you're talking about, Abbey." Ara doesn't even blink when he says, "I don't know why I ever became friends with you. You must get your kicks out of all the drama. Well, don't mess with my family, and don't ever bother me again."

Abbey watches Ara's figure fly out the classroom door, and with it, her crush on him disintegrates. She can't believe she even fell for someone who could accuse her of lying, who couldn't see the truth right in front of him. *Ara's so stubborn. He*

136

tried to kick me out without looking at the facts. And he thinks that I'm a drama queen?

In a twist of irony, she sees a taped paper on her locker advertising drama club auditions for the next day. The posters are randomly placed, as she sees copies scattered at various intervals around the hallway, but she still laughs at the coincidence. When she stops grinning, she examines the flyer again.

Lisa

Now that Ma's sick, Lisa spends more time with her mother than she ever did as a girl. She's surprised that she doesn't resent her mother as much as she'd imagined during this confinement period, although she's still disturbed that Ma never told her the reality about her father. Somehow, though, the continuous stories of truth have overshadowed the one lie.

The mere fact that Ma is finally opening up to her, connecting with her, improves their entire relationship. The climax came the other day, though, when Ma said, "Your father would have been proud of you."

Lisa almost laughed at the incongruity of the situation. She'd been decked in ratty clothes, rubber gloves on her hands, bending over the toilet. "Not like this, he wouldn't. Besides, he didn't even know me. I was born in the States, and he died back in Taiwan."

"It's true that he never knew I was pregnant." Ma sank down and sat on the tiled floor. "He very much wanted a daughter, though."

"How do you know?"

"One day, he made a special gift for his imagined future baby. He cut the cuffs off his old socks—we didn't have money to buy new materials—and painted five tiny red bats on them."

"Red bats, huh? I can just feel his enthusiasm for a child."

"Red bats are very lucky symbols, and five of them represent the Five Fortunes: Good Luck, Prosperity, Wealth, Happiness, and Longevity. He attached little pieces of oyster shells to the home-made bracelets using fishing line, to make them jingle. He said he'd been inspired by the aborigines on the island—they're equivalent to the Native Americans in this country, having lived in Taiwan long before other cultures invaded."

"I've never seen these special bracelets that you're talking about. What happened to them?"

Ma laughed, a wet rattle in her throat. "They were very sweet but impractical. After several days, the oyster remains started to stink up the apartment. The deep red color bled off onto the furniture. I had to throw them out. Besides, you can't give babies sharp pieces of shells to play with. Your father didn't know the first thing about children, despite all his dreaming."

Her mother rubbed her hands together, and Lisa saw Ma's dry skin—another side effect of the chemotherapy—flake off onto the floor. "I asked him why he wanted a girl. Girls wouldn't carry his name, and they would end up absorbed into their husband's families. They're essentially useless. That's what both tradition and my parents had taught me."

Lisa pulled off the cleaning gloves with a sharp snap. "I hope he thought differently."

"Lu said his daughter wouldn't be useless. She would be the essence of me, another muse for him. He got that part wrong, though. You remind me of your dad. You two have the exact shade of brown eyes, a light tan color." Ma pulled herself to her feet, wobbled, and cupped Lisa's chin. "He loved you before you were born, before you even existed in my womb. But this is the reason I know that he would have been proud of you: because I'm proud of you."

For once in her life, Lisa felt loved by her mother, that her personhood mattered. As though the emotion itself possessed a physical form, she almost saw the bond of empathy forming between them.

"Thanks, Mama," Lisa said, using her childhood term of endearment.

*

Illness colors their every interaction, but Lisa enjoys the forced mother-daughter bonding. Because of the aggressive nature of her mother's condition, the oncologist recommended "neoadjuvuntchemotherapy," or chemotherapy prior to surgery.

The first time Lisa and her mother went to the clinic, Ma sat upright in the recliner chair. Despite the rigid posture, her mother didn't utter a word of complaint as Lisa watched the dripping of the IVs. Lisa had brought along a book, but she found herself staring at the Kool-Aid red liquid entering her mother's body instead.

Lisa remembered the summer she turned eight when she had begged for the cherry drink. It seemed like every kid she knew guzzled the stuff, and she thought it was unfair that all her mother bought was 100% apple or orange juice. No matter how much she pleaded, Ma refused to buy the beverage. By sheer luck, on that Labor Day weekend before school started, there was a neighborhood block party. Anybody living in the vicinity could attend. Lisa snuck into the event and homed in on the giant jug of cherry Kool-Aid on the refreshment table. She drank until she had finished half the pitcher. That night she experienced a painful stomachache along with a massive headache. She tried to eat a few forkfuls of food at dinnertime, but the meal came back up, burning her throat. Her vomit permeated with the sick sweetness of the drink.

Whether it was from trying to escape that recollection or from the monotonous raindrop rhythms of the machines, she fell asleep for the rest of Ma's initial chemotherapy session. She awoke to find her mother still ram-rod straight in the recliner. Ma joked, "Even as a sick woman, I have more energy than you." The chemotherapy sessions after the first one, though, took a toll on her mother.

On this day, Lisa's not surprised to find her mother sleeping in despite the late hour. She decides not to wake her up until the last possible minute. They still have plenty of time to make it to the hospital in time for the surgery. Her mother has opted for a mastectomy, the removal of her entire left breast. "Just take out the whole damn thing!" her mother said. "I'm sick and tired of worrying about it."

Lisa goes into the bathroom to pick up the hair clogging the bathtub drain and covering the tiled floor. She notes the black wig on the mannequin head on the countertop. They went shopping for fake hair the other day. Usually Lisa's mother doesn't mind people staring at her scarf-covered head. For the surgery, though, Ma had insisted on a wig. "I don't want the doctors to stare at my bald head instead of completing the right incisions."

Lisa knows the real reason, though. Her mother wants some control of the situation. It's scary for Ma not to know what's going on and not to have any say while she's unconscious during the surgery. Lisa spots the telltale emerald green tube on the countertop, which confirms her suspicion. The lipstick is a frosted pink that Ma wears on every important occasion. She calls it her "good luck makeup." Lisa has seen it worn at her own childhood birthday parties, her high school graduation, her first job, and at Abbey's birth.

A new makeup item rests next to the prized lipstick. It's an unopened cylindrical compact containing brow powder—something her mother never needed before. Ma plans on using it to simulate eyebrows on her now satin smooth skin.

Lisa heads into the kitchen to make her mother breakfast. She's careful not to wake her mother up by making a lot of noise. *Honestly, though, how much sound can I make opening up cups of yogurt and packets of popsicles?* Ma can only eat the softest foods. Lisa hopes that Ma's mouth sores disappear and that her mother regains her appetite soon.

Her mother appears in the archway of the kitchen, and Lisa startles in guilt. She didn't hear the light footsteps walking down the hall. She sees the gaunt shape of her mother, as though Ma's skeleton is trying to emerge through the skin, and she hides her concern in activity. She pushes the kitchen chair back for her mother, grabs a bowl to contain the now-melting popsicle, and selects a delicate silver spoon for the yogurt. "Do you want peach or pear today, Ma?"

"Peach." Her mother takes two bites of the creamy substance before she pushes it away. "Will Abbey be at the hospital?"

Lisa shakes her head. Her daughter doesn't like seeing Ma receive medical treatment. Lisa thinks it reminds Abbey too much of her grandmother's mortality. Her daughter much prefers seeing Ma at home, so Lisa arranges all her mother's medical appointments during school hours.

Lisa gives Abbey some credit, though. When her daughter first learned about the news, she reacted with stoicism, as opposed to Lisa's own outburst. Abbey asked questions about the diagnosis, and after gathering all the facts, she nodded her head once. Then her daughter didn't bring up the topic ever again. That one conversation ended the matter for Abbey, as though the technical medical details wrapped the condition up in a nice neat bow.

On the other hand, Abbey has immersed herself with school things. Lisa notices that her daughter's joined some extracurricular activities at school. Maybe Abbey is keeping herself busy in an attempt to disguise the grim uncertainty of Ma's fate. Lisa recognizes it as the same coping mechanism she uses.

"Are you all done?" Lisa asks her mother. She dumps the barely eaten yogurt into the trashcan. She cleans up the minimal breakfast dishes. She herself only has a coffee mug to wash. She has no appetite this morning, so she loaded up on caffeine.

She knows her way around her mother's kitchen now and can track down any object. In fact, Lisa and Abbey have moved in with Ma for the time-being. Her daughter didn't complain, and it's easier for Lisa to stay in one household to take care of them all.

She enjoys doing the small things around the house. She fluffs the pillows, adjusts the thermostat, and uses tiny actions to bring comfort to her mother. Sometimes her delight in these tasks reminds Lisa of her time with Jack.

The same concern colored her devotion to his well-being. In the end, though, she had pretended that it was a business relationship she could cut off. She had even called Monroe Senior Home and reported his whereabouts. She'd been furious with Jack at the time, believing he'd been responsible for her family's downfall: her mother's alcoholism, her daughter's near-rape. If only she hadn't been distracted by taking care of him, or indulging in fantasies about him as her new father, things could have been different.

Looking back, she realizes that she really cared about Jack. He *had* filled the void of a missing father to her. Even though she now knows more about the history of her real father, everything remains in the past. Jack's fatherly care, though, had resided in the present.

She finds herself thinking about him sometimes and wondering how he's doing. She heard from Abbey the other day that Jack has stopped showing up for work at Atchison Elementary. His absence worries her, but she has no time to check up on him. She doesn't even know if he would welcome her back after her abrupt departure.

"Is it time to go now?" Ma asks.

Lisa's hand jerks, and the coffee mug hits the side of the sink with a clink. She's chipped its slate grey edge. She can't believe she's been reminiscing about Jack with her own mother's health at stake. Guilt heats up her cheeks, and she's glad she's facing the sink with her back turned to her mother. She cleans up the broken shard with a swipe of her fingers, not caring if she bleeds. "You're right, Ma. Let's leave."

On the way to the hospital, Lisa worries. She's scared about the outcome of the surgery. Has her mother waited too long for the operation? Will the cancer disappear?

Another concern surfaces in Lisa's mind. She's anxious about her financial situation. She used up all of her earnings from her employment with Jack to cover staying with her mother. She's now subsisting on the finder's fee that Monroe Senior Home gave her for giving them the information about Jack.

She glances over at her mother during a pause at a stoplight. She sees the crease in Ma's forehead, the worry line that's etched in. She squeezes her mother's hand, and the wrinkle fades a little. *I'm doing the right thing staying with Ma. I can survive on Mac-n-Cheese if need be, but I can't survive without my mother.*

Silk

Silk can't turn around in her house without spying presents everywhere. Lisa informed Silk's boss at Lincoln Vineyards about the completion of her mastectomy and the encouraging words of the surgeon: "The surgery went beautifully, and I don't see anything in the lymph nodes." In turn, Gus spread the word to everybody at work, to Silk's shame. She doesn't want her body's failure with its irregular breast cells made public. "But we're family at Lincoln Vineyards," Gus had said when she confronted him.

Now all her co-workers believe that the surgery's a milestone in her victory over cancer. When she looks at the array of items, a tottering pile of flowers and teddy bears, she doesn't have the heart to tell her colleagues the truth: someone becomes a "survivor" only after they've passed the magical five-year mark.

On the other hand, she does feel like a veteran of the cancer field. She has gone through chemotherapy before and can anticipate the side effects from the current round after the surgery. The breast removal, though, is new. The first few days she felt like a display for the circus, a lopsided freak. It didn't help that she carried around surgical drains on her body. The tubes and grenade-like containers sucked away liquid junk to prevent any infection from the procedure. She still finds it disturbing to see her distorted chest and the nine-inch scar in the mirror. It's the reason why she asked Lisa to go to the store today.

When they arrive at the shop, it reminds her of an expensive boutique store with its muted lighting and soft classical music. Except for the prescription she holds in her hand. She releases the thin sheet of doctor scrawl to the store owner, who deciphers the words, "breast prosthesis," and gushes. "I'm the best fitter," the woman says. "I'll find something that will match you perfectly and feel oh so natural."

Silk feels herself blush. She cringes inside, thinking about a stranger assessing her body in such an intimate manner. At once, her daughter steps in. "My mother and I were hoping to find something privately. Thank you for your offer, though." Silk relaxes, relieved to see Lisa both recognize her discomfort and handle the situation for her.

Silk, intimidated by the myriad choices offered at the store, gapes at the array of supplies, but Lisa exhibits infinite patience. Her daughter continues to sort through and offer different artificial breasts in an assortment of shades and sizes. Despite the potential for awkwardness, Silk feels comfortable passing back and forth the silicone shapes to her daughter. Lisa diverts any embarrassing moments by keeping a steady stream of small talk.

After two hours, Silk reaches a decision. She tucks the breast form into her bra for a final viewing. The teardrop shape almost mirrors her real right breast, but its perkiness destroys the illusion. After giving birth and breastfeeding Lisa, Silk's breasts have gravitated in unique directions.

Silk eyes the drape of her shirt over the restored symmetrical chest. She cups the fake breast. *This is how I used to look and feel.* She remembers the tight-fitting red phoenix qipao she wore at her wedding reception, the way its tight contours brought out a sensual side to her. She recalls rejoicing in the power of her own curves. She remembers walking around the guests' tables at the wedding banquet toasting her friends, with Lu whispering urgently in her ear, "Let's skip the toast and go to our room."

It's been a long time since she's been touched or looked at with desire. *I wonder if I should have remarried.* She's felt lonely over the years, although she filled up her time with increasing hours at work. She debates whether it was worth it to hold on so long to the memory of a man.

She hears a rustle outside of the dressing room curtain, where Lisa sits in a chair waiting for her to emerge. Silk understands that being a single mom meant having little time with her daughter while she was growing up, possibly contributing to Lisa's rebelliousness and looseness. She worries if the lack of a father figure led Lisa to form broken relationships like that with Paul, the biological father of Abbey. She wonders if single parenthood can be passed down like black hair and brown eyes.

She takes off the prosthesis and lays it down in its fancy beribboned box. Apparently, she can still experience mother-daughter time. Perhaps it didn't need to be too late for Lisa to have a fatherly figure in her life as well.

Silk exits the dressing room and addresses her daughter. "I think you should talk to Mr. Chen again."

Lisa almost falls out of her chair. "What are you talking about, Ma?"

"I know I kicked Mr. Chen out of my house, but he reminded me too much of the past and my grief involved with the 228 Massacre. His comment about Chinese and Taiwanese people being identical angered me."

"So what's changed, Ma? He still thinks the same way."

"I'm different. Since I've opened up about your father, I feel more forgiving toward Mr. Chen. After all, he was practically raised in this country, with no direct ties to the massacre."

Silk strokes the smooth ribbon of the fancy box with the new breast form inside. "Lisa, I really enjoy this time of recovery with you. I feel like it's brought us closer together as mother and daughter, but Mr. Chen offered you something that I never could and never can—a fatherly love. It's not right for me to deny you that."

Lisa issues a rapid series of blinks, and Silk understands that her daughter and Jack Chen must have formed a deep bond during their time together. Even as a child, Lisa used that gesture to hold back her emotion. "Remember, I tried to erase your father's memory and that hurt me, you, and Abbey. Please don't do the same." Silk places a hand on Lisa's shoulder. "Besides, you need to tell people what they mean to you before it's too late, or you'll regret it. Trust me."

"Yes, Ma." Lisa nods. "You know best."

Jack

Jack examines the lilac bush. Two weeks ago, he couldn't have imagined himself in the garden at Monroe Senior Home. Then again, he had lived at a shoddy hotel room in Los Angeles until five days ago.

Jack possesses a black thumb. He's the first to tell people not to bring him houseplants or flowers because he'll kill them all. Fei wasn't much better, but she enjoyed looking at them and receiving a bouquet on special occasions.

It was her memory that spurred him into the garden the day after he visited the home to ostensibly clean out his belongings. He woke up in the enormous bed, content. He lay constrained to his "side of the bed" although he could have stretched out in the remaining expanse. He liked the niche, though, and he had felt the warm memories of Fei wrap around him.

Outside he saw the glow of sunshine and heard the birds trilling. He decided to walk in the garden to visit the plant that corresponded to his room color. When he spotted the same hue in the bush adorned with slender purple stalks, he breathed in its sweet scent. He touched the soft heads with gentle fingers. When he spotted the odd white splotches disfiguring the green leaves, he frowned. Since most of the residents stayed in the climate-controlled interior, the gardener didn't need to come very often. Still, Jack took offense at the drooping lilacs with their mottled leaves; their sad state seemed like a personal affront to his relationship with Fei.

At the library outing scheduled for the next day, he loaded up on gardening books. He learned that lilacs were hardy plants that required little besides weeding and mulching. He also discovered the name of the offending disease: *powdery mildew.*

He took to spraying the bush with a mixture of water and milk to attack the mildew—the bacteria that sours milk also prevents mildew spores. At first, the other residents peered at him through the home's shiny glass windows, agape at the strange sight. Later, some of them joined him outside. They asked what he was doing, and soon a regular crowd monitored his efforts.

Their presence is the reason why he doesn't notice Lisa appear as he scrutinizes the glossy leaves for signs of damage. She taps him on the shoulder to draw his attention, and Jack excuses himself from the group of fellow residents. He leads her to an iron wrought bench in the shade, but his annoyance builds during their short stroll. Why did she reappear in his life when he'd achieved a sense of tranquility? He rearranges his features into a polite stranger's smile. "Lisa, how are you?"

She digs the toe of her tennis shoe in the dirt and takes a deep breath. "Jack, I've come to apologize. It was rude of me to leave you in the lurch, and it was wrong of me to sever our tie."

"It was very sudden." His fingers tighten against the bench arms.

"You know that I didn't grow up with a father, and you acted like one to me. I really appreciated it, and I want you to know that."

He releases his grip on the metal and examines the new indentations on his palms. "Thank you for saying that."

She braves a smile at him. "I'd like to continue our relationship."

He wants to connect, too, but he doesn't know to what extent. What if she hurts him again? Besides, he'd been kicked out of Silk's house. "Would your mother approve?"

"Actually, she suggested it."

He opens his mouth in shock. How had Silk's animosity toward him disappeared?

"Breast cancer and dealing with mortality has changed Ma's attitude." Lisa talks about Silk's diagnosis and her recent surgery.

"Oh, I'm sorry to hear about her illness, Lisa," he says. "Please give your mother my sincere wishes for her good health."

"I will." Lisa gestures around her. "How are you doing, Jack?"

His nostrils flare. "How do you think I am? How did you imagine I'd handle it when you forced me to move back to where my wife had died?"

Lisa shrinks back. "Yes, I told Tina the receptionist where to find you. I know, I shouldn't have said anything."

"You promised me you'd keep quiet when I hired you."

"You don't understand. I was having all these problems—"

"What about my troubles? A broken leg, a dead wife, my shattered peace of mind?"

Tears well up in Lisa's eyes, and she flutters her lashes to block their fall. "My life went to pieces around me. At the time, I blamed you—I thought that you had distracted me from Ma and Abbey, so I retaliated."

He rubs his temples. Tension causes his headaches to flare up. "You know, Lisa, I didn't want to return to Monroe Senior Home at first, but I find it peaceful now."

"You're okay here without Fei?"

He sighs, a sound as ancient as his bones. "I thought I'd have to wrestle with deep sorrow when I came back, but it's been the opposite experience. Sure, I feel lonely, but I take joy in knowing that this is where Fei wanted to end her days. Plus, I focus on the simple things." He points to the lilac bush.

"It's lovely." Lisa touches the soft petals, careful not to damage them.

"I'm starting to take care of the plants around here and soak in the sunshine. It's a nice change of pace from being a janitor. In my old job, I would deal with decay a lot, like rotting trash and rusting pipes. It's nice to create instead and to grow things now."

He shows Lisa some cracked blocks next to the sandalwood deck. The bricks cover a rocky patch of dirt that has never yielded any plants. Recent minor earthquakes have fractured the blocks, leaving dangerous uneven ground for the residents to walk across. He intends to remove them and grow something on the stubborn earth. He's already asked for permission from the management and awaits their approval. "So you see," he says, "by making me confront my grief, you also exposed me to a nice hobby and a new method of coping."

Lisa looks relieved. "I'm glad it's worked out that way. I felt like I did the right thing by Ma and Abbey, but I constantly worried about you."

"I thought about you, too." What else could he say? He *has* thought about her tenderness while caring for him, but he's also reflected on her coldness during their last phone conversation.

She must take the statement at face value, though, because an emotional torrent unleashes from her. She launches into all that's happened to her since their last contact. She talks about Abbey's drugging at the party, Silk's alcohol abuse, and her father's true story. Lisa also reveals her mixed emotions about Silk's cancer: her sorrow about the diagnosis, her joy at a renewed chance for bonding with her mother, and the combination of hope and fear for the future.

He doesn't add or evaluate the flow of Lisa's words. He's too busy trying to figure out whether he's acting as a mere sounding board for her. With her family in tatters, maybe he's the only person she can turn to.

Lisa seems unfazed by the growing silence. In fact, through her tears, she says, "Thank you for listening to me. I feel like I've taken a load off."

He shifts in his seat as he tells the lie. "You're welcome." He's not sure how to respond to the overflow of words, but he feels Abbey's situation tug at his heart. He recalls the tiny girl eating lunch alone, near the trash bin. He knows how loneliness feels, too—after Fei died and when Lisa abandoned him. "How is Abbey doing?"

"Abbey's moved on from the incident at the party. And she's dealing well with my mother's cancer. She's very mature, much better than I was at her age. I think it helps that she

155

busies herself with schoolwork. Abbey also recently joined her school's drama club, and it keeps her occupied."

Lisa clears her throat. "Speaking of Atchison Elementary, do you think you'll go back to work? The principal keeps calling me. Remember, Principal Marshall believes that I'm your daughter. She's wondering how long you'll be out on your leave of absence. Do you think you'll go back?"

He had requested a temporary leave of absence in order to settle his affairs at Monroe Senior Home. He surveys the garden and steps closer to the vibrant lilacs. He sees how his touch has transformed near death into life.

He turns back to Lisa. "Now that you ask me, I don't think so." Besides, he doesn't need to run away anymore, since he's found his home. With the decision made and voiced, an interesting idea blossoms in his head.

Abbey

From her comfortable seat in the stage wing, Abbey imagines the sweat running down the poor drama club member who's controlling the spotlight. She bets the mandatory black attire would trap in the heat that rolls off the huge light like waves. Abbey's been assigned to handle the props for the evening. She darts back and forth across the stage, setting the scene whenever the curtains come down between the acts. Earlier, she had applied stage makeup on the principal actors in the play. She remembers swiping candy apple rouge on the cheeks of Tess Bourke.

Thirteen-year-old Tess serves as the star of Atchison's Drama Club. Her head's scarlet waves fly up whenever she moves. *Even Tess' hair makes a statement.* Despite Tess' small 5'2" frame, her voice can boom across an auditorium.

Abbey first spotted Tess, planted on center stage with a completed Rubik's cube in her hand, at the drama club's initial meeting. She wore a blazer paired with a T-shirt and jeans. A red paisley tie looped around her neck. Next to her, a lean boy with a runner's physique sat cross-legged. He flung one arm around her shoulder, in a casual but protective manner.

A motley group of students, arrayed on relocated cafeteria benches, circled the girl and boy. Abbey noticed with relief that none of them were in her grade. Abbey chose to position herself in the far back, but before she had settled in, Tess' clear voice urged her to come closer. Abbey felt both a flush of embarrassment and pride as she advanced forward—usually nobody noticed her at school.

"Take a seat up here, if you'd like." Tess patted the wooden stage. "I won't bite."

Abbey shook her head and settled on one of the nearby benches.

"Welcome to the Atchison Drama Club," Tess said. "I'm glad you could make it here today. The drama club is not supported by school funds and is run by a volunteer system of students. Currently, I'm serving as the president." She touched the knee of the boy next to her. "This is Drake Blakely, the vice-president of the club. He's also my boyfriend and co-conspirator."

Drake smiled at the introduction and looked over the crowd. "I'm glad to see a lot of new faces. I know that the drama club has a reputation of having only 7th and 8th graders, but we're actually open to everybody. I don't even know where we got that stigma, except that an eighth-grader started the club a few years back. So welcome, everybody."

Tess clapped her hands once, a ringing vibration. "Let's start with some icebreakers now. Then we'll talk more about the specifics of our group."

They started with a round of charades and "Two Truths and a Lie." At the end of their time together, the group felt so comfortable that they even practiced voice projection exercises. They formed a circle, with each person lying on top of someone else's stomach. Everyone produced belly laughs to work their diaphragms, and people ended up in fits of giggles afterwards.

Abbey enjoys the anonymity of Atchison Drama Club, with its lack of fifth graders. She finds the older kids unfazed by peer pressure and academic achievement. They all seem cool and down-to-earth, as if their greater age or their closeness to leaving Atchison provides them immunity against school stress.

Out of respect for the older students and because of her shyness, Abbey declined auditioning for a role in the current production. She wanted to be on the sidelines providing support. In fact, she jumped at a chance to participate as a crew member.

Now, Abbey sits on the side watching the story unfold before her. The play revolves around a family drama, complete with raised voices, stomping, and slammed doors. The golden daughter turned rebel, played by Tess, storms out of the house in one scene. Abbey finds it ironic that Fairview with its upstanding citizens (a place where divorce is known as the "D-word") relishes this sensationalist fare.

Abbey prefers the obtuse angle in which she views the actors. She breathes in the closeness of their larger-than-life characters, embodied in their expansive movements, intense emotions, and caked-on makeup. She feels like she appreciates the play's artistry and technicality more from this vantage point.

The close view enables Abbey to see Tess when she stumbles. Tess, running out of the pretend door frame after a boisterous argument with her parents, catches her full skirt on the nearby umbrella stand. The upended container spills out its contents all over the floor. With one step of her loafers, Tess slips and falls face-first against the wooden stage.

Someone draws the curtain, and Abbey rushes to Tess' side. A large bump is rising fast on Tess' right cheek, and her lips drip blood.

Drake runs in with a pack of ice. "Do you need a doctor, Tess?"

Words slur out from beneath Tess' injured mouth. "I feel a little dizzy, but I'll be fine."

Drake forces Tess to lie down. "No, you can't go back onstage. I'll find someone to cover for you."

Tess motions to Abbey. "You can take over for me."

"I don't know the lines," Abbey says. She starts backing away from Tess.

"You're at every rehearsal, and you're like a sponge, Abbey. You correct us all the time. You even fed me my lines once."

Every sound from Tess' mouth makes her grimace in pain, so Abbey agrees to take her place.

*

In costume, with heavy makeup applied, Abbey creeps onto the stage with stiff legs. Terrified of seeing the crowd, she almost closes her eyes, but then she realizes the blessing of the huge spotlight. She looks straight into its pervasive, bright glow to drown out all the people, but a rapid movement attracts her attention.

Beyond that dazzling orb, one figure detaches itself from the back of the room. It moves closer down the aisle until she distinguishes her mom's figure, a thumbs up curved into one hand. Abbey had told her she'd be staying late after school today for the play's opening night, but she didn't know that her mom would come. A deep comfort warmer than the brilliant spotlight enfolds her. She feels herself relax and unleash the lines she already knows by heart.

Lisa

Lisa weighs Abbey's piggy bank in her hand. The ceramic pig feels light, with only a soft tinkle of coins hitting its side when she shakes it. She realizes that her finances are running low and that she needs to find a paying job soon. Besides, her mother insists that she's "doing fine" and wants Lisa to "not hover over me anymore." Lisa can't bring herself to do it and puts the hammer away.

Feeling guilty that she even thought about stealing her daughter's savings, Lisa returns to reading the classifieds. She circles all the help-wanted ads within walking distance—no use wasting their little money on gas—and goes job hunting. During her fifth attempt of the day, the manager at Coffee and Crullers offers her a trial run on the spot. She needs to memorize the extensive menu of over fifty beverages offered at the upscale store, aimed at Fairview's high-maintenance residents. The customers who waltz in don't order their drinks by name but by the number off the menu. Lisa also discovers that Coffee and Crullers' patrons speak a secret language:

"snowstorm" involves a mound of whipped cream on top of the drink; "more moo" means heavy on the milk; and "pixie dust" requires rainbow sugar sparkles mixed in. By the end of twenty minutes, her head hurts and she's messed up three orders, but the supervisor still nods at her and says, "You'll do."

Since it's a doughnut plus coffee shop, the baker arrives well before dawn to fashion his decadent treats, so Lisa can request the morning shift from 3:30 am-7:30 am for work. She wants to start very early in the morning because she figures that she can return home before Abbey starts school and her mother wakes up.

*

It's eerie roaming around before even the sunlight wakes up. Lisa feels like a prowler lurking in the streets, and she startles at every rustle in the darkness. When she reaches her destination, she finds comfort in the coffee shop's warm glow. She runs inside Coffee and Crullers, where a sweet fragrance greets her.

She meets Ray, the plump taciturn baker, who grunts to communicate with her. Her job involves securing toppings for the puffed circle treats. She finds rhythm in dipping the doughnuts into the spreads before her: cocoa, white chocolate, sprinkles, cinnamon sugar, peanuts, and glaze.

The first customer ambles in at 4:00 am. The woman orders a no-frills black coffee. As Lisa hands over the piping beverage, she recognizes an unlikely reflection in the woman before her. The similarity lies not on the outside, but comes from the inside. At first glance, the tall swan-like woman with undulating hazel hair and grey eyes seems very different from her. Beneath the veneer of makeup, though, Lisa spots the familiar tired eyes, the ghost-like pallor, and the invisible weight dragging

164

down the woman's shoulders. Lisa sees the same physical signs of the mental stress she suffered before she spilled her secrets out to Jack.

The woman's fingers brush against Lisa's wrist as she's reaching for her order. Without realizing it, Lisa says, "How *are* you doing?" She doesn't ask in the false manner in which she's handled customers before. It's easy to get into the routine of things and forget that patrons are people instead of orders to finish up before the day's end. Lisa inquires, not as though she's a following a required script, but with an earnestness that digs deep under the question's surface.

The real concern that Lisa conveys unlocks the woman's lips, and she pours forth her story. Maggie lives with her husband, her daughter, and her mother-in-law. In contrast to the stereotypical horror stories, Maggie loves her mother-in-law Lucille. However, Lucille recently broke her hip, and Maggie finds it difficult to take care of Lucille and her five-year-old daughter Tracy at the same time.

Lisa empathizes with Maggie in the right spots. She talks about taking care of Jack before, and her mother and Abbey now. Lisa even offers some tips in dealing with insurance companies and adaptive equipment.

"Thank you so much for your information and for listening to me," Maggie says. "I'm so glad that I ran into you."

"I'm happy to be here for you, Maggie. I feel like we're going through something similar. It's hard when you can't talk to your family about it because they're the ones that cause the strain. It's tough to carry that kind of burden alone."

Maggie nods with fervor and asks, "Do you think you might want to have lunch with me sometime? None of my girlfriends understand, and you seem to relate better to what I'm experiencing."

"Maggie, I'd love to."

They exchange phone numbers. Lisa sees a happier Maggie leaving the shop. *It's so much nicer to really connect with the people who come in.* Lisa smiles as she waits for her next customer.

Silk

Silk counts it out on her fingers. She's been back at work for ten days. The number signifies rebirth in Chinese symbology, but she feels hollow inside. It seems like she's acting a part beside her fellow workers.

She feels relief, though, for the disappearance of the initial emotion at Lincoln Vineyards. The exuberance at her return died down after the formal celebration her boss held for her. Gus had thrown her a party in the secluded vineyard location typically reserved for weddings. Under a canopy of sparkling stars, she and her coworkers had feasted on an array of dishes made with grapes: the fruit stuffed with goat cheese, speared in chicken kabobs, and caramelized for a sweet dessert.

Today the routine of work resumes; nobody even glances in her direction. She reaches up to clip another grape cluster off the vine. Her fingers are rough and calloused by the years of work, and she can no longer remember the delicate fingers of her youth. In the fading light of dusk, her hands remind her of Lu. At this image, she drops the fruit.

Cursing herself, she stoops down to recover them and presses a hand against her aching back. *I'm too old for this.* With shock, she realizes that she means more than just the physical hardship of the vineyards.

She feels happy to drop the emotional weight she's been carrying for decades because of Lu. He's no longer shrouded in mystery for her daughter and her granddaughter. Silk can indulge in past happy memories and talk about her husband freely. She still bears a burden, though, because confessing about Lu solves only part of her emotional issues.

She stretches an arm high above her head to reach a laden branch, and she feels her artificial breast shift awkwardly. Ironically, the uncomfortable motion brings her a sense of accomplishment. She has waged war with her own body and survived. *I can face any problem and move forward.*

She knows that she must confront the fear she's held onto ever since the 228 Massacre. She has never returned to Taiwan because she's been afraid. The same KMT government still rules the country. She's tried to pass on the Taiwanese language and traditions to Lisa and Abbey, but she's never taken them to see their homeland. Silk has always invented an excuse for not visiting, mostly surrounding the lack of time or money. The truth is that she was afraid to return to a place that featured in her recurrent nightmares.

How odd that her nation can inspire both pride and fear in her. Intellectually, she knows that the massacre belongs to the island's past, but she can't bring herself to go back there. She thought about it once when Lisa was twelve, an impressionable age. At the time, Silk wondered if she could locate some distant relatives, even though she had lost touch with everybody. Maybe Lisa would have gotten into less trouble growing up if she had encountered her real roots at an early age and connected with more family members.

Silk had even set aside money for the adventure. She had created a savings account, nicknaming it the "Culture Cultivation Account." It had taken all of Silk's courage to even store away the money. In all these years, she has never dipped into it.

She realizes that solid logic can cure her of her foolishness. After all, she challenged her bias against Jack Chen through intellect. She knew that he had matured in the United States and that his family had no direct part in the violent history of Taiwan. She hasn't spoken directly to Jack since removing him from her house. Instead, she extended her forgiveness to Jack through a third party. She had allowed Lisa to reestablish a relationship with him.

Silk wonders if her psyche is strong enough to overcome the phobia of traveling back to her home country. She toys with the idea of retrieving the funds from the Culture Cultivation Account—the original amount plus interest would well cover travel expenses for the entire family. She fills up her crate to the brim with plump grapes and wipes her brow. *No, I'm too old to travel.*

She spots a plump raisin in one of the branches that she has gathered. She plucks it off and pops it into her mouth. Despite its shriveled appearance, the raisin sprays a burst of sugar onto her tongue.

*

During her lunch break, Silk walks into her boss' office, a wondrous display of glass architecture. Expansive floor to ceiling windows backlight his desk. The scenery shows a calming view of purple and greens from the vineyards, disrupted by the occasional scurrying worker.

She calls Lisa during her hour off, as they agreed upon. Since she's been back at work, Lisa expects a call every noontime to get an updated report on how Silk's feeling. Lisa greets her with the usual pestering questions, and Silk brushes aside her concerns about the harsh sunshine and the heavy boxes.

"Look, Lisa, I have something new to tell you."

"What, are you all right? Do you feel faint?"

"No, it's nothing concerning my body. It's about something for my mind and my soul. I need to go back to Taiwan."

A crackle down the line. Then Lisa says, "I think you should go. It would be very healing for you. Besides, I've always wondered about my relatives there."

Thankful that Gus, her boss, went off the premises to eat, Silk closes the office door for more privacy. "Lisa, don't get your hopes up about any extended family."

"I don't have any aunties or uncles there?"

"Probably not. You see, something happened..." She sits down in Gus's swivel chair and spots the newspaper's front page. "It's like that Mt. St. Helen's eruption. The plume of smoke that's captured in the headlines? The bombing looked like that."

"When was Taiwan attacked?"

"During the war." She remembers the ashes drowning out the sky. "The airport disappeared near where I lived in Kaohsiung."

"I thought your family was from Taipei."

"Yes, all my birth family stayed in Taipei, the capital city, and it took the brunt of the bombs." She had known even before the refugees fled across the island, escaping from the north to the south. She questioned all the arriving pig farmers and sugar planters. They confirmed her suspicion that Taipei, the heart of Taiwan, had liquefied like so much ô-á-chian, that gooey concoction of egg and oyster. "I don't think anybody survived. All I had after that for family was your father."

"And nobody after he died in the massacre."

"No, not true." She flips the newspaper on its back to hide the volcano's eruption. "The most important member of my family survived. I still had you."

Jack

Jack finds Will in the same spot near the stoplight, almost in his old position, holding the tattered sign. The Army surplus jacket and oversized jeans appear to have collected more grime since Jack's last visit. He pulls his Rambler over to the side of the road and beckons to Will.

Will shuffles over, and Jack hands him a piping hot rotisserie chicken meal. He asked one of the kitchen staff at Monroe Senior Home for an extra dish "for a friend." They didn't bat an eyelash before wrapping it up in aluminum foil; they even added a beverage to the take-away bag.

Will gobbles the meal down with such ferocity that Jack wonders when the man last ate. After he finishes, Will burps and speaks. "Thank you. That was so delicious. I didn't think I'd see you again, though. People break their promises to me all the time."

"I don't go back on my word." Jack points to Will's creased cardboard sign asking for work. "I have a question for you. Is that for real? Would you really take any job?"

"Yes, sir, I would." Will's eyes light up. "Do you need something done?"

"I know of an open position…"

Will shakes his head. "I won't be able to do any formal work. I've tried before, but every workplace has rejected me."

"I can put in a good reference for you. I used to work there."

Will's blue eyes dim. "You mean well, but when employers look at my pacemaker, they think I'll drop dead with an ounce of work."

Jack tries another tack. "Do you follow the news?"

Will guffaws. "Now how would I do that?"

Jack pictures the large color television in the posh entertainment room at the senior home and feels a spark of guilt. "Never mind. Do you remember when the government passed the Rehabilitation Act seven years ago? It provided rehabilitation services for the handicapped—"

"I'm not handicapped. I'm able to do all sorts of work, and I don't need rehabilitation."

Jack holds up his hands. "I'm not saying that you do. Please let me continue."

"Okay, I'll hear you out."

"This bill required federal jobs to hire and train 'the handicapped,' people who aren't able to work and need vocational services. This year, they passed an amendment, expanding the definition to include people who suffer from any type of physical or mental impairment which would affect their quality of life. This new revision could apply to you."

"You have a government job in mind?" Will asks.

"I worked at Atchison Elementary School. The school's supported by federal funds, and the principal there seems very wary of lawsuits." Jack knows that Maureen Marshall holds his position open, fearing that if she closes it, she'll be accused of discrimination against the aged.

"It's a janitorial position." He checks Will's face to spot any negative reaction but finds none.

"I'll take it." Will pumps his fist in the air. "But where would I stay?"

"I can put you up at my place until your first paycheck. I live in a senior home, but I can request special visitation rights." In fact, Jack's already run the possibility by the staff, and they appeared fine with it.

Will offers up a hopeful smile. "Then I'll apply for the position."

*

Jack's at work in his vegetable garden at Monroe Senior Home when Will surprises him. He spins Jack around and hugs him. "I got the job!"

Jack smiles from under his wide-brimmed hat. "I told you so. Now, wait a moment while I finish up with these plants, and we'll go inside together."

Jack turns his attention to the tomato plants and carrots that have sprouted from the rocky soil. He eyes the other seedlings that surround his neat row. When the staff took away the cracked blocks near the sandalwood deck, it revealed such an extensive area that he knew the space could house more than one gardener's efforts.

After making the ground fertile, he offered up spots to the other residents. Now he leads the Monroe Gardening Club at the home. He's glad to see the results of their work paying off through the tiny green buds in the plot. He takes a quick peek at the lilac bush on the other side of the garden and brushes the dirt from his hands. "I'm done, Will."

Jack leads the way back to the suite. He's traded in the giant bed for a more compact version, although he keeps the comforter from his married years. Will sleeps on a camping cot, now folded out of sight.

Jack rests one hand on his old oak dresser. "I have something to give you, Will."

Jack reaches into a drawer and pulls out his blue uniform. The shirt is neatly pressed, and Jack's name has been erased from the upper left chest area. One of his female neighbors removed the lettering and positioned a badge with Will's name on the faded spot.

Will's voice falters as he thanks Jack. He's heard the history behind the shirt. "This means a lot to me, Jack. I'm really grateful for all you've done."

"It's my pleasure to help out friends. Good luck with everything," Jack says as he hands over his most treasured possession.

Abbey

Abbey basks in the limelight provided by the school's drama club productions. She loses herself in the characters she plays and enjoys inhabiting different eras and remote countries. She's not sure if she finds delight in the unleashing of her imagination or in the escape from her everyday pressures (an ailing Ah-Mah, jeering peers, Mom's money worries). In any case, for the last play of the school year, Abbey starred to thunderous applause.

She feels relief for the end of school. Maybe she can put this tumultuous time behind her. She also looks forward to summer because, instead of enduring a dull academic break, she's scheduled to participate in two major activities.

She'll be attending a summer arts camp located in the San Bernardino Mountains. Her mom hesitated, even though Abbey received a scholarship to cover its fees. After Abbey vouched for the staff's credentials—prescreened counselors, all alumni of Atchison Elementary, run the Creative Arts Camp— her mom finally relented.

The other major event involves a planned vacation to Taiwan (insisted on by Ah-Mah), a journey Abbey feels ambivalent about. A certain part of her wants to examine her Taiwanese heritage closer, but she also feels nervous about going there. She worries that when she opens her mouth, people won't understand her carefully practiced Taiwanese.

The final school bell rings for the year. Abbey gives Tess a quick hug in the freedom of the summer sunshine. "See you next week at camp," Abbey says. Starting Monday, they'll be sharing a cabin in the woods with four other strangers.

Abbey feels so full of joy that she high-fives Will on her way to the parking lot, where her mom waits. She knows all about the janitor's story through her mom. Will looks startled by her touch, but he recovers. In fact, he holds out his hand for another slap. Abbey laughs at his goofiness. All the other kids like Will, too. She respects Jack Chen a smidgeon more for helping Will find a job at Atchison.

*

"Welcome to Creative Writing." The printed font marches across the portable blackboard at the back of the mess hall. The prim script dims Abbey's spirit. She's come from a fun spontaneous improv session during her free time, and she isn't ready for a rigid class yet.

The camp counselor leading the session, Miss Vickers, wears preciseness like a cloak. Everything from her stick-straight brown hair to her uncreased uniform screams control. The only anomaly in Miss Vickers' image lies in her cute button nose, but the teacher's piercing amber eyes compensate for it and demand seriousness and attention.

"The outdoors offers a wonderful source of inspiration," Miss Vickers says. Her voice sounds clipped, each word pronounced with sharp diction.

Abbey feels a spark of hope at the woman's words. *At least we get to go outside.* Several other kids near Abbey stand up to leave, but Miss Vickers stops them.

"However, nature also provides distraction. Today you will learn about the discipline of writing. You don't need to be inspired to create," Miss Vickers says. "You can use your past experiences to tell an intriguing story. Your assignment is to write about why you're here. What made you attend this camp? You have thirty minutes." Miss Vickers passes out lined paper and sharpened pencils.

Abbey wiggles in her plastic chair to find a comfortable position and chews the eraser on top of her pencil. She finds it hard to concentrate with all the faces around her. Besides, they're seated at round tables already set for the upcoming lunch, and the smell of chili wafting through the kitchen doors distracts her. At the next table, she spies Tess, who contorts her features into a silly face at Abbey.

Abbey looks down at her blank paper to avoid laughing. She composes herself after several deep breaths and writes, "I'm at camp because of my school's drama club." With that penned thought, her words flow. She reveals her exploits in drama and her love of the stage. She tells about the origins of joining the club—the comment from Ara about her being a "drama queen."

Then to Abbey's surprise, she exposes herself on the page, describing the drugging by Vance. Her cheeks burn while writing the words, but at the end of the paragraphs, she feels calm and collected. She hands the assignment to Miss Vickers, who raises her eyebrows. It's taken a full fifty minutes, twenty minutes over the allotted time, for Abbey to sort through her emotions.

*

In the middle of Abbey's lunch, she feels a tap on her shoulder. Miss Vickers holds her essay and says, "Come with me." As she leads Abbey to the staff's office, Abbey's thoughts tumble in confusion. *Did I say something wrong? Was my story too racy for the tight-lipped Miss Vickers?*

The counselor closes the door and sits across from Abbey. She rustles the paper with one hand. "Is this story true? Are these allegations real?"

Under Miss Vickers' intense scrutiny, Abbey can't speak a word. She can only nod.

"Can you describe this Vance that you encountered?" Miss Vickers asks.

Abbey stutters as she talks about Vance's broad shoulders, his stout legs, and his drooping eyelids. She wonders if the counselor will turn on her too, like her peers. Maybe she'll get kicked out of arts camp for telling lies.

Miss Vickers' eyes cloud up for a moment. "About seven years ago, I was molested by a man named Vance. I didn't tell anyone."

Abbey examines Miss Vickers. Because of her solemn aura, she looked old to Abbey at first. At second glance, though, Abbey recalculates Miss Vickers' age and adjusts it to the late teens.

"It's the same man. I had no idea he would ever touch another child again." Miss Vickers' amber eyes glint with resolution. "I'll make sure to do something about it this time around."

Lisa

Lisa unfolds the newspaper, sees the headline, and spits out her morning coffee. It stains the luxurious Egyptian-cotton bathrobe that she's been saving for this stay-in Saturday. She blots the soaked newsprint with napkins and reads the article that's startled her:

AROYAN FAMILY DEFAMED

Friday brought a shocking accusation against the respected Aroyan family. Katherine Vickers, 19, filed charges of molestation against Vance Aroyan, brother of Melik Aroyan, our town's revered pediatric dentist. Vickers, an alumna of both Atchison Elementary and Fairview High, claims that Aroyan's unwelcome advances occurred in 1973 when she was twelve years of age.

At the time Vickers did not come forward. Vickers stated that she didn't talk because she was "too ashamed" and "scared to talk against an honored family in the community."

Vickers' recent change of heart is due to an anonymous source who tipped her that Aroyan continues with his questionable practices. Vickers'

181

allegation falls within the statute of limitations for molestation cases, and the police will investigate the matter further. The Aroyan family could not be reached for comment.

Fairview News is a tiny newspaper but avidly read by all the residents in town. In fact, everybody quotes tidbits from it during their daily run-ins with each other. Instead of asking, "How are you?," they greet each other with, "Did you hear about...?" The relaying of juicy news creates a sense of connection within the community.

Lisa jumps up when her mother arrives in the kitchen. She spills her coffee on the kitchen table.

"What are you reading?" Ma asks, as she mops up the mess with a towel.

"There's a controversial article about the Aroyan family."

Her mother speed-reads the piece in two-minutes-flat. Ma looks at Lisa. "Should we tell Abbey?"

"Tell me what?" Abbey's groggy voice pipes up from beyond the kitchen archway.

"Nothing. It's nothing." Lisa's surprised that Abbey's awake. Her daughter returned from camp two days ago. It's summertime. Don't kids sleep in anymore?

Lisa sees Abbey narrow her eyes. Her daughter knows her too well. "What are you hiding from me?"

Lisa taps her fingers against the coffee mug in a quick rhythm. "Um, we were wondering if we should go to the Pancake Barn for breakfast. If we leave now, we'll beat the lines."

Abbey shakes her head and yawns. "No, thanks. I just want some cereal. Besides, it doesn't look like you're ready to go out." Her daughter eyes Lisa's coffee-stained robe with amusement.

Abbey grabs a bowl and fills it with cornflakes. She pulls up a chair at the table and says, "Oh good. You got the newspaper."

"That's right," Ma says in an aspartame voice. "Here you go, Abbey."

When her mother hands Abbey the comics section, Lisa knows their cover's blown. If Abbey behaved like Lisa, she would devour the funnies and leave the other sections untouched. Her daughter being Abbey, though, frowns at the two of them and reaches for the front page. "What's going on with you guys today?"

A minute later, Abbey knows the answer. Her face blanches while she's reading the article on the Aroyans. Both Lisa and her mother flutter to Abbey's side in concern. "Are you okay?"

"I...I'm fine." Abbey grinds down her cereal with a spoon, crushing the flakes into corn dust.

Lisa waits to see if her daughter will say any more, but Abbey remains shuttered. "You know what? I'll whip up some homemade pancakes even better than the Pancake Barn." Lisa sees her mother pacing a few feet away, wringing her hands. "Want to help, Ma?" Keeping her mother busy will help Ma's unease.

Lisa and her mother make the fluffiest pancakes, worthy of being captured on film. In fact, they do take a few photographs of their labor. Lisa offers Abbey a heaping plate of the moist buttermilk layers, but she pushes the pancakes away.

"You need to eat breakfast, Abbey," Lisa says. "It'll make you feel better, take your mind off that dreadful day."

"That's not it, Mom." Abbey looks up at them and points a shaking finger at the newspaper article. "I'm the unnamed tipper. This Katherine Vickers worked as a counselor at my arts camp. I wrote about the party with Vance forgone of her writing assignments."

Lisa sees a mixture of emotions flit across Abbey's face: surprise, fear, and relief. She gives Abbey a long hug. "Whatever happens, we'll get through this together." Her daughter nods and manages to swallow a tiny bit of pancake. Lisa closes her eyes. *I'm so glad we're going to Taiwan tomorrow, far away from this emerging drama.*

Abbey

The Taiwan humidity hits Abbey like a slap in the face, and the incessant car honking attacks her ears. Despite her cramped legs from the fourteen-hour flight, she launches herself into the taxi's claustrophobic but air-conditioned interior. The driver's risky maneuvers along the crowded streets scare her, but she notices that Ah-Mah remains unmoved by the constant zigzagging. Abbey looks out the window and focuses on the gray sky, overcast with storm or smog. The buildings stream by, a blur of dull browns, as if sprung up from the dust of the ground beneath them.

Taiwan's capital, Taipei, marks the family's first stop on the island. They plan on traveling north to south in a dizzying three-day itinerary. Abbey's not even sure if it's worth the trip, to get trapped in the airplane, a flying sardine can, for two whole days (on the way to and back) for such a short visit. She yawns, her tenth one since arriving because she didn't get much rest in the air. She pops in a breath freshener and crunches down, hoping the mintiness will wake her up. She organized

185

the itinerary for the day—each family member gets one whole day to do whatever they wish—and she wants to make the most of it.

She intends to spend the majority of the day at The National Palace Museum. Drama club's inspired her to see the world through creative lenses. She supposes that she should have gone to some historically significant place like the Fort San Domingo, which guarded the initial European settlers in Taiwan: the Spaniards, the Dutch, and the British. She didn't want to stare at a bunch of crumbling mortar, though. Besides, she thinks art can reflect a nation's history, and what better place than a building with the word "national" in it?

The museum's sprawling grounds overwhelm her. The wide lawns evoke a sea of green. Two parallel rows of trees border the walkway to the multi-gabled building. When Abbey enters, she unlocks a labyrinth of artwork. The collection boasts approximately 650,000 pieces, so many that the curators can display only a small portion at a time. She takes her time looking at all the paintings, sculptures, and ceramics. Her mom and grandmother linger behind her and rest on the supplied benches. She hears them chatting in quiet tones while keeping her in their sight.

Sometimes her mom comes up to her, and they look at a piece together. This happens when Abbey stares at a chunk of jade shaped like a cabbage. Mom finds it amusing to see a piece of vegetable captured by art. She doesn't understand how the intricacies in the variations of green jade enable the stone to mimic a real-life cabbage. Ah-Mah, on the other hand, avoids all the exhibits. She keeps folding and refolding the crisp brochure given to them at the front desk when they paid admission for entry, her eyes fixed on its tiny print. When the building closes, Abbey tries to involve her mother and grandmother deeper in uncovering the museum's beauty.

"Which piece of art did you like best?" she asks.

"The fake cabbage, of course," her mom says. "I did find the pair of grasshoppers hidden in the leaves before you did." She dances a little jig, several hops with her right foot and a punch with her left fist.

"What about you, Ah-Mah?"

Her grandmother stands on the staircase outside the building, peering at its locked doors. "You know, this whole place wasn't here when I was around. It came later when the KMT showed up. They took all this mainland Chinese stuff and stored it here." Ah-Mah hands her the crinkled brochure, worn down with twists. "Here you go, I don't want it. This is supposed to be our *national* museum, not a mainland Chinese art locker."

Abbey feels a sense of shame holding the mutilated brochure. She meant to show her grandmother the wonders of art and impress Ah-Mah by picking a place that seemed so reflective of patriotism. Instead, she had managed to make her grandmother more aware of her hurtful past.

Abbey trudges along in the sun's fading rays, glad that the spreading darkness hides her sadness. She's not sure she wants to deal with a jostling mass at night market right now. She wants to return to their hotel room and drown her embarrassment in sleep. She suggests canceling their next stop, but her grandmother assures her that "it'll be fun," so Abbey drags her body into another dangerous taxi.

En route to the Shilin Night Market, Abbey hears music. It's a raucous tune filled with drums and cymbals. She sees its pied piper effect bringing a throng of children in front of an elaborately painted van. "Wait, can we stop here first?" She glances at Ah-Mah, who nods in permission. Maybe the folkloric music will cheer her grandmother up.

They get off to stand around the car painted with dragons and inscribed with good luck characters. A makeshift stage borders one side of the vehicle, where intricate puppets dance in rhythm to the songs. Each figurine appears painted with sharp features and rouged cheeks. The dolls wear elaborate headdresses with tassels and beads. Abbey can't understand the music, but she likes the flashes of bright colors and the way the puppets swirl to the heady tunes. She claps until her hands hurt at the end of the show and sees the same reddened hands on the girl next to her. The other girl, wearing a polka-dot rainbow bow in her hair, smiles at Abbey.

Abbey and her family walk a block down to the bustling night market. Encouraged by her connection to the unknown local girl, Abbey feels excited again. She can't wait to try all the delicacies. It seems like every treat under the sun is sold by these shouting vendors, crammed together on an asphalt lot. She cranes her neck, watching some workers create little pancakes crafted into different shapes: ducks, guns, elephants, and more. Ah-Mah sees her interest and pays for a piping hot batch from the seller.

"I'm glad you're here to try our Taiwanese treats," her grandmother says.

"Thank you for asking me to come along." They smile at each other, and Abbey takes the pancake.

Feeling forgiven, she bites down on the hot goodness with eagerness and feels a pair of eyes on her. It's the same girl from the puppet show. Abbey grins at her and passes over a fresh pancake shaped like a cat. The girl takes a big bite and mumbles something with her mouth full. Abbey thinks she's saying thank you. *"Biánkhek-khì,"* Abbeys says in Taiwanese. The girl stops eating and steps back a little. Abbey repeats the words, "You're welcome." The girl almost spits out the dough at Abbey.

Abbey turns to her grandmother. "Did I say it wrong?" she asks.

"No, you said it perfectly fine. The girl grew up under KMT rule. She probably never got taught Taiwanese and understands only Mandarin."

Ah-Mah scuttles Abbey away from the girl who's now pointing in their direction and laughing. A fruit vendor, an older gentleman with juice-stained hands, blocks their way. "For you, miss," he says in Taiwanese. He hands Abbey a bell-shaped fruit. It's a deep red, and its waxed skin reminds her of a cross between an apple and a pear. She bites down, enjoying the crispness combined with a rich juiciness which floods her mouth. She stops as she discovers the middle, a flavorless weave covering a hard seed. She feels like this bell fruit, looking Taiwanese on the outside but with a woven façade hiding the core of her inner Taiwanese-American dual self.

Lisa

Lisa rubs her feet as the morning light streams into their Taipei hotel room. It's a quaint room, only slightly smaller than her studio back in Fairview. Her mother and she share the hard "therapeutic" wooden bed while Abbey sleeps on the rollaway cot. Lisa swings her legs off the bed and tests her blistered feet against the floor. They spent the night walking among the crowds in the murky dark, battling the lines to eat tidbits of savory food. They ate and ate: oyster omelets, three cups chicken, grilled sweet sausages, mochi, bubble tea, shaved ice...all delicious.

Abbey opens her eyes and stretches her arms out. "What are we doing today, Mom? You're the boss."

Lisa shuffles over to the window and peeps through the grimy glass. She spies the breakfast cart below. She knows what she wants right now. A nice piece of warm sesame scallion bread washed down with sweet soy milk. Could that count as the cultural expedition for the day? "I want to go downstairs and walk around."

Abbey moves next to her and looks out, too. "Oh, do you mean to those buildings over there?"

Lisa follows her daughter's pointing finger to a plaza decorated with three buildings, a white one in the back and two ancient red-columned buildings in the front. They seem important. They're also stationed kitty-corner from the sesame bread seller. "That's exactly what I was thinking."

The trio makes their way out, and her mother orders the desired succulent breakfast treats. Munching on their crispy goodness, Lisa finds the energy to start at the farthest building first. She climbs the mountain of stairs to enter the impressive building, with its blue-glazed tiled roof and its arched gateway.

They enter a large hall with cool marble floors. Chinese characters scroll across the back wall. An impressive statue stands in front of the words, flanked by a set of Taiwan flags. The sculpture shows a man sitting on a throne. At first glance, Lisa thinks of the Lincoln memorial, despite the fact that the statue wears a dark brown coating instead of the pure white seen in the Washington, D.C. version.

Her mother starts shaking next to her, and Lisa wraps an arm around her to stop the trembling. "Are you okay, Ma?"

Ma points to the metal figure, shakes Lisa off, and scoots away from the statue.

Lisa sees Abbey step closer, touch the base of the podium, and read the inscription. "It says that this is a memorial hall for Chiang Kai-Shek who died in 1975."

A Taiwanese guard approaches them. "Please don't touch." Lisa didn't notice the line of official-looking men standing at attention alongside the walls.

Ma startles at the man's voice, widens her eyes at his uniform, and sprints down the hall, almost sliding on the smooth floor in her haste. The soldier grunts his disapproval at her lack of reverence but doesn't chase after her.

Lisa finds her mother clinging to a tree on the manicured lawn outside. "Chiang Kai-Shek brought the KMT over to Taiwan, and his son rules now." Ma bangs her fist against the bark. "The KMT are still in power."

Lisa plucks a leaf that's fallen onto her mother's disheveled hair. She spins the delicate piece of plant in her hand. "Let's go somewhere with good memories for you, Ma."

Ma makes a sound between a laugh and a cry. "And where would that be, Lisa?"

*

Yangmingshan National Park holds a numerous trails, each covered with different types of flowers. No cherry blossoms, though. Not the season for them, her mother tells Lisa. Still, Lisa likes picturing her mother and father wandering the scenic place, lost in love. She spots a couple of waterfalls and calls out to Abbey. She once took Abbey to see a waterfall in Yosemite, and she thinks her daughter might like the refreshing spray of these Taiwan ones, too. Lisa sees Abbey's brow furrow as she approaches the rushing water. They hold hands, and Lisa feels Abbey tighten her grip. Her daughter watches the splashing with a forced smile and then leads the way back to Ma, who's resting in the shade.

"Ah-Mah, can you take us to where you met Ah-Gung?" Abbey asks.

Her mother doesn't even consult a trail guide. Silk leads them with sure steps to a spot near a pond. Lisa sees their images reflected in the deep water, three faces in succession on the placid surface. She sees the same smooth obsidian black hair and the high cheekbones passed on down the line from

193

grandmother to granddaughter. Lisa keeps gazing at the still-life portrait of her family until her mother asks for some privacy; she wants some alone time with Lu's memory.

Silk

Silk feels like they're false tourists on a pretend vacation because sight-seeing hides the actual goal of this trip. She wants to embrace this country as her own, even after the decades of absence. She had hoped yesterday that Yangmingshan Park would provide a deeper connection for her. When she stepped into the idyllic location, despite all the years, her feet knew how to take her to where Lu and she first met. She spotted the shaded bench, like a familiar friend, overlooking the pond. Asking for privacy from her family, she walked close to the water's edge. She could almost sense Lu's footsteps resounding against the path. She saw a swan preening in the emerald water and leaned forward to admire its elegance. Startled, the bird flapped its wings and hurried off. In the aftermath of the ripple, Silk caught a reflection of her aged self, and all illusion of Lu's nearness disappeared.

Back in the city proper, and in charge of the day's schedule, Silk wonders if she'll find any remainders of her old family home. They hail a cab, and it pulls up to the address she's given the driver in no time. When Silk gets out, she feels disoriented and scans the area for familiar landmarks. She sees the crowd stepping around her, focused on their own destinations, and panics. She doesn't belong here in this strange city with these people who know where they're going and what they're doing. Then she spots the implausible, good old Fortune Pharmacy—it must have been rebuilt after the war—on the southeast corner of the block, mere steps away from her childhood house.

She hurries along, snapping at Lisa and Abbey to follow. She frowns when she can't see the familiar weathered row house. It shouldn't surprise her that her old house has disappeared, just like its former residents from her life.

Although she grew up with two older sisters, the huge ten-year-gap between her and the next sibling made Silk feel like an only child. By the time Silk arrived in her parent's lives, they were too busy working to care about the baby of the family, and her sisters were too mature (at least in their own minds) to play with her.

In short time, her sisters married off, and she rarely heard from them. "That's the way it should be," Silk's ma told her. "We women enter our husband's households and integrate into their families." In turn, when Silk married Lu, she knew that her parents were secretly relieved to stop providing for another useless daughter who would not take on the family name. Even so, she wonders if they would have wished to remain in touch—until the World War II bombings took away any possibility of contact.

Silk feels a tap on her shoulder. "Ah-Mah, I think I found the address."

Silk looks up—to find a restaurant where her old home once stood. *And it's not even a Chinese restaurant. It's called USA Chicken.*

"Ma, is this the right place?" Lisa asks.

Silk checks the number on the front of the building. "This is the correct address." She glances up and down the street. "It looks like they turned this whole block into businesses."

"I am a little hungry," Abbey says, her stomach rumbling.

The three of them enter a bright red room, and Silk asks to speak with the owner of the establishment. The proprietor sports a goatee, wears thick glasses, and dresses in a white suit complete with a bowtie. The only deviations from a complete Colonel Sanders' knock-off are his thinning black hair and Asian complexion.

Silk, using Taiwanese, tells the man that she used to live in this exact spot and wonders if he knows anything about its previous residents. The man stares at her and then blinks. He takes off his heavy glasses, dusts them with a handkerchief, and proceeds to speak to her in slow Mandarin: No, he doesn't know anything about any house on this lot. He doesn't care about what happened to its old occupants. Now, did she want to eat some chicken or not? Silk swallows down the last of her unfounded, lingering hope to find evidence of her family's survival.

*

Silk rolls the greasy chicken in her mouth, dissatisfied. "I think there's something wrong with this chicken," she says.

"No, it's okay," Abbey says between noisy mouthfuls.

"I agree with you, Ma," Lisa says. "There's an ingredient here that doesn't taste quite right."

The bus boy stops sweeping near their table. He speaks to them in broken English. "Secret ingredient. Bitter melon."

Silk throws her half-eaten drumstick into the garbage, a symbol of her distaste with the whole Taipei experience. They leave the capital, taking the train down to the southern part of the island. The last leg of the trip happens in Kaohsiung. From her recent disappointment at the restaurant, Silk retains little optimism. She prepares her mind to relinquish her married home as lost. Still, she searches the street where Lu and she lived when they were married and ends up tracking down the old apartment.

The building still stands, with the same cracked façade. In the upper left corner of the wooden door, she spots the two intertwined doves that Lu carved onto it when they first moved in. He wanted their home to carry a permanent symbol of their union, and he picked the tranquil birds as a metaphor of lifetime peace in their relationship.

When she knocks on the door, a tall striking man and a sweet-looking petite woman peek out. Silk notices that they don't wear wedding bands on their fingers. The two appear to be in their late twenties, and they introduce themselves as Donald and Rebecca. After hearing that she used to live in the apartment, they invite her in.

Although the apartment's outside remains familiar, the inside has changed. The large wall between the kitchen and the living room has been knocked down. Silk used to hang Lu's artwork on its smooth vast surface. The tiny kitchenette is filled with sleek and modern appliances. The carpet in the living areas has shifted from a muted gray to a pulsing orange. Oversized furniture, decorated with inordinate fringes and extravagant ruffles, crowds the apartment and clamors for attention.

Silk forces the corners of her mouth to lift up in a polite smile. "It's a very nice place you have here."

"Thank you," Rebecca says. "It's very modern, isn't it?" She touches the shiny hood above the cooking range.

"It's all Western," Donald says. "My interior decorator studied in America and assures me our home imitates the height of style over there."

Silk detects a faint snicker from Lisa, but when Silk turns to glare at her, she sees both Lisa and Abbey intent on admiring a plump footstool.

Silk ends the visit. "Thank you for letting us come in." Nothing in the apartment reminds her of her married days, and she feels happy to escape to the nearby park.

When Silk stands on the grassy knoll, she finally experiences a slight sense of homecoming. She can see the harbor from her vantage point and is transported by the view. The boats bobbing on the indigo water greet her with tiny curtseys. The gentle breeze revives her spirits, and she closes her eyes to drink in the moment.

"Ma, we've found something!" Lisa calls out.

"Ah-Mah, you need to come take a look at this." Abbey's voice holds both surprise and fear.

Silk reluctantly opens her eyes and moves closer to the rest of her family. At first, she doesn't see it, even with her daughter and granddaughter pointing. A clump of brush hides a tall stone. Silk moves aside the branches and examines the stone plaque, a memorial for the 228 Massacre. It seems constructed in haste, no doubt because of the KMT leaders' continued control over the country. The wobbly writing, though, spouts poetry: "We mourn for our loss, the depths of which we can never measure. 02-28-47."

She sinks down on her knees at the stone's base, while Lisa and Abbey stand to the side with their heads bowed. Silk realizes that this monument is the closest thing to a burial Lu will ever receive. She wants to express a tribute to her late husband, and a million things flit through her mind. She longs to speak about her sorrow, her despair, her hurt at the tragedy. Instead, she decides to focus on the most important thing at that moment, reconciliation: "Lu, I've brought your daughter and granddaughter to see you."

A moment passes by in silence. Then Silk feels Lisa's hand on her shoulder. "Dad, I'm sorry I never got to meet you," she says. "I'm sad I didn't ask enough questions about you when I was a child, but I know that I will never forget you now."

Silk hears Abbey's voice next. "I'm so glad to be a part of the Lu family, and I'll strive to make you proud, Ah-Gung."

Abbey's use of the Taiwanese word for grandfather fills Silk's eyes with tears. She lets the salty rivers weave their course over her weathered cheeks. She blinks to renew her vision and spies a patch of wildflowers nearby. She uproots them without thinking and places them gently on the memorial.

The gap left in the dirt by Silk's spontaneous act stares back at her. She takes a moment to rummage in her purse to retrieve her canteen. She drinks the last dregs of water and fills up the entire container with the rich chocolate earth of home.

Jack

Will left a week ago, and Jack feels the emptiness in the cavern of his room. Lisa and her family's departure for Taiwan compounds the absence. In this expanse of solitude, Jack ponders his relationships over this past year.

Jack realizes that he's invested deeply in other people. He has careened from Fei to Lisa to Will, experiencing purpose in connecting to these individuals in his life. He wonders if he needs to link to any person—no matter how fleeting—to cultivate meaning in his life.

As usual, he decides to check on his vegetable plot early in the morning, greeting the other members of the gardening club with a jaunty wave of his hand. As he bends to check the texture of a ripe tomato, Rose Sweeting sidles up. Rose is a charming seventy-year old woman with a penchant for oversized floral hats. Her skin glows milky white, and she makes sure she dons lengthy gloves and long layers in the sun, to protect her lily complexion.

"Jack," she says with a sweeping smile, "could you come and look at my flowers?"

He walks over and looks at the colorful petals. "Those are some fine-looking petunias, Rose."

"Not as handsome as your vegetables, I'm afraid. What's your secret, Jack?"

She seems like the last person who needs to ask this question. She gets stacks of gardening magazines carted to her suite every week. He knows this because she lives two doors down from him. So he remains silent.

Rose saunters over to his patch of plants, employing a slight sway of her hips. She plucks up one of his carrots. She runs a slender figure down its sleek side and locks eyes with him. "What a fine specimen you have."

He stares at her. He knows that at Monroe Senior Home he's outnumbered by a 3:1 ratio of women-to-men. He'd been hit on before and after his wife passed away, but in more subtle ways. Female residents asked him over for tea or a game of cribbage, and he had always managed to finesse his way out of the invitation. At this interlude with Rose, though, Jack freezes.

She seems to take this as an invitation to progress. She puts the tip of the carrot to her lips. Her mouth appears soft and dewy. For one instant, he toys with the idea of a fling with her. His eyes move down from her fair face, assessing her body. Despite the complete covering up of her skin to block out the sun's damaging rays, he sees the appealing hourglass curves of her figure hinted at underneath the clothing.

Then she takes a bite of the pointed carrot, and the temptation passes. Something about her skull-white denture teeth chomping into the dirt-encrusted root frightens him. He backs a step away from Rose, and his voice returns to him.

"Maybe you could ask Bill for advice on gardening," Jack says. Bill's the actual hired hand for the home's landscaping. "He's the professional. I'm an amateur." Jack bids Rose a good day and moves away.

He brushes his rough fingers against the lilac bush before going back inside. He looks back once through the glass patio door at Rose. She remains standing where he left her, her expression unreadable under the awning of her giant sunflower hat.

After the exchange, Jack hurries to get out of Monroe Senior Home. He can't believe that he even considered Rose's offer. Does he need to fill the void of Will and Lisa so much that he would turn to a transient relationship?

He rests his hand against the well-worn steering wheel of his Rambler. He doesn't even need to concentrate as he takes the familiar route. Before he knows it, he's arrived at the local cemetery with its rolling verdant hills.

He locates the plot where the gravestones form a right triangle. One headstone needs to be placed, after his death, to complete its intended original square shape. He plans to be buried alongside Fei, one row beneath the mounds of the parents he respected.

He clears the area of weeds and stares at the green mass in his hands. The bothersome plants remain the only living things in the area, surviving above the pits of bones. He wipes down the markers, the granite chilling his fingertips. *What does it mean when your closest relationships disappear? Do you still exist when the people you love are gone?*

Abbey

Abbey picks up the phone on the second ring. The sharp shrill noise jarred her from slumber, but she sprang to the living room to grab the receiver. She knows that her mom and Ah-Mah need more rest than she does. In fact, her mom acts like a bear under the influence of jet lag.

Tess' exuberant voice surges down the line. "I'm so glad I got through to you. Guess what Drake told me?" Tess' boyfriend Drake had scored an internship at *Fairview News* for the summer through family connections and provided emerging news to Tess on an ongoing basis.

"I don't know." Abbey muffles a yawn. "What?"

"Oh, sorry. I forgot that you came home yesterday. Welcome back, by the way."

"Thanks. What's going on?"

"It's about Vance." Abbey had confided the whole story to Tess during camp, and now even Tess' voice drips with anger at the man's name.

"Is this about what Miss Vickers said?" Abbey asks.

"Yes." Tess sounds triumphant. "Vance admitted it."

"He did?"

"Apparently, once word got out about Miss Vickers' charges, other women stepped forward to complain, too. There are fourteen women in all, including your red-haired friend from New York who was at the party. She ended up reversing her story."

"Why did she lie in the first place?"

"She didn't accuse him in the beginning because she wanted to forget about the whole incident. Since she lived miles away from Fairview, she just wanted to move on with her life."

"That wasn't fair to me!" Abbey wraps the phone cord tight around her pinky. "Or any girls living right here who could've been hurt by him."

"Well, I heard that she received pressure from her cousin to shut up. You know, Ara's on the same basketball team as him."

"You don't say." Abbey lets the telephone wire spring back. "I can't believe Vance owned up to it."

"It just goes to show how one person's courage can change everything. All the allegations must have gotten to him, the scaredy-cat, because Vance confessed to all the charges today." Tess gives a long whistle. "He'll be put away for a long time."

Vindication floods through Abbey's body.

"Not only that, but the Aroyan family will be issuing a public apology." Tess sounds elated, like a little kid jumping up and down. Abbey hears breathlessness in her voice. *Maybe she's bouncing with joy for real.*

"Thanks for calling. I really appreciate it," Abbey says. "Let's talk again tomorrow. Same time?"

"Sure thing," Tess says.

Abbey places the phone back on the hook, dazed.

Two minutes later, the phone rings again.

"Tess?"

"No, it's Michelle Adams from school."

Abbey rubs her ear with her thumb. Had she heard right? "Michelle? Why are you calling me?"

"I heard about Vance's confession. I'm sorry I signed that petition against you."

"It's okay. I forgive you."

"Great. Now let's talk business. I want to do an exclusive interview with you, complete with details about the wild party and your undeserved petition."

"Sure." Abbey agrees to the front-page story planned for the fall edition of the school newspaper.

After Abbey hangs up the phone, she hears a rapping on the door. She opens it to find the local postal worker holding a stack of letters and a small oblong parcel. She places the mail for her mom and her grandmother to the side and discovers that a cream-stock envelope and the package are addressed to her.

The letter relays a formal apology from Principal Marshall. Next to the note lies a check made out to her mother, and the memo line labels it as Abbey's scholarship fund. The money's "for further studies after the excellent education provided at Atchison Elementary." Abbey bites her lip. She isn't sure what to do about it, so she ignores it for the moment.

She retrieves the package and turns it around in her hands. It feels empty, but removing the wrapping reveals an elegant velvet box. Inside, a glittering tennis bracelet snuggles next to a cotton cushion. The diamonds shine with a rainbow gleam. She finds a scrap of paper, too, written in a steady handwriting. The black letter soldiers march straight across the blue-lined paper.

She recognizes Ara's handwriting in an instant. "For any inconvenience you may have suffered," he writes.

She feels disgusted by the impersonal note; Ara should have apologized in person, and to a greater length. She's also disturbed by his gift. He can't seem to see beyond gender stereotypes. She doesn't even like jewelry. She thinks about chucking the whole thing—box and all—into the wastebasket but reconsiders. She picks up her telephone and dials a familiar phone number.

"Hey, Tess, do you know of a good pawn shop?"

Lisa

When Lisa returns to work after the Taiwan trip, she sees Maggie, her first customer ever, march through the door. Maggie wears the same worn expression Lisa noticed at their first meeting. When Maggie spots Lisa, though, her grey eyes change and start to sparkle.

"I heard you were on vacation. I'm so glad that you're back."

"It's good to see you, too, Maggie. Let me get your coffee for you." Lisa makes the plain brew steaming hot and places the Styrofoam cup in Maggie's hands.

"Thanks." Maggie stays in place, and a look of wistfulness crosses her face.

Lisa picks up on her vibe of loneliness. "We never did have lunch together. When do you want to meet up?"

Maggie decides on a place for later in the day. Lisa's glad on two counts for the fast decision: she wants to be a friend to Maggie, and she wants to avoid eating alone at home. Ma took the day off for grandma-granddaughter bonding time. She has gone on these outings every other week since Abbey's been around for the summer. Their latest adventure entailed getting manicures, the first time for both her mother and Abbey.

To Lisa's surprise, her mother enjoyed the pampering, although the nail polish won't last five minutes in the vineyards. In contrast, Abbey hated the experience. She didn't like the stink of the parlor, the trimming of the cuticles, or the jabbing of the orangewood stick. Still, the two bonded over choosing the most outrageous colors available at the salon ("pink elephant" for Ma and "orange orangutan" for Abbey) and finding decorations for the nails. Her mother chose delicate sprays of cherry blossoms, while Abbey opted for miniature zebras to fit her zoo-themed color.

*

Lisa and Maggie share lunch at a local spot, the Café Fresca. The place specializes in gourmet sandwiches, made to order. Lisa bites into her entree, truffle-lined prosciutto wrapped in crisp focaccia. "How's your day so far, Maggie?"

Maggie groans. "Please don't ask. I never like to talk about work. It's horrible in RMA."

"What's RMA?"

"Return merchandise authorization. Basically, I sit at a desk and answer phone calls, and people complain to me about defective products they receive. All I can do is apologize and act as their personal punching bag."

"That bad, huh?"

Maggie spears the pickle on her plate with a fork. "I'm used to it, though. The job gets routine after awhile. Plus, it's a nice change to have problems that deal with things, like a piece of plastic or a metal object. Relationship issues are much harder."

Lisa nods. "People are complex."

"Or stupid. No, not people. *I'm* stupid." Maggie's brow wrinkles in frustration.

"I don't think you're stupid."

"You didn't see Tracy at school the other day," Maggie says. "I was supposed to chaperone a museum field trip, but I plain forgot. I was half-listening to a customer on the line and drawing up a chore list when I finally remembered. I arrived to see Tracy leaving the museum. How could I do that to my little girl?"

Lisa pats Maggie's hand. "It was a mistake."

Maggie moves away from Lisa's touch. "Tracy was looking forward to the trip together. She talked about it for weeks. Do you know what really drove the guilt home? When I wrapped my arms around Tracy, she didn't blame me. She didn't even ask me why I was late. Tracy smiled at me and said, 'Thanks for coming.'"

"Do you know what? I forgot to pick up my daughter, Abbey, once during a teacher in-service day. She had to call me to get her."

Maggie's shoulders lift up a little at Lisa's admission.

"In fact," Lisa says, "it was because I picked up my daughter late, that I stumbled onto Jack, the friend with a broken leg whom I helped out."

"You're kidding, right?"

"Nope." Lisa tells Maggie the full story of taking care of Jack, complete with the relationship break-up and the semi-reconciliation.

"I'm glad you two sort of reconnected in the end. And thanks for cheering me up."

"No problem. I like sharing stories," Lisa says. "I wish I had someone like you to talk with before."

"Well, I definitely appreciate your talking with me now."

"Do you know what, Maggie? Maybe we could meet regularly."

"Yeah, we'll be a support group for, for..."

"The sandwich generation," Lisa says, holding up her meal. "We're sandwiched between taking care of our children and our elders."

"Excuse me." A petite blonde woman in a white lace blouse and black slacks walks over to them. She carries a tray with an eggplant sandwich and a steaming cappuccino. "I couldn't help but overhear you two. Did you say that you're holding a support group for caretakers? When do you meet?"

Lisa starts to correct the woman but sees Maggie give her head a slight shake. *Why not? The more, the merrier.* "We'd love to have you join," Lisa says. "Why don't you give me your contact information, and I'll let you know about our next meeting?"

Silk

Silk splays her destroyed nails in front of her face for inspection. The "pink elephant" color, reminiscent of Pepto-Bismol, shows jagged edges and holes. Her fingernails parallel how she feels. She's exhausted after two hours of work, so despite the long drive into town to see the doctor, she relishes the respite. Even against the cushy driver's seat, though, her back hurts. She placed a heating pad on it last night, clucking her tongue at her advancing age. Today, she found herself wheezing as she carried a crate of grapes around.

She arrives at Dr. Eggleston's office for the routine blood test. She jokes to the doctor about the aches of her aging body. As usual, Dr. Eggleston remains quiet. The physician's typical reserve irks Silk now. *She could at least crack a smile.*

The phlebotomist at the laboratory works in a quick, professional manner. Silk's wrinkled, sun-spotted arm sometimes hides her veins. Unlike some of his other colleagues, though, the man pokes the needle in on the first try and removes her blood.

On her way back to work, she wonders when her results will come in. The laboratory that diagnoses the blood samples resides upstairs in the same building. She sometimes manages to receive her numbers one or two days after a visit. As she steps onto the premises of Lincoln Vineyards, Gus comes out to meet her.

"Silk, you have a call from Dr. Eggleston. Come on into my office."

She pauses to catch her breath after her walk from the car and picks up the phone. "Dr. Eggleston? I just got in."

"Mrs. Lu, we need you back in the office to discuss your results," Dr. Eggleston says.

"You received my blood work results already? The lab must be having a very slow day."

"Actually, I asked them to expedite the testing," her doctor says.

"Whatever for?"

"I'd really like to talk to you in person…"

*

Apparently, Dr. Eggleston acted on a hunch when she heard about Silk's recent pain. The doctor didn't dismiss them as mere signs of aging. In fact, she ordered Silk's blood work to be evaluated immediately. The results show the tumor markers growing exponentially, doubling every week.

Silk sits upright, shocked, on the examination table. She hears Dr. Eggleston talk about recurrence, but all she can process is the annoying crinkle of the thin paper underneath her. Through a haze, she understands that Dr. Eggleston wants to order a CT scan, a MRI, and a bone scan. Her doctor promises to alert Silk's oncologist and her surgeon.

Silk doesn't understand these actions. She had a clean bill of health a month ago. In fact, Silk's trip to Taiwan left her feeling more vibrant than ever.

"Dr. Eggleston," Silk says. "The numbers must be wrong."

"The technician ran the test several times, Mrs. Lu." Dr. Eggleston says this in a tone of martyred patience.

"That can't be right. My last check-up turned out fine."

"Yes, but I'm sorry to say, your prior results don't guarantee immunity for the future." A small frown surfaces on her doctor's typically tranquil face.

Silk forces out the next words: "How much time do I have?"

"It's hard to say." Dr. Eggleston's fingers clench at her pure white smock, leaving sweat stains on its hem. "It's possible that the cancer has progressed from your bones—that would explain your constant aches—to your lungs. You also mentioned that you experienced some wheezing today. When cancer reaches the lungs or the liver, five percent of patients live for a year, and two percent live for two years after the diagnosis."

Silk stifles a gasp and gives her doctor a thin smile. "I think I have some phone calls to make then."

Jack

If Jack were in school, the comment section in his report card would read, "Meets expectations." He feels like he's followed everyone's desires to the letter. When he was a child, he listened to his parents and heeded their every command. He figured that they were decades wiser than him, and he always trusted their advice. He never even considered a rebellious period during his teenage years.

When he met Fei, he transferred all his devotion over to her. He served as the friend, the lover, and the provider that she needed. Even with Lisa, he conformed into the father figure that she wanted. The rift in their relationship, caused by her sudden departure, still remains a fracture between them.

He can listen to all of Lisa's woes and worries, but he wonders if she could ever be a daughter like the one he once dreamed about. Likewise, Abbey could never be the doted upon granddaughter. Whenever Abbey sees him, she acts courteous but distant. At least, Abbey's intense previous grudge against him has passed since the arrival of Will at Atchison Elementary.

At this juncture in his life, he realizes that the only expectations he hasn't met are his own. In fact, he has never been concerned about his own welfare. He wonders if you can experience a mid-life crisis at the ripe age of 66.

He decides to go over to his vegetable garden to analyze his thoughts further. When he looks through the patio glass and sees Rose, though, he retraces his steps. Ever since her proposition, calm flees from him in her presence.

He turns around, hunts down his car keys, and shuffles over to his Rambler. He tries the ignition, hears it stutter, and hits the dashboard in its sweet spot to start the engine. *I know one thing for sure; I never want a new car.* His Rambler has been his companion for so many years, it's like a dear friend to him. He knows all its quirks and capabilities.

He drives past his usual coffee shop haunt, driving farther than he ever has before. He wants to get lost in the momentum of driving because it always clears his mind. He winds up in a section of town known as the "poor side." Even the shoddy part of Fairview (which "true" residents point out possesses a Fairview mailing address without the city services—getting them from L.A. County instead) seems encouraging. He spots zero hoodlums or drug dealers. Instead, he sees stout women bustling to collect laundry off lines and children in frayed, but modestly patched up, clothes.

He doesn't want to park in front of somebody's home, so he settles into a dusty vacant lot. The dirt appears dried and caked in; even weeds don't dare to intrude on the baked earth. Five minutes pass before a congregation of local boys and girls arrive. Not one looks older than twelve.

The children give Jack a curious glance as they enter the lot. Their ringleader, a tall tanned boy, tells them to focus. "Come on," he says, "let's play!" The leader bounces a beaten soccer ball up and down, alternating between his left and right feet.

A memory emerges in Jack's mind: Eric, a student from the local college, would chit-chat with him on a regular basis. One time, Eric talked about his upbringing in the undesirable part of Fairview.

"People wonder what it's like to be born on the poor side. I don't think I ever thought of it that way. I just knew that my mom and dad worked hard at their jobs, and I figured I should do the same at school."

"So you don't feel out of place here?" Jack motioned to the clean-cut students dressed in fancy clothes.

"No. I think people are all basically the same everywhere. We had nice folks, mean folks, smart folks, stupid folks, and crazy folks. The only difference I see here is the grass."

"Did you say *grass*?" Jack asked.

Eric spread one of his massive hairy hands across the green growth of the lawn. He plucked a blade and seemed to memorize its contours. "It's so *alive*. All we had growing up near our apartments were crusty, yellowed lawns overgrown with weeds. Nobody had the space, the time, or the energy to putter in the outdoors. In fact, I remember playing soccer on this dry, dusty piece of land. Whenever you fell, your skin scraped right off."

Jack hears a shrill scream through his car window. As though his memory has turned alive, a little mousy girl tumbles and skins her knee. She reminds him of Abbey, with her small elflike face. She cries for her mother, but the tall ringleader moves in and bandages her up. He whispers a few words into her ear, and then she gets up and goes on with the game.

What if the children had rich, lush grass? When they landed, the children would roll on the softness of the turf and laugh instead of weep. It wouldn't take too much work. Jack begins creating a list of the necessary materials in his head.

Abbey

Abbey imbibes the ambience of downtown Fairview. She likes what she sees. It feels like a far cry from the usual spots she frequents, with their glossy exteriors and moneyed airs. Downtown Fairview possesses an urban, gritty feel. A mixture of Fairview residents and Los Angeles neighbors jostle each other down its concrete paths. She feels safe, though, with feisty Tess by her side and Tess' mom working at the bank around the corner. As if in tune with her thoughts on danger, Abbey hears Tess' pager beep—Abbey's mom checking up on them, no doubt.

Abbey sneaks an admiring glance at Tess strolling next to her. Tess, a frequent visitor of the area, glides down the busy sidewalks adorned with mom n' pop stores and sleek chain invaders. A rusted bronze statue of Fairview's first founder stands guard in the middle of the pedestrian square, a half-hearted attempt to instill some culture in the commercial district.

They find the pawnshop they're looking for, a tiny storefront with a heap of mismatched items overflowing its display window. Abbey peeks past the wobbly tower of goods. Inside, the organization system appears haphazard: scarves drape over stereos, pillows mix with toasters.

"Are you sure this is the best pawnshop in town?" Abbey asks Tess.

"Absolutely. I've found the most useful items here, like an authentic flapper's dress."

"That's a helpful item for you, huh?"

"It is for any *aspiring actress*," Tess says. "Anyway, Sal offers the best prices around."

Tess pushes open the door, to a silver bell's merry tinkle. Sal looks lean, his gaunt features chiseled into a walnut complexion.

"Good to see you back, Tess." Sal grins, and crow lines appear around his wide-set eyes.

"I brought someone because I love showing your place to people. This is my wonderful friend, Abbey. She's got something to pawn."

Abbey pulls out the shining diamond bracelet, and it slithers free from her palm onto the scratched glass table top. Sal emits a low whistle as he examines the stones under a magnifying glass. "Are you sure you want to pawn this?"

"Definitely," Abbey says.

*

Abbey and Tess leave five minutes later. Abbey fingers the bulging wad of money in her pants pocket.

"Don't worry," Tess says. "The office is just up the street."

The girls' strides match one another as they walk toward a drab green façade. Faded lettering across an awning marks the building as "Teen Might."

The lobby seems like a barebones affair with metal folding chairs set out. Air Supply's "All Out of Love" crackles out of a begrudging radio. Abbey approaches the front counter, staffed by a friendly redhead with braces.

"I'd like to make a financial donation to the center," Abbey says.

The girl smiles wide, and freckles dance across her dimples. "That's wonderful. Let me show you to our director's office."

She takes them to Pamela Darby's office. It's a tiny room with just enough space to fit a large metal filing cabinet and a coffee-stained desk. Abbey and Tess sit across from the director in hard folding chairs.

"I would like to donate some money," Abbey says.

"That's real kind of you." Pamela puts a hand up as Abbey reaches into her pocket. "Slow down, honey. Have a drink." She pours a tall glass of sweet iced tea for each of them and leans back in her chair. "How did you hear about us?"

Abbey appreciates the director's calm and easy manner. She likes the drawl in the Southern woman's voice and the tuft of honey hair that sweeps across one eye. "I had an *encounter*... so I went to the library and researched all the local non-profits that offered sexual assault counseling to teens."

Pamela nods with empathy but doesn't press Abbey about her history. "What made you pick us, darling?"

Abbey doesn't usually care for sugar-laden endearments, but the term seems genuine enough coming from the director's lips. Abbey hesitates. "Well, there aren't that many organizations to choose from in the local area. I like the objective of Teen Might to empower adolescents and the fact that young people can volunteer for the counseling positions."

Abbey takes the money out of her pocket and pushes it toward Pamela. The director doesn't even bat an eye at the sight of a pile of bills and coins advancing toward her. "Would you like a receipt, dear?"

"No thanks, and I'd rather be anonymous," Abbey says.

"Well, thank you for your generosity. Please take your time to finish the sweet tea."

Abbey nods but gulps down the rest of the syrupy liquid. Pamela hands each of them a brochure on their way out to explain more about the programs offered at Teen Might. She gives them each a hug and says, "You know, we could use a few more caring gals like yourselves around here."

Lisa

Coffee and Crullers seems different at night. The muted light lends a soft atmosphere to the scarred tables and scuffed-up chairs. Lisa's group, though, sits in the semi-luxurious "Reading Corner," the finest space in the coffeehouse.

An arrangement of overstuffed plaid armchairs crowds next to a rickety bookshelf carrying dilapidated reading material. The distance from the other tables and patrons, as well as the coziness of the furniture, makes it an ideal setting to chat about the group's family problems.

Lisa wonders if her mother felt this stiff at her first AA meeting. The introductions start out formal and dry:

"Hi, I'm Lisa. I have an eleven-year-old going on twenty named Abbey. I also take care of my mother, Silk, who has been battling breast cancer."

"Hello, I'm Maggie. I balance caring for my five-year-old daughter Tracy and my mother-in-law Lucille, who recently broke a hip."

The petite blonde from the café greets them next. "Hi, I'm Heidi. My son Adam is seven years old and has dyslexia. My father Carl is seventy years old and was recently diagnosed with Alzheimer's."

The women settle in with their caffeinated beverages. With each sip, their tongues loosen. They share the odds and ends of their past week. Maggie talks about the uncomfortable similarity in bathing her daughter and her mother-in-law. It confuses Maggie to see her powerful mother-in-law reduced to a childlike figure. Heidi relays the story of Carl wandering in circles around the neighborhood that he's lived in for forty years, unable to find his own house. It scares Heidi to see her father lost, and she worries about his future. Heidi also wonders whether his disease is inheritable and will pass down to her or her son.

"What about you, Lisa?" Heidi asks. Her baby blue eyes project a sense of youthful earnestness as she waits for Lisa's answer.

Lisa rubs her face with her hands. "It's been a long week," she says. "My mother's cancer has come back."

"Oh no," Heidi says.

Maggie, silent, places an arm around Lisa's shoulder and gives it a tight squeeze.

"The cancer has already spread to her lungs, and the doctors don't give her a good prognosis."

"When is she starting radiation again?" Maggie asks.

Lisa drops her head and speaks into her chest. "Ma's decided not to undergo chemo again. She says she's handling cancer a different way this time around."

"Is it an alternative method?" Heidi asks.

Lisa gives the ghost of a laugh. "You could call it that. Ma's way of dealing with the recurrence is to make a wish list of things to do before she dies."

Silk

Silk narrows the list again, crossing things out until her top three choices remain. She isn't sure how much time she has left, but Dr. Eggleston said that it would be "very short." Silk prepares for a quick departure from this world. She already quit Lincoln Vineyards and has expressed her appreciation to Gus and her colleagues. She even visited her local Alcoholics Anonymous meeting site and dropped off an ikebana arrangement to express her gratitude to them.

"What's this for?" the leader asked.

"It's a symbol of the serenity you provide people at these meetings," Silk said. "An emblem of the peace you gave to me."

What Silk didn't say was that the minimalist floral display reminded her of her unencumbered youth in Taipei, when the art form under Japanese rule blossomed in hotels, shops, and homes. She didn't reveal that ikebana was the closest she came to step eleven of the famous AA list, connecting with an unseen God.

This tenuous line to faith helps her feel at peace with death. She has decided once again to avoid aggressive treatment against her cancer. This time, though, she bases her choice on grounded statistics instead of nebulous notions of fate or karma. She understands the grim odds, and she prefers living the rest of her time active rather than chasing an impossible cure.

Making a bucket list, despite her daughter's aversion to the idea, isn't a morbid activity for Silk. She sees the checklist as a compilation of her ultimate goals. In fact, it feels more like a testament to *living* than to dying.

She reads her list one more time: 1. Travel to Rome, 2. Rent a Convertible, and 3. Act Like a Tourist.

She thinks about her number one priority goal: her first objective refers to a mutual dream shared by Lu and Silk. They always wanted to travel and joked that they would traverse the globe once Lu became famous from his scientific breakthroughs.

"Where would you go first?" they asked each other once while daydreaming about their future travels.

"Italy," they replied at the same time. They even agreed on exploring the same magnificent city, Rome.

"I want to see the history and the architecture there," Lu said.

"I want to people watch and experience their food," Silk said. She imagined that she would like a country filled with artists, creators of fancy operas and brilliant paintings. It seemed so fascinating and a good break from the scientific jargon her husband spouted. Besides, she loved noodles, and the pasta-eating Italians seemed like her sort of people.

She rifles through the paper statements on the table near her bucket list. She'll be pulling money out of her pension to cover the expenses of her goals. *Instead of golden years of retirement, I'll have golden weeks.*

Jack

Jack sits in his only suit—a wrinkled salmon Salvation Army find—clutching the numbered ticket. The brightly lit standard-issue government room appears almost empty. A few lumberyard types lounge on the hard benches, and the wait feels interminable until the staff calls his number.

The city official is dressed in oxfords and an arrogant smile. "Number 93, what do you need?" he asks.

"I'm not sure." Jack falters. "I think I need a city permit. I want to plant grass on an empty public lot. It's near Jackson Avenue and Maple Street."

The official wrinkles his brow, unsure of the coordinates. Jack bets that the man has never stepped into that part of town before. After a moment, the man shrugs and reaches into a tottering paper basket. "You'll need to fill these out and send us a $500 check. Next in line," the official says. Jack holds the mass of paperwork in his hands, already disheartened by the miniscule print.

He returns to Monroe Senior Home to brood in one of its velveteen couches. How will he start the project when he can't even brave the paperwork? How will he pay the fee? He lives at the home on the charity of Fei's old employer, and he has no money to spare.

While sitting there, he sees Rose pass by, an arm draped loosely around a stranger's waist. She stops in front of him. "What's wrong, Jack? The meeting's still in five minutes, right?"

It takes a moment for the words to register, and then Jack launches off the soft cushion with a jolt. The Monroe Gardening Club will be meeting in the Sun Room soon, and he has to preside over its proceedings. The club meets once a month, usually to sort over territorial squabbles. Members often complain about each other's crops overgrowing the individual set boundaries.

"Jack." Rose grabs his arm to stop him from bolting. She motions to the man standing next to her. "This is Charles Peters. He recently moved in, and I'm showing him around."

The tall stranger appears to be in his early eighties, but the man's back remains ramrod-straight and his gaze level. Dark brown eyes hide beneath white bushy eyebrows, and a thick mustache quivers as he speaks. "It's nice to meet you, Jack. Rose has been saying marvelous things about you. May I join your meeting?"

"Certainly, Charles. It's this way." Jack leads them to where the dozen members of the gardening club await his arrival.

After he mediates their squabbles, he clears his throat. "I need help," he says. "I'm trying to renovate an old lot near Jackson and Maple. I want to plant grass and make it a park for the local kids. The city, though, requires a mountain of paperwork to be filled along with a $500 fee. Can anybody help me?"

He hears shouts from all around him. The room echoes with excited voices. All the members want to assist him with plotting out the land. A previous lawyer offers to help Jack handle the paperwork. Another man explains that he can secure discounted supplies at the local hardware store. Rose suggests selling their own flowers and vegetables to raise money for the city fee, and other members want to give out of their own pockets for the cause.

Last to speak, the newcomer Charles booms out from the back of the room. "You know, Jack," he says. "My nephew is on the board of the city council. I think he can expedite this whole process." Jack blinks in surprise at the offer, and then he grasps Charles' hands in a warm shake.

Abbey

Abbey has never been scared of the telephone until now. The red device rests soft and sinister against its cradle. She curls her toes up to stop the tremors in her body as she looks at it.

She surveys the now familiar room to calm her nerves. The Teen Might call room consists of a bank of telephones arrayed on a vinyl folding table. The far wall is filled with letters of gratitude from adolescents who have been helped by the organization. A side table holds a platter of day-old pastries along with an enormous vat of bitter coffee. On her first day of training, she thought that the thermos contained hot cocoa and almost spat out the putrid liquid at Tess.

With several weeks left before school began, Abbey and Tess had decided to volunteer at Teen Might. All workers undergo a week of training from 9am-2pm. Five people, including the two of them, had shown up at the orientation.

The first few days passed in an easy rhythm of memorization, comforting to Abbey in its similarity to school. She learned about the difference between empathy and sympathy, and the importance of conveying real understanding to her troubled peers. She discovered active listening; during role-play, Abbey practiced paying close attention to the conversation and rephrasing the other person's statements, but Abbey felt like she parroted back the speaker's words.

On the second day of training, Abbey received a giant magnet with different emotions on it. The top of it read, "Today I am feeling…" A miniature square frame could be moved around the sheet to capture the day's emotion. The options covered sad, anxious, confused, happy, and hysterical, among others. In truth, she kept the marker centered on "content" most of the time.

One spot on the board was fill-in-the-blank, though. This morning, Abbey had drawn an anxious face and written the word "frazzled" in the open area. Before she had left for Teen Might, her mom had erased Abbey's work and doodled in a smiling face paired with the word "confident."

Abbey smiles at the thought of her mom's encouragement. Who knew they could connect in such a silly way? Feeling braver, she readies her hand on the telephone receiver.

The last activity for training week involves receiving a mock call from one of Teen Might's regular counselors. Abbey sits alone near the telephone, the other trainees watching her from the side near the refreshments table. Her pretend client remains hidden from Abbey's sight by calling from the director's office, making the situation seem more real.

She takes a deep breath and picks up the buzzing phone. "Hello? This is Teen Might. My name is Abbey. How can I help you?"

"Hi, Abbey." A stranger's voice travels down the line. "I'm Melanie. I wanted to talk to you about this party I went to last night."

Abbey's mouth feels like cotton as she repeats the words back. "You went to a party last night?"

"Uh-huh. I went with my boyfriend Jim, who's five years older than me, and he brought me to his frat house. Something happened there…"

Abbey's voice whispers. "Happened?"

"Jim left me to talk to some friends. I was the only high schooler there, and I was nervous, so I drank an entire beer before he came back. Jim placed a hand on my thigh and said, 'Let's go somewhere private.' He led me to a bedroom, where I saw two of his buddies inside, and then Jim locked the door." The caller bursts into tears at this juncture, and Abbey follows suit.

Abbey hangs up the phone with shaking hands. She can deal with her own drama, supported by her friends and family. She has somewhat processed through her emotions, and she feels closure from the outcome of the lawsuit against Vance. However, she sure isn't ready to delve into another person's pain and misery.

Tess travels to Abbey's side and holds her. The door to the call room swings open to reveal the director, Pamela Darby, and a concerned-looking brunette teenager with a "Melanie" nametag stuck on her shirt. *Oh, I really screwed up this time.*

Pamela runs over to Abbey. "It's okay, sweetheart." She hands Abbey several tissues, and Abbey uses one with great force, shredding it to bits.

Pamela considers Abbey for a moment and says in a soft tone, "You've experienced a *situation* before, right? Have you dealt with all your pain, dear?"

Abbey stops crying and looks straight into the director's eyes. "Yes, I'm okay with *my own* experience, but not other people's yet."

Pamela looks at Abbey and Tess, and says, "Well, there is another way you two girls can help at Teen Might…"

Lisa

The businesswoman edges closer to their group, her chair tilted at an angle to better listen. This is the fourth time Support Sisters (as they call themselves) have met at Coffee and Crullers. Lisa spotted the eavesdropper two weeks ago. The first time, the woman, dressed in a pinstripe ensemble paired with tennis shoes, had voiced an audible sigh and plopped in a recess upon entering the coffee shop. The lady had untwisted her chignon, freeing a cascade of curly caramel hair. While nursing a steaming beverage with one hand, the woman had glanced at their close-knit group.

At the next meeting, the manager had offered to save the Reading Corner for Lisa's group. He posted a sign saying, "Reserved for Support Sisters, 8pm-10pm." After it went up, Lisa noticed the mystery woman looking even more interested in their activities. The stranger tried to be subtle about her efforts, but Lisa noticed that the woman chose an increasingly closer table on each subsequent visit.

With the session now in progress and the woman sitting a few feet away, Lisa frowns. Her friends share intimate thoughts that require confidentiality:

"I can't carry a 140-pound woman out of the tub by myself. If only I could find a way to pay for a bathing assistant..."

"My dad's Alzheimer's sometimes makes him scratch and bite me. I don't know what to do."

"Let's stop for a moment," Lisa says in a low voice.

Lisa appears at the mystery woman's side and startles her. "We're having a private discussion," Lisa says. "We would appreciate it if you didn't listen to our conversation."

The woman turns a bright red. "I'm so sorry."

Lisa stares hard at the stranger. "You've been watching us for several weeks now. What makes you so interested in our group?"

The woman blinks her cat-green eyes in surprise. "I didn't know I was so obvious. I've been trying to find out what kind of group you're running to see if I could be of any help." She reaches into her faux leather briefcase and pulls out a business card.

"Marla Jones," Lisa reads. "Administrator at Families First. What's that?"

"We're a nonprofit that offers resources to families who are caring for sick relatives."

Lisa cocks her head to one side, thinking. "Well, your organization would be helpful to us. We're an informal group of caregivers who stumbled upon one another, and we're not aware of all the services out there."

"Families First is a great resource," Marla says. "I'm really sorry I disrupted your meeting. I wasn't sure how to best approach you."

Despite Marla's mature title and her professional outfit, Lisa realizes that Marla is younger than she first thought. The girl seems just out of college.

"I accept your apology," Lisa says. "I'll try to visit your office soon."

Marla's sweetheart face smiles at the promise. "I'd like that. Thanks."

As Marla disappears through the door, Lisa returns to Support Sisters. She explains her delay, and the ladies all concur: Lisa needs to visit Families First as soon as possible.

Silk

Silk has eaten pasta at every meal for the last four days in Italy, although only a few bites at a time because of her diminishing appetite. She never realized that pasta came in so many disguises. She has tried pasta in squid ink, pasta alla carbonara, and pasta with *guanciale* (cured pork cheek), among other dishes.

Still not tired of it, she looks at the menu and orders. When her meal comes, she realizes she asked for a soup instead of a dry noodle dish. The pasta e fagioli arrives in a steaming bowl. Despite its overabundance of beans and its distinctive short tube noodles, she is reminded of her old days with Lu.

She packed her husband's lunch every day. In the decadent days, before the food shortages under the Kuomintang rule, she made noodles with tender stewed meat and crisp verdant vegetables. Later on, her recipes devolved to noodles with a sprinkling of scallions. They say that love can exist on an empty stomach, but her heart wept to see her husband's lean and hungry frame. Eventually, she and Lu could only afford sweet potatoes, those Taiwan island-shaped symbols of poverty. Sometimes, she salted the potatoes with her tears.

She pushes the hot bowl of pasta soup away from her. She pays for the untouched food and leaves. She will find another restaurant, devoid of noodles and empty of sad memories.

The way she finds a place to eat in Rome is by wandering. She doesn't have much choice, since she's directionally-challenged. On the first day of her trip, she attempted to follow her guidebook and became utterly lost. The labyrinth of streets confused her—besides which, some of the alley names lay obscured, carved into the far recesses of brick walls. At the end of each day, she hails a cab to take her back to the hotel. The ease of returning home fast outweighs the extravagant cost.

She toes one of the cobblestones beneath her feet. The unevenness aggravates her back pain, but she likes the pedestrian-friendly city and enjoys the quaint European feel that pervades the area. Italy vibrates with so much history, on every stone that she treads upon. She glances at the picturesque piazza surrounding her.

The open square boasts a small fountain displaying frolicking nymphs at its center. She stops to watch the bustle of people: tourists draped in heavy cameras gasp in delight at the scenery around them, and locals decked in effortless fashion whistle as they stroll by in leisure. A delicious aroma wafts in the air, making her salivate. She follows its scent and steps around the corner, brushing up against one of the many tiny Italian cars jam-packed on the side streets.

She looks in surprise at the tiny storefront advertising pizza *al taglio*, "by the slice." She sniffs again, in doubt, but the perfume leads straight to their counter, where a number of patrons stand waiting. She gets in the line. When it's her turn, the multitude of options overwhelms her. Finally, she orders a piece of pizza *bianca*. Still unfamiliar with any Italian words, she has to gesture with her hands to indicate how big of a slice for the man to cut. She takes the odd version of pizza and examines it. It doesn't contain cheese or sauce but uses olive oil and salt instead.

When she tries it, the piping hot pizza delights her tongue. She blows on the slice in rapid successive puffs to hasten the cooling process and eat it faster. She goes back in line for seconds. *They don't make pizza like this back in America.* Nevertheless, she knows that she'll hold back any bitter remarks the next time Lisa orders from Antonio's Pizzeria in Fairview.

Silk spends the next two days hunting down every pizza place in sight. She finds that she likes the fast bakery shops rather than the sit-down restaurants. She likes to eat a slice while wandering outside. At the end of her two-day pizza rampage, she splurges on a gelato. She uses lazy licks to taste the creamy pistachio-flavored treat as the sun sets and drowns the neighboring buildings in crimson. In the ruddy warmth, she experiences both a happy stomach and a joyful heart.

She reserves the last day of her trip for architectural exploration, in honor of Lu. She prefers the open outdoors over stuffy interiors, despite the excellent artistry found inside many of Rome's historical buildings. Given her likes, she selects the Roman Forum and the Colosseum to visit.

Il Foro Romano was the bastion of Roman culture. Walking among the pitted stones, she finds it hard to visualize it as the past epicenter of Rome. She gazes hard at the remains of the Basilica Giulia, but she can't picture a hundred judges filling its space. She shakes her head, knowing that she will never appreciate the arches, the history, and the legacy of the place as Lu would have. However, she can pretend that her husband's spirit walks beside her as she picks her way around the marble fragments.

She experiences a slight sadness that the rocks are the only remnants of numerous old temples, shops, and palaces. In spite of the destruction, she sees a mass of people milling about. She can see that the Forum remains honored in the hearts of the Italian people. *Perhaps, Taiwanese people can also be like that. Although the 228 Massacre destroyed the country's elite, Taiwan can remain strong and continue to honor their lives and contributions.*

Her next stop is the Colosseo. She skirts the dressed-up gladiators pouncing on the tourists to purchase admission tickets. She doesn't know a thing about the Colosseum, so she tags behind a tour group, one of the many scattered along the area's perimeter.

She fixes herself in the back of a Japanese tour group. She retains a clear understanding of the language from her schooling in Taiwan during Japan's occupation. The guide relays the Colosseum's sordid history. Silk can't believe that the arena housed gladiators and wild beasts, pitted against each other for people's amusement. She discovers that the Colosseum changed into a sacred place, with the Vatican preserving the arena in order to honor the memory of martyred Christians.

After the games stopped, she learns that it became a depository for materials, which looters then stole. These supplies were later used to build Renaissance churches and palaces. How could so many lovely places come from such guilty beginnings?

Despite the knowledge of Rome's violent history, she views the city as one of beauty. She thinks that Taiwan can be described in the same manner. In spite of the 228 Massacre, Taiwan can still be the *Isla Formosa*, the Beautiful Island, to her.

Jack

Jack stands with the rest of the Monroe Gardening Club, admiring their work. The dusty lot on Jackson Avenue and Maple Street has been transformed into a lush green oasis, with several saplings lining the edges. He can already imagine the trees full-grown, their abundant foliage shading picnicking families.

Rose stands next to him, but for once he doesn't mind. Since the last gardening club meeting at the senior home, she has started dating Charles. Jack no longer feels anxious passing her in the hallways. He can see her eyes fixed on the iron gate leading to the park despite her oversized purple felt hat. All the club members wait in anticipation for the local boys and girls to arrive.

The children jostle one another as they run through the gate. They smile at the dew beneath their feet and pull in hungry breaths of the fresh grass scent. He sees their tall leader walk in last. The boy pauses on the border between street and field, looks in Jack's direction, and gives him a slight nod. Then the youth moves onto the lawn, bouncing a soccer ball high and shouting, "Let's play now!"

Residents on the nearby streets don't walk up to see the new development. Instead, the men loiter out of their windows, flicking ashes from their cigarettes in the park's direction. Some of the women look up from stringing their laundry on their balconies and flash the seniors a brief smile. Their emotion lasts mere seconds before they reach into their bulging baskets to pull out another damp shirt to hang on the line.

Jack knows that the woman walking with bold steps toward their group isn't native to the area. The lady's got a glued-on plastic smile, and she's dressed in a severely pressed shirt and slacks. The trim and efficient brunette introduces herself as Natalie Waters from *Fairview News*. "I'm doing an article on the park," she says. She whips out a pad and pen. "Now, whose idea was this?"

*

The interview lands in the dreary middle of the newspaper, next to the "News of the Weird" section, but Jack glows with pride. It's the first time he's ever been mentioned in print, and he reads the short piece over again.

"FN: What inspired you to create this park?

Jack Chen: I had a student named Eric when I was working at the local college. Eric couldn't get enough of the outdoors because he grew up on the poor side. He told me about this piece of dusty dried-up land.

FN: What has been the reaction of the residents nearby?

Chen: They haven't said anything to me about it. Then again, what's so special about grass? In my opinion, they should have always had a park.

FN: Do you think you'll complete other projects?

252

Chen: Who knows? I never dreamed that I would pick up gardening as a hobby at the age of 66.

FN: Anything else you'd like to tell our readers?

Chen: I couldn't have done this without the help of my friends at the Monroe Gardening Club."

Jack places the newspaper in the Monroe Senior Home dining room, a strategic location for all the other residents to see the article. Then he wanders down the home's hallways. He hears the television set blaring from the entertainment room. He turns down its annoying volume and notices that the station is set to the local news broadcast.

A newscaster interviews a younger-looking version of Charles. *It must be Charles' councilman nephew.* "In fact," the councilman says, "I thought of the park idea myself."

The interviewer looks surprised. "I thought *Fairview News* correspondent Natalie Waters cited Jack Chen as the originator of the beautification plan."

Charles' nephew leans closer to the news anchor. "Sometimes older people get their facts mixed up. I actually *requested* the man to do the job, along with the rest of his crew at Monroe Senior Home."

The reporter nods her pretty head. "So you mean he worked on your behalf? Thank you so much for clarifying this matter, Councilmember Peters."

Politicians. Jack shakes his head. He picks up the remote control and turns off the TV.

Abbey

Teen Might's director, Pamela, introduces the organization to the group of bored students. The kids smack their gum, shuffle their feet, and roll their eyes. Abbey takes a deep breath and almost chokes on the stench of sweat socks and crammed bodies. Her eyes sweep over the Jefferson K-12 School students as she and Tess walk to the center of the open floor. Abbey realizes that the first four grades are missing for the school assembly, probably because of their talk's content.

Abbey and Tess sit across from each other and act out their prepared scene. Abbey serves as the victim, and Tess plays the concerned friend. Abbey feels comfortable in the role and more honest as a hurt teen than a mature support-giver. The role-play is supposed to help the students understand how to listen to one another when trouble arises and how to get help—from Teen Might, among other options.

Pamela wrote the script, along with Abbey's input, and it unfolds much like Abbey's own experience, with a few identifying details removed. Abbey had insisted on staying close to the truth. She felt that the crowd would feel the authenticity that way, and she could act with more confidence. She's grateful for her drama club experience, which makes role-playing a better fit for her than over-the-phone counseling.

As Abbey starts to talk about the pretend happenings, she experiences déjà vu. It's as though she's sharing her real story with Tess again.

"How was the party last night? Sorry I missed out," Tess says.

"I was nervous going to Andy's house. I mean he's so popular, elected homecoming king and all."

"Did you take something to help you relax?"

"Someone offered me a drink there, and then I started feeling dizzy..."

Abbey freezes at this moment. She can't tell everyone the naked truth. The sweat gathers underneath her lucky headband, a stretchy purple piece with a tulle tulip on top. She pats the frilly flower, and feels a thread jutting out. It's a bump where smoothness should exist, and she remembers when Ah-Mah repaired the seam.

Her grandmother, unable to locate her scissors, had run the violet string through her mouth and snipped it with her teeth.

"Did you break that thread with your teeth?"

Ah-Mah blinked at her. "Oh, I'm used to it."

"Cutting things with your teeth?"

"No, just thread. I did it all the time after I turned in my scissors to the government."

"They asked for your scissors?"

"Sure, scissors, screwdrivers. Anything that could help the war effort."

World War Two, her grandmother had meant. Ah-Mah had been through more than she had. Her grandmother had endured a painful history and continued to thrive. Abbey touches the headband one more time and projects her voice even louder. She continues with the script, and to her surprise, it doesn't hurt Abbey to speak about an experience similar to her own. Instead, it's freeing, and she's glad she told the truth to her mom when it first happened and didn't let the genuine version fester inside her.

At the end of the dramatization, the students sit in silence. Every head turns toward Pamela for her concluding remarks. When the principal thanks Teen Might for coming, the students offer up sincere applause. A beeline of people arrives to take informational pamphlets from them.

Abbey hands out a brochure to an Asian girl in braids. The girl, who seems a couple of years older than Abbey, folds her pamphlet in half in slow motion before meeting Abbey's eyes. "I'm glad you came today. I went through something like that a year ago, and I didn't tell anybody. We don't talk about things like that in Asian families."

Abbey holds the girl's gaze. "Silence can hurt more than you know." Her family's own experience echoed that statement.

"I thought I was too young, and nobody would believe me." The girl squares her shoulders. "Trust me, I'll be telling somebody right now."

Abbey watches as the girl moves over to Pamela and asks to speak with her in private. Abbey's heart gives a silent cheer. She's so glad that the director asked Tess and her to become speakers for Teen Might.

Tess glances over at Abbey as the last student files away. "I'm glad we're not in Los Angeles going to a year-round school like Jefferson. It's nice to have the extra week before school starts up."

"Actually, I can't wait to return to Atchison," Abbey says.

Tess raises her eyebrows.

Abbey smiles. "I have an appointment with Michelle Adams that I don't want to miss."

Lisa

Families First hides within an enclave of similar dull suites. Lisa circles the parking lot twice before spotting its location. Inside, the office appears to be a warehouse, complete with exposed rafters and frigid air. Marla ushers Lisa over to a space heater and hands her a cup of steaming coffee. "Don't worry, your body will adjust," she says. Indeed after a few minutes spent defrosting, Lisa feels ready to tour the place.

It takes a brief walk to see the whole operation. The space is divided into one open area and three cubicles. The cubicles belong to the director, the Helpline operator, and the marketing assistant. The director, Rob, a man with graying hair that matches his slate eyes, continues talking on the phone as they approach. He gives a brief wave with his free hand. He holds up one finger and mouths, "Give me a minute."

The next cubicle belongs to Susie, the Helpline operator, who fields calls from the general public. She looks like a librarian in her beige cardigan set, with her eyeglasses hanging from a beaded holder. In fact, Susie does provide information on anything and everything that caregivers require. The buttons on her phone are all lit up and blinking on hold, and she's rummaging through a cavernous file cabinet for the necessary materials. She gives them a hassled grin as they pass by.

Next door, the marketing assistant, George, sits in a sea of white envelopes. "Hello, ladies," he says. His craggy face peeks over the mound for a second before he reaches to fill another envelope.

Finally, Marla leads Lisa to her own desk. There are two long, rectangular tables in the open space, but only one of them seems filled. Marla gestures for Lisa to sit in the adjoining empty office chair. Separate plastic bins, color-coded for efficiency, shelter all of Marla's documents.

Marla pulls out a folder marked, "Lisa," and explains its contents. She's put together a basic package with information on Families First, with the Helpline phone number, brochures on caregiving issues, and a list of support groups in the area.

"If there's anything else you need," Marla says, "let me know."

Lisa looks through the sheets. "I think you've covered everything. Thanks a lot, Marla. I can't wait to give the information to the other ladies in the group." Although Lisa feels uncertain how long she'll be in Support Sisters, given Ma's precarious health. Soon enough, she may not act as a caregiver.

"We don't need this one." Lisa starts to hand over the support group listings but pauses. "Why is the facilitator's name crossed off?"

"She quit. That happens a lot around here. It's a small organization with few benefits and a high potential for burnout. Rob's covering all the groups right now, but he's stretched thin. In fact, I wanted to talk to you about—"

"Did I hear my name?" Rob walks in. "I'm Rob Hawthorne. It's nice to finally meet you, Lisa. I've heard so much about you. What do you think about the proposal?"

Lisa looks from Rob's expectant face to Marla's sheepish one.

"I was going to tell her," Marla says. "Lisa, I've been impressed by the way you run Support Sisters, and I told Rob all about you."

Rob jumps into the conversation. "I trust Marla's judgment 100%. We happen to have an opening for a Support Groups Coordinator. You seem like a perfect fit, and goodness knows, I have my hands full without a second position. So how about it?"

Lisa's jaw drops. "Are you offering me a job?"

Rob nods. "It pays slightly above minimum wage, and it offers mediocre benefits, but it's such a worthy cause." He puffs out his chest with pride.

Lisa watches the two waiting faces and stammers. "I have to think about it. My mother's not in very good health right now."

"I understand," they both say, and for once, Lisa knows that the people uttering the words are speaking the truth.

Silk

Silk touches the classic fire engine red polish of the car with caution. She turns the key in the door and slides into the leather seat. The Camaro retains that musky new car aroma. She looks at the automatic gear stick and regrets not learning how to drive a manual transmission. The convertible would seem a sportier thrill using stick shift.

She starts the engine—a smooth purr erupts under her fingertips—and exits the rental car lot. Her daughter thought it strange that Silk would want to drive a convertible. Lisa said to her, "Ma, you loathe driving even five miles over the speed limit." Silk just shrugged.

She doesn't care about seeming strange. She shakes out her sensible bob and cranks down the window. She rolls along at the speed limit and revels in the breeze tugging her hair.

She always liked driving. She enjoys the control of maneuvering a car. It turns where you want it to go and moves at the pace you like. In fact, she hated the plane trip to and from Italy. She kept gripping the armrests and shutting her eyes, particularly on departure and landing.

Another reason she likes driving is the freedom it offers. Once, she almost capitalized on its promise. When Lisa was an infant, a well-meaning neighbor dropped by.

"I'm new to the area and wanted to say hello to my neighbors." The woman offered Silk a basket laden with homemade blueberry muffins. A piercing wail started reverberating throughout the house. Silk ran to grab a hysterical Lisa from her crib and returned to see the neighbor still standing in the kitchen.

"Thank you for coming by," Silk said. The woman didn't budge. "Um, please sit down."

Silk hadn't been to the grocery store in awhile, so she didn't have anything to offer her guest. Meanwhile, Lisa kept screaming, making it difficult for Silk to think. Finally, Silk asked, "Would you like some water?"

"That would be lovely."

Silk handed the drink to the lady. Only after she placed it in the woman's hand did Silk realize that she had filled up a baby bottle with water on reflex. "Sorry," Silk said.

"No worries," the woman said. "Here, let me hold the baby for you."

Lisa quieted down in the woman's arms, gazing at the stranger's amazing green eyes.

Silk filled a glass with water and placed it on the kitchen counter. "Can you hold the baby for one more minute? I need to make some formula." Formula, another failure as a mother. Silk breastfed her daughter for a month before her supply had run low. She remembered Lisa's angry cries at discovering the shortage. Ever since then, Silk had invested in artificial milk.

She rummaged through the cupboards, but she couldn't find any formula. She then remembered using the last can in the middle of the night.

Seeing Silk's panicked face, the neighbor asked, "Would you like to hurry down to the store? I wouldn't mind holding this precious one a little longer."

The drive to the store took all of two minutes, and Silk found what she needed fast. Leaving the parking lot, she dreamed about fleeing in the opposite direction from her home. She could keep driving until the gas ran out. She could lose herself in the hum of the engine and the passing scenery.

She felt drained. Lisa stayed up all night, robbing Silk of any rest. She was tired of all the crying, the never-ending spit-up, and the explosive poops. Sometimes Lisa also reminded Silk of her dead husband. It would physically hurt her to look at Lisa's eyes. More often, though, Silk merely missed Lu. They had dreamed about raising a family together. Without him, Silk felt incomplete and incompetent. Even a stranger could handle Lisa better than her, as evidenced by the neighbor's visit.

Despite her escapist thoughts, though, Silk found herself in her own driveway. Her body's muscle memory had led her straight back to duty. The neighbor stayed for a few more minutes before leaving. Silk would have liked getting to know her better, but the woman moved away three months later.

Back then, Silk had no ties to Fairview. She had rented her old house. She didn't have any friends. She subsisted on odd jobs at weird hours, shifts that didn't mind a tagging baby. Now, though, Fairview has stamped itself in her heart and in her head.

For example, only locals know about Creek Drive. Silk pulls the Camaro into the posh neighborhood boasting million-dollar homes. Its real treasure glitters in the line of maple trees decorating the front of each house. Their leaves burst into radiant colors every autumn.

Silk gets caught in the kaleidoscope of jewel colors: ruby, garnet, and topaz. Whether it's from the dazzling riot of hues or her sudden splitting headache, the car jumps the curb. She barely misses smashing a Grecian urn filled with gliding goldfish. She lies panting for several moments before steering back to the rental place.

Jack

The news broadcast with Councilman Peters gives the politician more fame and Jack more work. Contracts pile up on Jack's doorstep, especially since he and the gardening club provide free landscaping (minus the cost of tools and plants). He finds himself placing maple trees in the city hall's courtyard, pruning ivy at the community college, and adding hydrangeas in front of the local hospital. Amid the onslaught of desired projects in Fairview, he asks for one special assignment. He refuses any assistance, and it takes him two weeks to complete the work.

*

It's an easy task to hunt Will down during these late summer months. With school out, Will remains in the comfort of his own home, even while working during the hot and dry season. He tutors a handful of students eager to get an early academic head start. Jack knows Will's schedule because he calls him every other week to chat.

Jack scrutinizes Will's residence. Although he's phoned Will numerous times, he hasn't dropped by in person until now. The yellow stucco building is gated with an intercom box. Despite the security measures, Jack sees a brick wedged under the bottom of the glossy white door, holding it open a few inches. He steps inside to find apartment number ten. He locates his friend's home in the back, past a tiny courtyard filled with potted ferns. The noise of the main street, a mere block away, retreats as he steps inside Will's abode.

The place appears spartan, almost military in its sharp lines and simple furnishings. A large shadowbox serves as the apartment's only decoration. Its massive black frame houses Will's most cherished mementoes: his brother's Army jacket, his father's plus-sized jeans, and his mother's delicate silver necklace.

Will himself sits at a small oak table, a half-eaten slice of toast in one hand. An open textbook, splayed out on the wooden surface, doesn't quite cover the second place setting at his right elbow. Gleaming silverware wrapped in linen line up next to a clean, white ceramic plate.

"I already ate," Jack says.

"The plate's not for you." Will wiggles his eyebrows. "I always forget that Yvonne's a heavy sleeper. She probably won't be up for another hour. We'll have plenty of time."

"Oh," Jack says. He looks around and spies a pair of red stilettos winking at him in front of the bedroom door.

"So, what do you think of the place?" Will asks while chewing his charred bread.

Jack turns toward him. "It's simple and tidy. I think it suits you."

"I'll take that as a compliment." Will shoves the remaining bread into his mouth. "Tell me. Where is this mysterious place that you're taking me to?"

Jack's unwilling to reveal the location both during their walk to the Rambler and inside the car. They sit in silence the whole ride there. When they arrive, Jack pulls in so close that he rubs the car's tire against the curb, making a vivid black slash on the concrete.

"Do you recognize this spot?" Jack asks.

Will swivels left, then right. "What did you do to the place?"

Jack motions to the massive tubs that line the sidewalk. "I put in these planters to commemorate the spot where we met. Fairview and Los Angeles squabbled over the boundary lines, but the two cities ended up working it out and giving me permission to beautify the area."

Jack touches one of the bright orange-headed plants in the pots. "They're birds of paradise. I figure they'll last a long time in this climate. Do you like the new look?"

Will pats a concrete urn next to him. "I wish this had been here before. It would have made one hell of a urinal."

Jack bursts out laughing but quiets down as he looks at Will. Despite the joke, there's seriousness etched on Will's face. It wasn't very long ago when Will had stood on that same corner, homeless and friendless.

"Thanks, buddy," Will says. "First, you planted friendship and purpose in my life. Then, you revived the forsaken areas around Fairview." He clasps Jack on the arm. "Come on. Let's get back, Johnny Appleseed."

As Jack drives to Will's apartment, he thinks about how the tables have turned. Now, Jack envies Will. Jack enjoys beautifying the city and serving as an upstanding Fairview citizen, but he feels a twinge of pain thinking about their different situations when they return to their own affairs. Will goes back to his lady friend, while Jack looks forward to a mountain of paperwork.

Abbey

Abbey rolls the smooth No. 2 pencil against her sweaty palms and tucks it into her jacket pocket. Every year she asks her mom for one new item on back-to-school day. It gives her more confidence to enter a new grade with a shiny unscratched folder or an unblemished pink eraser. Her day so far has gone well. She enjoys the new classes and her teachers.

Also, sixth graders at Atchison achieve special seniority status. It's the unofficial year marking their entryway into the upper echelons of the school and the mysteries of adolescence. She receives more than her fair share of admiration because of her stance against Vance Aroyan. Michelle, the school journalist, predicts that Abbey will be flooded with devotees after her article prints.

"People flock toward courage," Michelle said after their interview this morning. "They adore a heart of justice, too. I imagine Teen Might will gain a lot more volunteers soon."

Abbey reaches into her coat and brushes the soft rubber tip of the pencil with her thumb for good luck. Then she pushes the principal's door open. She plans to do one more thing before the day ends.

Principal Marshall looks up from her desk, startled at the interruption. "Why hello, Abbey. Welcome back to school." She peers at Abbey in confusion. "Do we have an appointment?"

"No, Principal Marshall," Abbey says. "Don't worry, this will only take a minute."

Abbey pulls out the check for the "scholarship fund" and slides it across the table. "I don't need this."

The principal raises her eyebrows. "It's for your future studies. I think it'll come in handy."

"Thank you for your concern, but I'll manage."

"You deserve it, Abbey," Principal Marshall says. She gives Abbey a brilliant flash of white teeth. "You're one of our best students after all."

"Has anyone else ever received a scholarship check before?" Abbey asks.

The principal averts her eyes.

"I thought so."

Principal Marshall crosses her arms over her chest. "Well, young lady, does your mother agree with this decision?"

"My mom and I are in 100% agreement."

Principal Marshall looks at the rectangular piece of paper on her desk but doesn't touch it. "It's a gift, Abbey, and I'm not going to take it back. You know, when one receives a present, it's polite to graciously accept it."

"Let me ask you this, Principal Marshall. After somebody gets a gift, can they do whatever they want with it?"

"Of course," the principal says. "Except return it to the giver. That would be in poor taste." Principal Marshall pushes the paper back with a wooden ruler.

"Okay," Abbey says. "I'll take the check and do what I want with it then."

Abbey picks it up and proceeds to tear the check into tiny pieces. She drops the remains in the wastebasket next to the mahogany desk. Principal Marshall's mouth remains wide open even as Abbey leaves the room.

Lisa

Lisa rushes in through the front door. She places the rice in a pot, boiling it with green onions and ginger until it makes a watery gruel. Even after the long presidential voting line, she still made it in time to eat with Ma.

She sees her mother's flamboyant clothes, a Hawaiian-print shirt with orange linen pants. The piece de resistance is a grand straw hat, the color of pee, overshadowing Ma's face.

"Ma, why are you wearing those ridiculous clothes indoors?"

"I'm practicing my tourist wardrobe, remember? I'll be out on the town soon."

"Can you at least take off the hat? There's no sun indoors, and I think it'll interfere with our lunch."

Her mother removes the hat without a word and places it on the empty chair usually reserved for Abbey, who's out with Tess and the director of Teen Might at a speaking engagement. Lisa fingers the American flag pin on her silk blouse.

"Did you vote yet, Ma?"

"I can't. I'm not a U.S. citizen like you. I'm a permanent resident."

"Oh." Lisa feels grown up, going to her first election ever. "I picked Reagan. He seems so dashing, and he's from California."

"You should feel proud, Lisa. You belong here and—"

"You fit in, too, Ma."

"Partially. I'm still tied to Taiwan, but I admire this land of the free. When I chose the United States to immigrate to, I wanted to feel that liberty, a release from the past." Her mother touches the glistening red-and-white striped pin above Lisa's heart. "I saw this flag waving at me when I first arrived in San Francisco. The immigration officer there labeled me a *displaced person* under a special law. The act was meant to help people who survived the Nazis, but when he saw my protruding belly and the promise of you, he let me through."

"Why didn't you stay in San Fran, Ma?"

"All that water. It reminded me too much of Kaohsiung and the place I wanted to leave behind."

"How'd you pick here?"

"I chose Los Angeles first. Someone told me the name referred to 'angels,' and I wanted to sense your father watching over us in this strange country. I couldn't stand the tall buildings, though, the way the city brought to mind Taipei and my lost relatives. The faces from Chinatown, instead of comforting me, reminded me about the horror I'd left. I decided to come to Fairview, a place full of unfamiliar people to start fresh."

"I never knew, Ma." Lisa scoops two bowls of *mui* and places the sticky rice porridge on the table. Food, the Taiwanese language of apology. "Please, eat this."

Lisa blows on her portion to cool it down. "Ma, I wanted to ask your opinion about something. You know that I went to Families First to get some resources for Support Sisters. When I was there, the boss offered me a job."

"Really? What kind of work is it?"

"It's the coordinator position for all their local support groups. Do you think I should take it?"

"Well, how do you feel about it?"

"I like facilitating support groups—at least, I like being a part of Support Sisters. Plus, it's something that would help a lot of people, and I haven't had a chance to do that too often. Working to survive is one thing—at the grocery store, the diner, and even at the retirement home—but working to help others is another concept altogether. The only other similar experience I had was taking care of Jack."

"Then it sounds like it would be a good fit," her mother says. "What's the problem then?"

Lisa spoons some *mui* into her mouth to buy time. She notices that her mother has been dipping her spoon into the bowl and dropping the porridge back in place. It's a ploy to pretend to eat, as her mother's appetite has plunged in recent days.

"I'm not sure it's good timing," Lisa says.

"Because of me? Nothing is ever good timing. Not happy things like babies and not sad things like illness...Or the 228 Massacre."

"Ma, please don't think about stuff that will make you feel worse."

"No, I'm ready to talk about it now. I need to tell you the rest of your father's story. It's not complete with just the beginning and not the end." She drops her spoon against the bowl with a hard clink, focusing on the words at hand. "Taiwan had transitioned from Japanese rule, which had held sway for fifty years. You know, that's why your father went by Lu, his Taiwanese name. His first name, Tarou, was Japanese, but he wanted to continue and honor his Taiwanese roots."

"How did the Chinese become involved in Taiwan again?"

"The Chinese KMT army from the mainland, rousted by the Communists, fled to our beautiful island. The country changed for the worse under their harsh rule. We starved under them. Then the native Taiwanese rose up against them starting on February 28, 1947. The KMT government responded by locking down the civilian leaders first. Then they targeted those considered threats to them, the intellectuals—your father, as a scientist, was included."

Lisa's voice shrinks. "Did you see him die?"

"No. He disappeared."

"How can you be sure he's gone then?"

"If there had been any way possible, he would have come back to me or sent me a message. I knew that his very silence meant death."

"How long did you wait?"

"Until my belly bulged out like a ripe watermelon. When I saw the first child murdered and lying in the street, I fled for your sake. I didn't ever want any danger like that threatening your life."

Lisa stops sipping her porridge. "On second thought, Ma, your hat completes the effect." She perches it gently on her mother's head. Lisa tilts the brim up, so that she can look into her mother's eyes. "The hat looks great," she says. It's the closest to "I love you" that she can get to and that her mother would accept.

"Lisa, you should take that job." Ma's own verbal display of affection. Her mother, eyes locked onto Lisa, takes a brimming spoonful of porridge and swallows it.

Silk

Sometimes you get so used to a thing that you're blind to its existence. Silk feels this way about Fairview. She has a certain fondness for the town. It's her step-home after all, different from the land that birthed her, but a place that still sustained and nourished her. It's the reason she wants to be a tourist for the day, to appreciate Fairview more. She knows that Lisa doesn't understand her motive, but then again her daughter's generation had more time to explore places and enjoy life.

Silk has lived in this city for three decades, and the route she takes is well-worn. Her haunts are the vineyards, her front door, and the various schools Lisa attended when she was younger. Silk glances at her mulberry-stained front door. Booked at a local hotel for the night, she pats the dull brass handle in consolation before locking it and heading into the unfamiliar.

She starts at the origin of the town, Fairview Hill. She's heard of the place, if only because of the numerous jokes based on it, the most common being, "Fairview. It's a dump."

Fairview founder, Ned Turner, sculpted the hill, turning the original landfill into a grassy knoll.

In the winter, a truck hauls in piles of snow from the mountains and dumps it onto the mound. The winter wonderland becomes rife with kids zooming down sleds and pelting one another with snowballs. Of course, she never took Lisa—it was far too dangerous. Lisa might have fallen down the steep incline and broken her bones. A packed snowball might have disfigured her face.

In the spring, a gentler time emerges, with wildflowers invading the hill. Kids cut classes to laze outside. Families visit on the weekends to collect blooms and place the fragrant buds as centerpieces in their homes.

Summertime calls for downhill racing, the school-aged kids egging each other on. They roll down the hill together to see who lands at the bottom first. Summer nights find couples cuddled together at its peak, an exquisite make-out point. She heard all these stories second-hand, through her gossiping coworkers.

Nobody comes in autumn, though. The breeze picks up at the top of the hill, and few look forward to braving the wind. The kids stay in school, still optimistic about the upcoming academic year, not ready to play hooky yet.

Silk encounters a few stragglers coming down the hill as she climbs up. The other visitors carry large heavy-duty cameras to capture the vista. She catches her breath at the top of the incline. She wonders if this is what Ned Turner experienced.

The grassy hill seems an island in the sea of the city. She feels like she can pluck one of the birds out of the sky at this height. Silk looks down and sees the geometric rows of houses and buildings that make up Fairview. If she peers under lidded eyes, the lines blur and she can picture the open expanse that Ned Turner saw before he built his dream city. It's a place full of possibilities, a beautiful image, a fair view, indeed.

The next logical stop lands her at The Fairview Fryer on 22nd Street. The owner, Bobby, is said to have descended from the original Ned Turner. The diner serves the famous local specialty, "The Fill." Most people think it refers to the hefty meal, but the dish really suggests the origin of Fairview, a landfill.

The man with the "Bobby" nametag wears a uniform slick with grease and displays both a bulldog size and face. "What can I get for ya?" he asks.

"I'll take The Fill Challenge," Silk says.

"You? Really?" The man barks out a gruff laugh. "Well, it's your funeral."

"It certainly is."

"What's that?"

"I said, extra special sauce, please."

Bobby isn't joking with the funeral comment. The staff requires participants in The Fill Challenge to sign a waiver form. Eaters have taken ill before and been rushed to the hospital.

The plate comes piled high with ground meat patties plus two thin buns unable to sandwich the whole mess. Extra bamboo skewers hold the concoction together. The Fill boasts twenty different patties, gleaned from exotic animals like ostrich, snake, and alligator. The special sauce glistens, and to her palate, tastes like ketchup and mustard swirled in grease.

To finish the challenge, she must consume the monstrosity within thirty minutes. Looking at a discarded newspaper in the corner of her booth, she reads the same headline over and over again to distract her from the oily taste. A minute before the time's up, she wipes her mouth and signals to Bobby. He looks at her empty plate and whistles. Then he whips out a Polaroid camera and takes a shot of her.

She knows she will be remembered in Fairview now, no matter how small. Her grinning face will be posted on a bulletin board next to the restrooms. She also gets to take home a trophy for the accomplishment, a bright white T-shirt emblazoned with the enormous all-meat plate declaring, "I had my Fill at The Fairview Fryer."

After the meal, she doesn't feel like going to the next landmark, Rejuvenation Waters, but she wants to cross it off her to-do list. She calculates the distance in her head. She can make it there on foot in twenty minutes. Plus, it'll be good for her to walk off the food.

After the trek, her tummy settles, and she feels ready to plunge into the baths at Rejuvenation Waters. She enters the locker room and notices the sign posted: "Please shower before entering our pools." She steps into the shower area where identical stalls stand covered in frosted pastel-colored glass. A narrow table takes up the walkway and displays jars of shaped soaps, colorful bath beads, and miniature shampoo/conditioner sets.

She grabs a handful of bath items and makes her way to a cotton-candy hued stall. She relaxes under the gentle water pressure and inhales the sweet steam. *Maybe I should stay here and skip the hot mineral waters. But I paid the entrance fee already. I need to use all the amenities to make my money count.*

Three large porcelain tubs contain the mineral water, looking remarkably like regular hot tubs. She gravitates to an empty pool, the one heated to 102°F. She sniffs the air around it. She worries that there might be a sulfuric or medicinal smell, but she detects nothing. Although the water seems hot and not boiling, she still feels like a lobster in a cooking pot. She leaves ten minutes later to take a cool shower and regulate her temperature.

The rejuvenating waters advertise a blend of minerals to reverse the aging process. However, after her dip, she feels even older than before. Her skin puckers from the water and seems coated in a slimy substance. She walks with halting steps back to her car parked at the diner, wiping her brow every five minutes.

Silk rushes to the five-star hotel she's booked for the night to recuperate. The suite appears spacious and elegant, but she doesn't notice anything except the pitcher of ice cold water on the bedside table. She gulps it down with zest.

She eyes the thousand-count Egyptian cotton sheets and the feather pillow with pleasure. As she makes her way over to the bed, though, the ground trembles beneath her. *Earthquake*. She looks around for something sturdy to hold onto or hide under. When she sees a brilliant orange color flash from behind the window blinds, she stops searching.

She remembers that one of the features of the luxury hotel is its rotational properties. At sunrise and sunset, the hotel turns on its axis, providing its guests with breath-taking views of the radiant sky. At the moment, though, the sharp color irritates her. She closes her eyes to block out the brightness. Immediately, she regrets this decision because the tilting motion becomes even more pronounced. She feels nauseous and dizzy. She stumbles out of the room, escapes the hotel, and finds solace in her car situated on a flat, stable parking lot.

She takes several deep breaths to reorient before driving home. Everything remains quiet in the house. Lisa and Abbey are probably out enjoying their mother-daughter time, or maybe Lisa's running a support group and Abbey's out with her friend Tess. Silk hopes it's the former.

She smiles as she sees her own creaky twin-sized mattress with its tattered quilt and sunken pillow. She collapses on the bed, exhausted. *Home sweet home. I could sleep here forever.* She smells the faint scent of cherry blossoms before her eyelids slide shut.

Jack

"You would think that I would own one black blazer at my age after all the funerals I've been to," Jack says to himself. He dusts off his salmon-colored suit. He wonders if people will notice its color or whether others will even see the wispy old man hanging at the edge of the service. At Fei's funeral, he wore a black polo—he wanted to show his obvious sorrow with the single piece of dark clothing he owned, and he knew she wouldn't have minded the informality of short sleeves.

When he enters the funeral parlor now, he sees twenty other people crammed into the small room. They're already gathered in a line to view the open casket. Everybody appears decorous in their black suits and dresses.

He sees Lisa look into the coffin, pat Silk's body, and wipe her eye with a discreet dab at her dress sleeve. The hidden tears must betray a deeper reserve of pain. He recognizes the shadow of grief over her face, the same one that warped his features at his wife's funeral. He reaches his hand out, but it's impossible to touch her from this distance. She moves on, but pauses as

Abbey, next in line, turns pale and freezes. Lisa has to gently urge the girl forward.

Jack saw the obituary in the paper a few days ago. He wonders if other people read the deaths section of *Fairview News* on a daily basis. It's not meant to be a morbid activity. In fact, he and Fei started the tradition a decade ago to scout for long-lost friends:

"Think of it like a free reunion," she said.

He snorted. "Except someone has to die for it to occur."

She shrugged. "We all die someday. We may as well be a cause for connection after our death."

He watches Lisa's petite hands try to direct Abbey down the aisle. A large silver-haired man barrels his way out of line and gathers them in a hug. They fall into the comfort of his arms.

Jack doesn't recognize the man. He wonders if Lisa would have found shelter in his embrace if he had stepped forward instead. He could have and should have been the reassuring male figure for her. Would a real father have turned his back on his child, even if she'd made a mistake? If she had tried to shut him out from her life? No, real fathers expected tiny failures and didn't retreat when their children hurt them. He would try again, if she'd give him another chance.

But the last time Lisa had kept in touch with him it was through a scribbled note. The handwriting, fast and sloppy, scrawled across a sticky "To-Do List" note read, "Jack, found a job running support groups at company called Families First. Abbey's good, Ma's worse. Hope all's well. Lisa." She used to drop by Monroe Senior Home, or at least call and chat. Then communication dropped to the occasional letter, which degraded to the most recent dashed note. It wasn't her fault;

wary of being burned again, he hadn't been quick to respond to her contact.

He reaches the open coffin. Silk rests in a quiet pose, her figure girlish in death. Faint blush and a hint of lipstick from the make-up artist give her a youth that didn't appear in real life. He only saw her the one time—at the botched meal—and he now notices tiny details about her. He sees the full eyelashes, a mole underneath her lower lip, and a faint square birthmark on her right hand. He realizes that he's practically at a stranger's funeral. There are so many things he didn't know about her, even on a surface level.

He feels relief to get away from the awkwardness of the funeral home and go to Silk's house for the reception. There's to be no burial because she had wanted to be cremated. The service acts just as a way for folks to pay their respects.

The house overflows with people, the space stifling with the massive amount of body heat. He lines up for the buffet, which consists of a large amount of pasta and chow mein. *Two dishes of noodles? Isn't that redundant?* He's wrestling with the slippery threads of the chow mein using a pair of oil-covered lacquer chopsticks when he inadvertently jabs the man in front of him.

"Sorry," Jack says.

The man turns around, bearish in his bulk. It's the same silver-haired gentleman who hugged Lisa and Abbey. "That's okay."

For a moment, the stranger's eyes rest on Jack's fish-colored apparel before he speaks. "Say, I haven't seen you around before. Silk worked for me for three decades at Lincoln Vineyards. I'm Gus." The man uses two hands to iron grip Jack's clammy fingers. "How do you know Silk?"

"I'm Jack." Jack looks toward Lisa, who stays huddled close to Abbey. Lisa's eyes, though, scan the room once in a while like a good hostess, checking to see if people need anything, but her eyes slide right over him.

His invisibility to her bothers him, but this year has been about release. Letting go of Fei to properly grieve, letting go of his career to let Will thrive, letting go of his expectations to discover landscaping, and now letting go of Lisa, so she and Abbey can rebuild as a family. "I don't really know Silk," Jack says. "I'm a very distant acquaintance of Lisa's."

Abbey

Abbey sets up the boxes in a precise order, already familiar with the routine. "We need to consolidate our things, not have them scattered around, so that we can move into one home," Mom had told her last week. Abbey finished inventorying their tiny apartment in two days, separating stuff into three requisite piles: toss, donate, and keep. Looking around Ah-Mah's place now, she notices that her grandmother's house can use the same organization.

Abbey wants to help her mom out with the task and keep busy during her leave of absence from school. Principal Marshall had insisted that Abbey take "two days off to properly grieve." She wonders whether the reprieve isn't for the principal, who still seems embarrassed when she spots Abbey in the hallways. Unfortunately, Mom couldn't take the time off from her new job and stay home, too. As a precaution, though, Mom asked a neighbor to check in on Abbey every afternoon.

Abbey sorts through Ah-Mah's clothes hanging in the closet. The shapeless outfits, loose and easy to put on, move straight into the donation box. Knickknacks take more time because they require dusting and examination. There are miniature Murano glass figurines from Italy, gourd carvings from Taiwan, and handmade clay blobs made during Abbey's childhood.

She moves onto the papers in the bureau. Waylaid coupons, discarded newspapers, and crumpled magazines take up the first drawer. The second one holds a bulging stack of cards. She recognizes the cheap dollar-store designs. She and her mom would mail them last minute to Ah-Mah on sentimental occasions, like her grandmother's birthday or on Mother's Day. Usually, the pair of them signed their names under the provided printed wishes. If they felt generous, they added a clichéd line like, "Have a good day!" or "Hope you're well."

Underneath the mound of greeting cards, she finds a wooden box. She lifts the lid to reveal love letters, rolled-up drawings, a black and white photograph, and a faded article. She blushes at the sight of the letters and puts them away. She opens the sketches and sees a younger version of Ah-Mah staring out at her; despite the unblemished skin, the crooked nose and high cheekbones remain. She peruses the photograph and article, thinking about the man in them, her grandfather.

She knows some stories about her Ah-Gung. She pestered her grandmother whenever Ah-Mah had the strength to talk. In fact, since her first attempt with the genealogy notebook, she has filled multiple journals with her grandfather's history.

She knows that Ah-Gung's fisherman hands came from working nets to catch and dry cuttlefish on his father's boat. She understands that those same hands sketched with lightning strokes everything his eyes saw. She remembers that he worked hard to get ahead in school, sometimes studying through the night without a pause to sleep. Ah-Mah talked about Ah-Gung's expertise with chemistry, how he liked peppering scratch paper with oblique formulas and shapes.

Most often, though, her grandmother talked about how the couple met at Yangmingshan Park. She talked about the bud of their love bursting into bloom over one short year. Their relationship contrasted with their peers' love affairs, since they lived on their own after marriage.

Ah-Mah had no in-laws to live with like a proper married woman because Ah-Gung's mother had died giving birth to her son and Ah-Gung's father had vanished in a boating accident several years prior to their courtship. They moved into the Lu family houseboat for a short time, though, because Ah-Mah wanted to assist Ah-Gung's relatives. However, Ah-Gung's uncles could care less for a female on board, especially one who vomited on voyages through any choppy water. Thus, Ah-Mah and Ah-Gung had lived together in their cozy apartment, falling deeper in love until the 228 Massacre.

228. The historical event that crashed into their lives and destroyed their personal world. Ah-Mah didn't talk much about 228. She mentioned the date (February 28, 1947) once and closed her eyes to block out the memories. "I'm sorry, Abbey," Ah-Mah had said. "228 is the reason I never wanted to talk with you about school. It's why I didn't even want to see your report cards or awards. You're too young to fold tragedy into your thoughts." She refused to speak any more about the matter, and Abbey knew better than to insist. She didn't like to upset her grandmother.

After finishing organizing the house, Abbey decides to research the massacre with her free time. The Fairview City

Library boasts an excellent collection and lies only a mile away. Besides, she wouldn't mind getting out of the house for a bit.

*

The library, covered in tiled flooring, gives even Abbey's light footsteps an echoing ring. Two librarians sit behind a massive oak desk. "I need some help researching a subject," she says. Her voice comes out as a soft whisper in the cavernous room.

The librarian closest to her nods his head. Ash-colored bangs sweep over his eyes with the bobbing motion. "I can help you. What are you looking for?"

"I need a book on Taiwanese history."

"Oh, a school project?"

She gives him a noncommittal murmur. "I want to learn about an incident called the 228 Massacre."

The librarian cocks his head, confused. "Never heard of it. Did you say Thailand?"

She shakes her head. "Taiwan. It's an island near China."

"You're looking for the Asian history section then. Follow me." The librarian sways from side to side as he walks, like a waddling penguin, and his shoes squeak against the floor.

They go down a narrow winding staircase to the lower basement. He leads her to a large shelving unit, which houses a mere eight tomes on Asian history. "Have at it," he says and leaves with a wave.

She looks at the books written by Chinese authors and peeks into the indices. None of them list Taiwan by name. She checks the Chinese history found in each volume, but they don't reference the 228 Massacre. In her frustration, she raps her hand against a stepladder. It flies to the side, knocking a dozen books off a nearby shelf. She places them back, but the last volume holds her attention. It's entitled, *The Comprehensive Modern World History*.

She flips through the numerous pages. *It's worth a try.* Taiwan takes up one page of the heavy tome, and the British author describes the 228 Massacre in three sentences. *It figures that only a foreigner could write about it.* The current ruling party must have prohibited all mention of the tragedy.

She reads about the turbulent background of Taiwan in 1947. She envisions the black market, the runaway inflation, and the food shortages under the Republic of China rule. One sentence catches her eye: "Leader Chen Yi killed up to 30,000 individuals, including a disproportionate number of Taiwanese middle and high school youths."

She thinks about her grandmother witnessing this scene. She understands now Ah-Mah's desire to block out academics from Abbey's life. She wonders if Ah-Mah worried about conjuring up images of the dead students by talking about school subjects with her. Or perhaps Ah-Mah was frightened about a massacre occurring in the United States with *its* brightest students.

Abbey snaps the book shut. She hates staring at the black wording. The calm print covers up all those innocent deaths. With one guileless sentence, the author obliterates her Ah-Gung.

She goes home and looks among her old school supplies. She keeps everything meaningful from the previous academic years in storage boxes. She roots around until she locates her genealogy project. The lopsided family tree tilts to one side, heavy with female names. She smoothes out the paper and touches her grandfather's name with reverence. *If only I can keep his name alive somehow.*

Lisa

I couldn't stand being in Ma's house anymore, Lisa admits to herself. When she told her daughter to pack up for one place, she hadn't meant her mother's house but a new location entirely.

"You could have warned me," Abbey said yesterday when the moving van pulled up to haul their stuff away.

"Sorry, I didn't tell you. It was all a big rush."

"Why do we need to leave now? Can't we stay here a little longer?"

Lisa yanked on the tape, making it screech, and sealed the last moving box. "How can you live in the same house where Ma died?"

Abbey jutted her chin out. "It's also where Ah-Mah lived."

Lisa stacked the last box on the heaving pile. She shook her head, the new stylish bob making soft swishes against her cheeks. "I should have known my world would fall apart after what happened to John Lennon. It was a sign."

"You and your stupid Beatles craze, Mom." Abbey rolled her eyes. "It's coincidence that your favorite member died."

"John isn't my favorite—Paul's got all the schoolboy charm. Anyway, all I'm saying is that Lennon got assassinated by a psycho who called himself 'The Catcher in the Rye,' and a day later, Ma died." She looked at Abbey with a sharp glance. "They're still banning that book from school, right?"

Abbey shrugged her shoulders. "I don't know. I think that's a high school level book."

"Don't ever read it." Lisa massaged her temples, the throb beneath threatening to explode. "What if we had come home earlier? What if—"

"What if we didn't need to move into this new place?" Abbey retreated to Ma's empty room and closed the door. She didn't answer Lisa's knocks on the door, and Lisa had left her to mourn.

Today, Lisa had dragged Abbey to the new house, the entire car ride paved with icy silence. To distract herself from thinking about her daughter's state, Lisa imagines the new owners opening the door of Ma's residence at this very moment. The keys were supposed to be handed over to them this morning. She's met the pair—they came to one of the open houses where the realtor had snuck vanilla candles in the bathroom and popped cookie dough into the oven.

They were a young couple, eager working professionals dressed in business clothes. The matching blond-hair blue-eyed partners would churn out the perfect family with 2.5 kids. They could probably even add the white picket fence to the yard. Lisa's own family feels like a mess in comparison, with its missing fathers and stranded daughters. Now, the glue that held them together—her mother—is gone, and Lisa feels

298

unprepared to step into the role. More than her fear, though, is the intense sorrow that's appeared since her mother's death.

Lisa visualizes the young couple (Gary and Ann?) walking through the entryway into the cozy living room, its matted carpet a deep sage green. Lisa hadn't had time to change the flooring. She wonders if they'll notice the sunken pits in the center of the room. The markings correspond to that god-awful plaid chair she hated. Its construction orange fabric captured layers of dust, fabric pills, and stray hairs with a magnetic pull. Her mother had occupied its seat every evening at ten p.m. to watch the news, even during the last days of her illness. As a child, Ma would not allow Lisa to sleep until she had accompanied her to watch the show.

Current events were very important to her mother—"so I can know what's happening in the world and how people are thinking in this country." Now, Lisa wonders if the time was meant for educating Lisa herself. She remembers that Ma would keep a running commentary on every news segment, inserting her own views. After each custom remark, her mother would say, "That would be the Taiwanese way of thinking."

In an hour or so, Lisa realizes that Gary and Ann will become hungry and explore the kitchen. They'll make something simple, something American. Deli sandwiches, she guesses. There will be a deep quiet in that room. Lisa's own memories, though, paint the kitchen as a bustle of sounds, despite her mother ceasing to cook in recent months. Lisa recalls the constant clanking of the metal wok, the snipping of chopsticks, and the soft hiss from the bamboo steamer. She misses the taste of her mother's specialties: homemade *xiao long bao*, with the warm soup bursting under the soft dumpling skins, and *jajiangmian*, the thick noodles hand-pulled.

For years, Lisa could smell the tang of ginger, garlic, and green onions whenever she walked through the door. She wonders if the sharp aroma remains. She thinks that houses permeate with unique scents, transferred onto them by their owners. She could never chop a clove of garlic without her mother's image appearing before her. Now, she can't peel one without crying.

Lisa continues on with her daydream and imagines Gary and Ann getting ready for bed. They'll probably call the yellow and white checkerboard tiles on the bathroom countertop "cute"— they did always bring a smile to Lisa's face. They'll comment on the gleam of the sparkling, pure white porcelain sink, never knowing how many times her mother vomited in it during her chemotherapy. In all honesty, Lisa enjoyed those moments when she held her mother's hair up and rubbed her back. She felt helpful then, like a good obedient daughter. During those times, she could block out memories of her own rebellious past, so disappointing to Ma.

Later, Gary and Ann would probably sleep in the master bedroom, the one her mother had died in. Lisa can picture her mother's face on that bed, resting in a peaceful pose with a half-smile played out on her lips. At first, when she didn't know, Lisa felt glad that Ma hadn't spent the night in that posh rotating hotel and had come home to rest instead. When she leaned in to cover her mother further with the familiar tattered quilt, though, Lisa had discovered the chill of the body.

She feels guilty about her mother dying alone. She plays the "what if" game a lot. What if she had insisted that her mother stay home that whole day? What if Abbey and her had eaten at the house? What if they hadn't gone to a movie later on a whim? These questions battered her every day she stayed at her mother's house after the death. The guilt and the thousand little memories that lived in that house had weighed Lisa down.

She looks around her new home. She likes its clean lines and the way it smells of nothingness, of promise. She enjoys the tiny reminders that this house is not her mother's place. The dishwasher gleams, and a full box of Cascade rests under the sink. Here, the dishwasher isn't a repository for clean dishes and glasses washed by hand, but serves as a functional machine.

She also likes the fireplace, the wall of logs near it stacked in a tidy pile. The fireplace fulfills a purpose, not like at her mother's house, where it had been transformed into a hollow for stacks of Chinese newspapers. She imagines the possibilities of the hearth's use on endless chilly nights: reading in a cozy chair, cuddling with Abbey, and cooking indoor s'mores.

Lisa startles at the drumming sound from behind her. She turns around to see Abbey positioning a picture, smacking her hands against the wall to flatten the tape.

"What are you doing, Abbey?" Lisa asks.

"I'm decorating the place."

Lisa understands. The walls remain a blinding white. "Abbey, do you like the house?" It's a little late to ask the question. She feels awkward thrusting a new home on Abbey on such short notice, and she still wants her daughter's approval.

Abbey shrugs.

"My friends from Support Sisters live around here," Lisa says. "They've introduced me to the other mom neighbors who have kids around your age. You could go over for play dates or sleepovers—"

"Sure, Mom, free babysitting for you, so you can do your new job. How long will you keep this one?"

"That's not fair, Abbey. I enjoy running caregiver support groups. I feel like I'm following my dream. I let you pursue your goals, and now you need to allow me mine."

"Sorry, you're right, Mom. You've let me do drama, Teen Might, a lot of things…"

"You still haven't said what you thought about the house. It's walking distance to your school. Plus, you get your own room."

"Cut it out. You sound like a real estate agent. We're already here, so I'll deal with it."

"Deal with it? Don't you like the house?"

"It doesn't have any character," Abbey says. "All the houses on the block look the same. The only difference is the number posted above the garage door."

"I don't understand, Abbey. For years, you complained about our apartment. You wanted more space, more privacy. You wanted the ideal three bedroom/two bathroom home in a nice tree-lined street to 'fit in' with your peers. Isn't that right?"

Her daughter narrows her eyes into cat-like slits. "That stuff's all superficial. I've changed, or haven't you noticed?"

"So have I. I'm proud to finally be able to own a house and not rent a dumpy studio apartment."

"Don't get me wrong, Mom. It's not that I don't like all the nice things here. I do. It just feels empty." Abbey wraps her arms around her shoulders and says, "I'm cold. I'm going to grab a sweater."

When Abbey leaves, Lisa notices the picture on the wall. It's not an abstract drawing, like she thought at first, but the genealogy project Abbey completed last year. Lisa sees that the names of her parents are bolder than all the rest. It seems like Abbey retraced them in ink before mounting the family tree on a homemade cardboard frame. Lisa stares at the contrast between the document and the stark wall. *While I've been trying to empty the house of ghosts, Abbey's been trying to invite them in.*

Jack

Gus slaps Jack on the back, causing Jack to stumble a little, and says, "Welcome back, buddy! You've done some fine work here." After weeks spent discussing and rearranging the land together, Gus seems to have developed an affinity for Jack. Jack smiles back at the vineyard owner's open, ruddy face.

"I asked Lisa and Abbey to come by today," Jack says. He steps back to reveal the two figures behind him, beyond the door to Gus' office. When they enter, Gus withdraws his smile, and he places his big bear hands on each of their delicate shoulders.

"I still can't believe Silk's gone," Gus says. "Do you want me to walk to the back with you? It's pretty busy today, but I can take a break..."

"No, that's all right," Lisa says. "We'd like to keep the ceremony simple anyway."

"I'll be here in my office if you need to talk afterwards."

*

305

Jack, Lisa, and Abbey wind their way out the building to find the ring of translucent stones laid out in a sunny spot. The brilliant rays overhead cause the rocks to sparkle like gems. In reality, various shades of polished quartz mimic the fancy jewels. Around the perimeter of the fist-sized stones, clumps of asters wave in the breeze. Their pretty pink, purple, and blue-flowered heads bob in curtsey.

A gaping hole remains in the center of the circle. Lisa places the urn, a blue and white porcelain container embossed with a serpentine dragon, in the pit.

"I wonder if this is legal," Lisa says.

"It's Gus' land, and you have his permission to use it," Jack says.

Jack *did* worry about the legality of the situation when the idea first struck him. He thought, though, that Lisa would appreciate having a nicer location for her mother's ashes than her mantel place. His desire for Lisa's peace of mind in her fragile state triumphed over his nervousness at skirting regulations.

The three of them cover the urn with the nearby dark upturned earth. He positions a stone plaque over the remains. It reads, "In loving memory of Silk Lu. Wife, mother, grandmother, and friend. January 12, 1925-December 9, 1980."

Lisa kneels down in the dirt, tracing the lettering of the plaque over and over again. Abbey stands beside her mother, stiff and rigid. Despite the constant caw of birds overhead and the shouts of surrounding vineyard workers, Lisa and Abbey seem enclosed in a bubble. He watches the motionless mother and daughter for a long time.

To his surprise, Lisa remains on her knees while Abbey turns toward him and breaks the silence.

"I think Ah-Mah would have liked this," she says.

"I hope so. I tried to make it look pleasant with the delicate flowers and sparkling stones."

"No, that's not what I mean. I think she would have liked the spot. She loved her job, and she really valued physical labor."

"I don't know about that..." *Silk didn't like me. Isn't a janitor as down-to-earth as you can get?*

Abbey looks him in the eye and says, "Ah-Mah eventually approved of you. If she didn't want my mom to be friends with you, she would have forbidden it. The fact that we're all standing here together proves my point."

He accepts her sweet interpretation and chooses his words of praise with care. He remembers Silk relinquishing her prejudice against him and urging Lisa to see him. He thinks about Silk battling cancer while keeping an upbeat attitude. "It takes someone special to overcome her past and thrive in the present."

The observation must resonate with Abbey because she bursts into tears and flings herself into his surprised arms. He hugs the girl tight, breathing in her complete trust. He whispers soft comforts until her heaving subsides. His shirt swallows her tears until Lisa gets up and pulls Abbey away.

Lisa pecks his cheek. "Thank you for everything," she says. The phrase sounds like a dismissal to him. The words seem full of underlying weariness and a desire to close this chapter in her life. She gives him a half-hug before leaving. *It's the kind of embrace suited for acquaintances pretending to be friends.* The loss he feels translates into a cold emptiness seeping across his chest.

Abbey

Abbey feels surreal returning to school after all the turmoil and adjustment of the past few days, but she enjoys the familiar environment. When nobody follows her to her locker at the end of the day, she exhales in relief. Her star status from Michelle's newspaper article has faded due to her forced absence and the knowledge of her grandmother passing away. She feels more comfortable at school now. She isn't anonymous by any means, but the other kids respect her from a distance.

While spinning the dial to her combination lock, she senses an overwhelming silence around her. She looks up because of the sudden end to chatter and squeaking sneakers. She spots Ara walking down the hall. Some students ignore him, while others fire accusatory glances his way. Although her own renown has diminished, he remains a pariah at Atchison Elementary.

This dislike weighs him down. His clothes appear ill-fitted, either from lack of care (the rumpled shirt, the dandruff-sprinkled black blazer) or from his slouched posture. He shuffles along with his head ducked down. She notices that his bangs cover up half his face. She wonders if he combs them over his eyes on purpose, the better to hide from the angry stares.

She still spies Ara up on the hill at lunchtime. However, an invisible magical circle drawn around Rosalind and her groupies excludes Ara. He sits a distance away, nibbling at his packed lunch, but the others never talk to him. Abbey imagines that Rosalind allows him to perch nearby only because his parents represent a certain socioeconomic status.

Abbey herself lunches with Tess. The drama club members stake out a bright area with concrete benches overlooking a quaint sundial. Sometimes she thinks of the group as a living Stonehenge wrapped around the ancient clock. A couple of times, Abbey has taken Tess to the elm tree, her old lunch haunt. Sometimes they see Will making his rounds there and talk to him.

Squeak, squeak. Ara's sneakers screech as he scoots down the hall toward Abbey. His mocha skin pales under the fluorescent lights, and his hazel eyes vanish beneath the overgrown hair.

"Hey, Ara." Her voice rings out in the deep quiet. "Come here a sec."

He moves toward her but stays a good three feet away.

She reaches into her jacket pocket to produce an unopened tube of bubble gum. She bought it on a whim; the wrapper reads "Tropical Boldness," and the mystery title intrigued her. She snatched it from the checkout stand and placed it with the other groceries before her mom could protest.

Abbey starts to pull the red string to unspool the roll and present Ara with one cube. Thinking better of it, she extends the whole packet to him. She leans over to bridge the gap between them and guides the bubble gum into his palm.

The moment she hands it over, she realizes her mistake. His father, a popular Fairview dentist, might not want his son chewing sugar-laden gum. She wonders how to redeem the situation when she sees him grip the gum tight. He rolls it between his palms, and the motion reminds her of the comfort found from gripping her lucky pencil.

A shy smile peeks out at her from his lips. He straightens his head and brushes the bangs away from his eyes. "Thanks, Abbey."

After he strolls away, head held high, she hears excited murmurs from the students around her. Her act will spread like wildfire in the school; everybody will know about it by tomorrow morning, if not tonight. She hopes that her action improves their attitude toward Ara because she understands an outsider's loneliness. Abbey opens up her locker and sees the stash of items filling its space. She stares at the wavering pile for a moment before emptying all the paraphernalia into her arms.

At home, she heads straight to the living room where she hears hammering. Mom's banging on the wall, half the time hitting her thumb with the tool and yelling.

"What's with all the noise?" Abbey asks.

Her mom points to the genealogy project, displayed in a new setting. "A lasting solid wood frame to honor our family history." She puts down the hammer and indicates a matching mounted shelf. "That's for all your school accomplishments."

Abbey kisses her mom full on the lips. Mom seems surprised by the sudden gesture, something Abbey had stopped last year when it seemed too babyish for a ten-year-old. Then her mom pulls her in for a tight hug.

Abbey organizes all her awards on the new shelf, displaying them with pride. Academic honors nestle next to programs from her drama productions. She grins over each achievement and dreams about her future. She wonders if she'll follow in her grandfather's footsteps and capitalize on her math and science skills. Or maybe she'll breach family protocol and become an actress. Or perhaps something else entirely, like a historian bent on uncovering global atrocities. A wide expanse of blank wall remains, a canvas of possibilities that beckons to her.

Lisa

Lisa steps into the foyer of Monroe Senior Home, her heels tapping out a confident beat. Unable to locate Tina the receptionist, Lisa opens the front desk's drawer and slips in the vanilla folder. It seems ages ago when she snatched the faded file about the Chens on her last day of work at the home. Nobody questions Lisa about her presence at the desk, and no one disturbs her as she walks down the intricate hallways. Her shoulder-padded caramel suit and steady gaze declare authority to all the residents and staff there.

She finds Jack in his room, his door ajar, staring out the bay window at the garden outside. His body, silhouetted by the sunlight streaming in, reminds her of his image the day she buried Ma's remains.

Overcome with emotion, Lisa had given him half-hearted thanks at the memorial site. If she failed to acknowledge him, perhaps she could also erase the memory of sticking a jar of Ma's ashes into the ground. Besides, with her mother's loss so fresh, did she even dare get close to him again? Near enough to allow her heart to break? After all, he was even older than Ma when she had died. He could disappear soon, too.

Lisa vowed not to look back as she left, but she turned around once. In that moment, he'd been outlined by the sun. She saw him down on his knees, his fingers rubbing the marker, no doubt to remove the dirt tracked from the burial. He polished the plaque like a relative, with slow careful strokes.

She turned away and saw Abbey looking at him, too. Her daughter's eyes remained red, a trace of her intense crying jag released in the shelter of his arms. She realized then that he really was family to them, even if he didn't know it yet.

Lisa knocks on the doorframe to draw Jack's attention. "I wanted to say thank you for the lovely memorial garden for my mother."

"You already told me the other day."

"I know, but I didn't do it properly." Her eyes slide away from his searching look. "You didn't know Ma well, and she even kicked you out of her house. It's really generous on your part to have planted the garden."

"It wasn't for Silk that I did it," he says. "It was to ease your suffering, Lisa."

"Jack, you've been kinder to me than I deserve. I know we've been through a crazy roller coaster ride of a relationship, with its many dips and peaks."

He shrugs and points to her full hands. "What are you holding, anyway?"

"This is my thank you present to you." She offers the tiny plant decorated with a hundred slips of paper. "It's a wish tree. I wrote down all the greatest hopes and best wishes I have for you in the years to come."

His eyes mist up. "Thank you, Lisa. I feel very appreciated."

"I know I've been neglecting our relationship." She fingers one of the papers. "I do hope to witness these dreams with you, if you'll let me. Will you, Jack?"

He grins, exposing his signature yellow teeth. "That happens to be one of my very first wishes."

She bows from her waist, her hands clasped together to show the deep extent of her respect for him. Then they embrace, a father and daughter reunited.

She travels to Lincoln Vineyards next. She found the canteen while organizing the items in her pantry. She didn't realize that it was the same container her mother had brought over to Taiwan until she opened its lid. She can't imagine going through such an atrocity as the 228 Massacre and then overcoming its emotional aftermath like her mother did.

Lisa stands near the plaque in the memorial garden and traces the word "mother" on it. She glides her fingers a few centimeters to the right and settles on the word "wife." Then she pours the rich dark earth of Taiwan out. *Finally*, she thinks, *my mother and father are together again.*

She straightens up and smoothes out her suit. From the outside, she looks like a professional Asian female, one who lives in a beautiful house and raises an intelligent daughter. She understands that people view others in their present state and not by their past. After she washes her hands, though, she knows that the clay from her mother's homeland will still cling to her. Its legacy will remain in the memory of her father drumming in her heart, and in her mother's courage coursing through her blood.

ACKNOWLEDGEMENTS

Deep gratitude for information from:

The 228 Memorial Foundation's Research Report on Responsibility For The 228 Massacre, George H. Kerr's *Formosa Betrayed*, The National Museum of Taiwan Literature, The Shoushan 228 Memorial Monument, Patrick Cowsill for his blog describing World War II, *Harvard Taiwanese 101*, *Nordie's at Noon: The Personal Stories of Four Women "Too Young" for Breast Cancer*, and Barbara Ehrenreich's *"Welcome to Cancerland."*

My heartfelt thanks to:

past English teachers who urged me to write, and my recent UCLA Writers' Program professors and peers for honing my craft;

online writer friends at Wordsmith Studio for solid community, and to Robert Lee Brewer who first challenged us;

NSLA supporters, especially the sharp eyes of Dan Kang and Christine Su, plus the inspiring creative minds of Abbi Chelian, Peter Cho, and Wesley Du;

MOMS Club members for providing me examples of caregiving at its finest;

Lany Avakian and her extensive cancer treatment knowledge (any health mistakes in the book are mine);

Siel Ju, Arthur Thuot, and Victor Trejo for their honesty and worthwhile suggestions;

my dear friends and critique partners: Robin Arehart, Sherry Berkin, Tracey Dale, Julie Daniels, Debra Davis, and Danielle Weinstock;

Kathleen Papajohn, my editor, who fine-tuned my efforts;

Melissa Newman and the rest of the staff at Martin Sisters Publishing for putting my words into print;

my family:
on the Chow side, especially San-Laung and Jue-Whei, for their tales and trips to Taiwan;
on the Ng side, particularly Daniel and Charlene for their love, and for Stan, who always believed in me;

and to my dear husband, Steve. May we leave a beautiful legacy to our children.

~ Author's Note

In 1995, then-President and KMT-chairman Lee Teng-hui made a formal apology on behalf of the Taiwanese government for the 228 Massacre.

ABOUT THE AUTHOR

Jennifer J. Chow, a Chinese-American, married into the Taiwanese culture. *The 228 Legacy* was inspired by the family stories she heard after viewing photos of a two-million-person human chain commemorating 228. She has traveled multiple times to Taiwan and visited places dedicated to the incident. Her experience with the elderly comes from a gerontology specialization at Cornell University and her geriatric social work experience.

Visit Jennifer online at www.jenniferjchow.com to learn more about her work.

Made in the USA
Lexington, KY
02 September 2013